SWEET
FURY

SWEET FURY

SASH BISCHOFF

bantam

TRANSWORLD PUBLISHERS
Penguin Random House, One Embassy Gardens,
8 Viaduct Gardens, London SW11 7BW
www.penguin.co.uk

Penguin
Random House
UK

Transworld is part of the Penguin Random House group of companies
whose addresses can be found at global.penguinrandomhouse.com

First published in Great Britain in 2025 by Bantam
an imprint of Transworld Publishers

A CIP catalogue record for this book
is available from the British Library.

ISBNs
9780857505262 hb
9780857505279 tpb

Interior design by Wendy Blum

Printed and bound in Great Britain by Clays Ltd, Elcograf S.p.A.

The authorized representative in the EEA is Penguin Random House Ireland,
Morrison Chambers, 32 Nassau Street, Dublin DO2 YH68.

Penguin Random House is committed to a sustainable
future for our business, our readers and our planet. This book
is made from Forest Stewardship Council® certified paper.

For Ben,
who never doubted

AUTHOR'S NOTE

More than anyone, I am indebted to the literary titan F. Scott Fitzgerald, whose collective works were hugely inspirational in the writing of *Sweet Fury*. In many respects, my novel is in conversation with his entire body of work and I remain so grateful to him for the profound and timeless literature he gave us.

Fitzgerald fans will find a number of Easter eggs of his poetic prose in the book.

Sweet Fury is, in part, dedicated to his legacy.

SWEET
FURY

SWEET

FURY

Show me a hero and I will write you a tragedy.

—F. Scott Fitzgerald, *The Crack-Up*

PROLOGUE

She stands there in the aftermath, trapped behind a wall of glass in a silent, seismic horror.

Outside, dawn is just beginning its purl, the sky over the Hudson a blooming bruise, skin of the water slate to silver, fingers of fog curling in. The world a milky calm, still unmarred by the carnage within. But she knows: nothing will ever be the same again.

Her stunned gaze travels down to her dress, stippled darkly with red. Her innocent hands, somehow sticky with blood . . . so much blood everywhere, so terribly bright . . .

Her stomach swills. She can't think of it.

She takes in the surviving remnants of the devastated room: the black book, the apocalyptic painting, the gold mask with its unseeing eyes. The knife. Beyond the glass, the clouds shift, and the blade flashes, blinding.

She won't look at the slump of flesh on the floor, puddle still spreading. The sick within her rising. No: she must put a stop to it, once and for all.

He's turned towards the balcony, backlit against the horizon's slow swell, one foot lunging before the other in a runner's stance. As though it might be any other morning, as though he might simply go for a jog, return with a coffee steaming in the early chill.

In the distance, one by one: the green lights of the shore beyond begin to blink out.

She must act quickly. Time is running out, and she's still in mortal danger.

She presses her palms to her ears—forces her focus to the sound of that soothing inner swirl. Draws within herself: a plucked chord singing to stillness. Breathes.

She opens her eyes, unlocks her phone; and then she places the call.

"Please help me," she whispers, and the tears begin to stream. "Someone's been stabbed. He's . . . oh god, I think he's dead."

Act One

INTIMATE
REVELATIONS

PRIVATE NOTES OF: J. GABRIEL

Patient: L. Crayne
Date/Time: June 10, 10:30 a.m.
Session: 1

New blood today. Famous film actress Lila Crayne.

Almost didn't accept intake. Nearly a year since I've had space for new patients, and wasn't familiar with L's work. But when I learned of her current project, and that our time together likely brief, my interest piqued.

First session. L entered office eagerly, extending her hand. Was initially taken aback— had expected withheld, sophisticated star. From open, guileless manner, would never have guessed L an American icon.

I offered tea; she accepted. Mentioned I'd come highly recommended from Brielle, close friend of hers. L quick to establish presence in space: slipped off shoes, tucked into couch corner. Presented as relaxed, self-assured; seemed almost unaware of therapeutic frame.

As I prepared kettle, L said she'd noticed diplomas in hall; she, too, went to Princeton for undergrad. We calculated I was three years her senior, so must have overlapped a year, though neither had known the other. Surprised I hadn't heard famous actress in attendance, but L explained hadn't acted professionally till after college. Seemed important to L to connect over our shared background, eating clubs, etc. I asked if comfortable working together despite commonality; L said she was.

L embarking on new film: feminist adaptation of F. Scott Fitzgerald's

Tender Is the Night, directed by L's long-term boyfriend, Kurt Royall (his name I knew). L also a producer, and will play leading role: Nicole Diver.

Here I confessed personal interest: Fitzgerald not only fellow Princetonian, also my favorite author (pointed out bookshelves dedicated to his work); and at this, L lit up. Told L Fitzgerald had written film treatment for *Tender*, but his version never made.

"It sounds like you're a real expert. I'm embarrassed to admit I'm still such a neophyte. Before this, I'd only read *Gatsby*."

Said while *Gatsby* overexposed, nevertheless my favorite. Read it every year.

"I can't believe my luck. It'll be so wonderful to have your guidance as I dig into his work." Interested in L's response to my knowledge of Fitzgerald. Does L need me to be an authority figure to feel sense of security? How will L respond in moments when I let her down or get it wrong?

Something disarming about L relationally; I was engaging in self-disclosure more than usual. Wondered at L's subtle lack of awareness of boundaries. An adaptive coping strategy? Sense of entitlement, or need for control? Or simply good initial rapport, and sign of strong therapeutic alliance?

Curious what drew L to adaptation, what personal resonance L felt in *Tender*, specifically. (All quoted conversation transcribed directly from preauthorized session recordings.

"I think my answer lies in the thesis of our film—what makes our adaptation different from the novel." Spoke carefully. "As I'm sure you know, *Tender* is typically read as Dick Diver's tragic downfall, due in large part to his patient, Nicole. Nicole is considered vampiric—in Fitzgerald's early outlines, her schizophrenia even triggered her to murder men! The popular read is that Dr. Diver, crippled by his savior complex, sacrifices his own needs when he marries Nicole and assumes all her problems as his own. She leeches on; and over time, she becomes stronger, slowly draining him dry. In the end she's healed, and she leaves her husband behind: a broken madman.

"But our adaptation reframes the story as Nicole's liberation." Paused. "Let me see if I can get it right. From the start, she's an innocent, isn't she? Her schizophrenia is the result of terrible trauma: after her mother died, her father raped her repeatedly. So her illness is reactionary: she's suspicious of all men and feels trapped, and desperately wants to escape. But when she's hospitalized, she's forbidden to discuss or process the abuse. Her father abandons her, and his reputation remains spotless. Then she meets and falls in love with her doctor, Dick."

I added, "Textbook case transference. Nicole immediately transfers her feelings of dependence onto Dick, seeing him as both lover and protector—a conflation of the romantic partner and paternal caretaker she'd found in her father."

"And against the guidance of the other doctors, Dick decides to marry her."

"Their relationship begins with an unstable foundation," I noted. "From the start, the power balance is skewed, and Nicole is dependent upon Dick for her own mental stability."

"So by believing himself capable of being both her lover and her doctor, Dick himself is responsible for creating the toxic relationship he ultimately blames Nicole for. And instead of helping her work through her trauma, he refuses to broach the subject of her past. He silences her."

"And then of course there's Rosemary."

"Right: Rosemary!" L said. "Dick's chronic wandering eye, his pursuit of these younger, vulnerable women, is intensely triggering for Nicole, given her past with her father. At the beginning, Rosemary's an impressionable, underage actress with complicated paternal baggage. And like Nicole, Rosemary falls for Dick, this much older man. And once again, rather than acting responsibly, Dick succumbs to Rosemary's desire for him to play lover and father both. When Nicole discovers their affair and has a schizophrenic episode, in that moment, her hero has become her ultimate betrayer."

Our eyes locked.

"You get it—I can tell," L said. "Our version of *Tender* isn't another tragedy of the tortured white man. It's a feminist story of healing, of reparations. From the very beginning, Nicole's mental illness was never her fault; it was due to the trauma she endured from her father, and from Dick himself. By the end of the story, she's only twenty-nine, and yet she's managed to become firmly grounded in reality and can finally stand on her own two feet. Dick has turned unstable and self-destructive, and is headed towards his own demise; but Nicole has overcome her trauma and reclaimed herself. She's free."

Had to admit: film's thesis impressive. If done well, adaptation would be sensational.

Asked why, with upcoming role in *Tender*, L sought therapy now.

Blushing, L explained reputation for being chameleon of an actor, disappearing so deeply into character she becomes almost unrecognizable. Further, given character's backstory, L felt it important to examine trauma in her own childhood. Sought out me, in particular, because of my specialization in trauma surrounding domestic violence.

Asked if she'd had therapy in past. L said I was her first—had always led busy life, hadn't seen it as priority. "Which probably meant I wasn't ready to look my trauma in the face. But I am now."

"That's brave of you."

"Is it? I don't think of it as brave. It's necessary."

L displays high level of self-awareness. Is astute, articulate, earnest. And entire time, L's unwavering focus fixed upon me; on doing the work, trying to be the good patient.

Asked L to tell me about her own childhood trauma. Curious how *Tender* might help narrate L's understanding of her own experience.

L told me father died in car accident almost twenty-five years ago, when L was eight.

"He was drunk," she said. "But then Daddy always was. I can hardly remember him sober."

"He was driving?"

Nodded.

"Can you tell me what happened that night?"

"I don't remember."

I waited.

"I can't remember any of that night," L explained. "And I was there."

"In the car?"

"Mother and I both were." Blew on tea, gathered herself. "I mean, I know the facts. I know what's in the report. It was late; there weren't many cars out. Daddy was weaving all over the road. And apparently he went onto the wrong side and collided with a truck. Mother broke an arm and a few ribs. I lost a tooth, and had a ton of stitches on my forehead, my cheek, my chin. I still have a scar—see? We both got concussions. But Daddy lost too much blood waiting for the ambulance to arrive. They couldn't revive him."

"And you don't remember any of this?"

Shook head. "Maybe it was the concussion. But I can't remember that night at all."

We'd landed on central event of severe childhood trauma. Uncovering repressed memory of father's death could be crucial to her healing. I hope in our time together to help L reconstruct this memory, bring it to light.

Before we ended, I returned to L's phrase: looking trauma in the face. Asked what that meant.

L studied me a moment. At last, quietly, she spoke.

"I want your honest opinion. If someone has done something terrible to you, can you ever truly heal? Or will you always have a scar? Is there a way to erase the scar itself—and more importantly, erase that person's power to hurt again?"

"What do you think?"

L smiled a little. "I don't know. That's why I've come to you."

"Well, I certainly believe in healing. I wouldn't be a therapist if I didn't."

L seemed unconvinced.

"Scars fade, Lila. They get less noticeable, and in time you forget they're even there. They become a part of you; eventually, you can't remember what you looked like without them.

"My professional opinion, since you asked, is that when someone has undergone a trauma, the best thing she can do is examine it. Get curious about it. As you said, look it right in the face. Only by doing so will it lose its power over you."

"Jonah." L watched me intently. "Do you think you can help me do that?"

"Lila." I smiled. "I do."

"**F**uck, you look good. If I could eat you, I would." He considered, then leaned down and licked her neck.

She laughed. "Don't tell me after all these years I'm finally turning you straight."

Freddie grinned. "If anyone could do it, it'd be you."

She turned to her reflection in the infinity mirror. Before her, an endless number of Lila Craynes radiated as far as the eye could see from her central solar hold. She shifted slightly to take in her image, and around her, thousands of Lilas shifted, too.

Her best friend wrapped his arms around her from behind. "I'm loving this," he murmured. "Very *All About Eve*."

She gazed at their image together in the low glow of the en suite bath. For all its sharp angles, its endless glass, this room was where she felt safest.

"Look at them," she said, smiling softly at their reflection. "Just look."

She'd first met Freddie James years ago in LA on the set of her break-out Kurt Royall film, *Waiting Game*. Back then, Kurt had already estab-lished himself as an industry tycoon, while Lila had still been a babe in the celluloid woods. Freddie, meanwhile, had had a couple films under his belt, and a couple accompanying cautionary tales.

It was love at first sight; in no time flat, they were joined at the hip and ready for the U-Haul. Lila had loved how attuned Freddie was, how keenly he observed, how sharply he listened. And she felt she understood him from the start. Most people were quick to put Freddie in a box, assuming a certain callous condescension in his sharp, dry wit. But Lila quickly saw past all that, and recognized Freddie to be someone loyal and kind-hearted—and in their industry, those qualities were near impossible to find.

When *Waiting Game* became a box office hit, Lila had instantly shot to stardom and earned the title of America's Sweetheart. Suddenly, every-one around her seemed to be *trying* so hard: to please her, to catch her attention, to lure her into liking them. Freddie was the one person who didn't change a whit. With him, there would never be any bullshitting. She would always simply be Lila: an equal, a friend.

While her career was exploding, Freddie was falling wildly in love with a man who owned the most respected PR firm in the business. The warning signs were textbook, and from the beginning, Lila had seen the situation for what it was. She herself understood toxic relationships all too well; and she would do anything to save Freddie from his. After three painful years of enduring the boyfriend's abuse, Freddie finally admitted she was right. And so—patiently, carefully—Lila had crafted a plan to help her friend escape.

Six months ago, *Tender Is the Night* was greenlit; and at Lila's request, Kurt had offered Freddie the role of Tommy Barban. The film would put three thousand miles between him and his ex, and (Lila hoped) would distract Freddie out of his terrible relationship for good. He'd packed up his life in LA, then flown across the country to New York, and into Lila's open arms.

"Don't be sad," he told her softly now. "We knew this day would come. I can't crash with the two of you forever."

She shrugged. "You know Kurt loves you—"

"Of course he does." Freddie grinned, then snapped into perfor-mance. "Honey. I'm the prototypical gay best friend. My very existence makes Kurt feel so . . ." He raised a brow. ". . . hetero."

Much as she hated to admit it, she knew this was true. In Kurt's presence, Freddie always assumed the role of the fabulous queen—and in the face of this pageantry Kurt inevitably relaxed, reassured Freddie harbored no illicit, underhand desire.

He nuzzled her neck. "Chin up. I'm moving to Soho, not Siberia. And besides: tonight, the birthday boy deserves to have you all to himself. I want you two swinging from the goddamn chandelier."

She smiled. "We don't have a chandelier."

"I expect acrobatics. Pyrotechnics! And in the meantime—" He smoothed his shirt, his hair. "—I've got a job to do."

She picked a speck of lint from his collar. "You're heading there now?"

"I am. Your overeager assistant has been texting me ad nauseum—if it weren't for you, I'd block the bitch. But don't worry: I'll play the part." He preened, examining his reflection. "I'll be golden and boisterous and perfectly coiffed, with equal amounts charm and snark. I'll win them over instantly, plying their patience, lubricating them with alcohol— getting them all good and ready for Kurt's enormous, red-blooded, gasp-worthy—"

Lila swatted him.

"—arrival!" He grinned. "Get that mind out of the gutter."

"Thank you, Freddie." She touched his cheek. "What would I do without you?"

"Lila." He took her palm, kissed its heart. "I literally owe you my life. This was the least I could do."

She pressed upon one of the reflected walls, and the invisible jib door swung open, releasing them from their sanctuary and into the waiting world. And as she and Freddie descended the stairs into the great room, she marveled all over again at her good fortune.

When she and Kurt had moved to the city, she'd found them a loft on the southern fringe of the West Village, glorious in its luxurious, yawning space, more Tribeca than Village in its gothic height, its long, stretched floor plan, its gleaming, naked design. The floors poured concrete, the walls a thick glossed white, the pipes artfully exposed: bloodred, glint of silver. The apartment was located on West Street, a stone's throw from the Hudson. She and Kurt owned the whole crown of the building, their ceilings twenty feet tall, encased almost entirely in shining slabs of soundproof glass. These transcendent windows, which looked down upon the city like enormous all-seeing eyes, seemed almost as though they might float off like divine clouds into the sky; but alas, the eyes remained earthbound, anchored to the ground by the pièce de résistance: the stunning private deck, which wrapped around the building's length in a single satisfied grin. The very bones of the home seemed to throw open to the easy reach of piers below, to the glittering water with its buoyed, bobbing boats, to the early-morning joggers swiftly flitting by.

After kissing Freddie farewell, Lila turned her attention to the birthday boy himself, waiting for her on the balcony. Kurt was leaning forward onto the rail, frosted martini in hand. A runner, Kurt: blood hot and humming, always hungry to race ahead, to win. Tonight he wore a starched white button-down open at the collar, fitted navy slacks, creamy leather loafers. Strong frame, thick shock of silvery hair, sun-soaked skin.

The quiet shush of glass as she eased open the balcony door.

"Freddie just left," she said. "He asked me to thank you again."

He turned, rested his elbows on the rail behind, and gazed at her, standing before him.

She'd picked a dress to make him wild: a backless champagne slip that clung delicately to the slender ribbon of her body. A naked dress: the type you'd glimpse from afar and do a double take, thinking she was traipsing about in the nude—the only bolt of color the bright slash of her lips.

"You look gorgeous, Crayne."

"Happy birthday," she said. "Boy, have I got a treat in store for you."

"I can see that," he said, sipping his martini.

"Later, stallion," she said, and he grinned.

"What's the surprise?"

She took the martini from his hand. "It wouldn't be a surprise if I told you, now, would it?"

His fingers moved to her hips.

"Patience, Mr. Royall," she said, and popped an olive into her mouth.

A quiet groan. "A few minutes. I can be quick."

"You? Never."

He laughed. "You're going to drive me crazy, you know that?"

She leaned in. Whispered, "My plan exactly."

They took the keyed elevator down to the street where Daniel was already waiting in the car, then drove through the leafy blocks of the Village, their security team following in their wake. When Kurt was momentarily distracted by a call from one of *Tender*'s producers, Lila texted Freddie:

ETA less than five. Assemble the boozy troops.

Copy that, Captain. Sloshed and sluiced.

As they turned down a cobblestoned street, Daniel slowed before a restaurant tucked into the base of a brownstone. Kurt looked up from his phone.

"That new French place?"

She kissed his cheek. "No shit, Sherlock."

"You sure it's open?" he asked as they stepped out of the car. "Looks pretty dark."

"They don't officially open till next week," she said. "I called the owner. Tonight, they're making dinner for just the two of us."

"How sweet," Kurt murmured. "Thank you, baby."

She turned away, smiling. Modesty just wasn't Kurt Royall's style. He craved the heady warmth of the spotlight, the roiling rush of crowds.

They opened the door, stepped inside.

"I wonder why it's so dark," Lila said, slipping her hand into his.

"Hello?" Kurt called. "Is anyone here?"

A stifled titter, and then at once the lights poured, bathing the space in a golden glow. Their friends leapt from their hiding spots, smiles bursting alight as they cried out to him, rushed to him, threw their arms around Kurt and Lila both.

"Happy birthday, Kurt, darling," they said; and yes it was happy, of course it was, for Lila had dreamed it into being, and it had happened without a hitch. She beamed at Freddie, sleek as a panther against the doorframe, all but licking his paws with satisfaction, and he nodded back, blew her a kiss. She'd done it yet again, knew Kurt Royall better than he knew himself. And the games had just begun.

The waitstaff waltzed in with fizzing flutes of champagne. Candles were lit, the room dimming and dancing in the shadows of the flames, the raw silk walls soaking in their glow. In the corner a cluster of musicians spun satin into the air while a jazz vocalist crooned in French. Beyond, arched windows opened to a dark garden dressed with fairy lights that twinkled like pinpricked stars against the velvety night.

The pressed linen tables had been arranged in a fat rectangle: a banquet fit for a king, for Mr. Royall himself. And the feast was exquisite: sautéed moules swimming in a shallow soup of lemon, butter, sage; robust and portly cheeses, placed plump atop beds of sharp, grassy greens, crusts splitting at the seams with their own luscious ooze. Baguettes, piping hot, flour sugaring the air, hiss of the dough as it stretched and pulled apart, soft slabs of unsalted butter swabbed generously on. Les escargots, simmering in individual pockets, parsley, salt, and oil swirling. Et le fois gras, the thick whip of it, so light and lush the guests dolloped it directly to their tongues. En fin les steaks, still sizzling, glistening and tender with their own blood. Tout était parfait.

When the main course had been served, Lila excused herself to the washroom to prime herself for the final coup de foudre. She gazed into the mirror, jostled her hair at the scalp so that it bounced thickly about her, lifted her erect nipples beneath the sheath of fabric, slicked on more lipstick. It was time.

Before she rejoined her guests she paused at the entryway, allowed herself to take them all in, the whole gorgeous gaggle of them. There were Bobby and Greta Starr, in their predictable matching black. Bobby Starr was head of Olympus Pictures, the distributor tentatively attached to *Tender Is the Night*. Lila knew Starr would use the evening's festivities to cajole Kurt into signing onto another unremarkable action flick. Meanwhile, Greta, the executive editor at *Vogue*, had her own agenda: she'd begged Lila and Kurt to pose for their August cover, and Lila had graciously agreed. Greta was a riot, especially when she was buzzed on cocaine, as she obviously was tonight.

To her right: Dean, the billionaire hedge fund mogul who invested religiously in Kurt's films (his contributions to *Tender* a record high), and his girlfriend, Yuliana, the model who posed for the occasional spread, but in reality spent more time enjoying her influencer status, frolicking and posing for her 300k fans. A few drinks from now, she'd be grinding her bony little ass up on Dean and Kurt, begging Lila to make out with her. (Lila, as always, would demur.)

Then Kaylee, the movie starlet Kurt had wanted to play the part of Rosemary, until Lila had finally convinced him otherwise. She was sure he and Kaylee had slept together at some indeterminate point in the past; and tonight Kaylee seemed to fancy herself subtle as she angled to be fucked by him again. To distract her, Lila had dispatched Freddie as diversion, and—despite the fact that Freddie's sexuality had never been a secret—Kaylee was already teasing her fingers high up his thigh.

Zev Winters, wunderkind actor and consummate skirt chaser, gracing almost all of Kurt's films (including an upcoming role in *Tender*), and his new (third) wife, Sarah—a lawyer, of all healthy callings. The fact that he'd gone plebian was a likely sign, Lila suspected, that his lothario act was still going strong. But Sarah was pretty, and seemed wickedly clever; and because of that, she most certainly wouldn't stick around for long. While Zev was charming as hell, he'd never been able to keep his dick in his pants.

The rest: all the same. Stunning, the lot of them, with their delicately threaded couture, their finely tuned bodies, dizzying wealth nearly shimmering on their skin. Some sharper, others more distinguished, others more charismatic. But despite these slight aberrations, they all pulled breathlessly in, prowling around one another's magnetic glow, purring with pride for the company in which they now found themselves, and ravenous all the same to climb to the very top. Eyes wet and gleaming, laughter pealing, hands alight, teeth glistening. They were rabid, every last one. Yet tonight, as ever, Kurt and Lila were set apart, revered; for in the eyes of the world, they were silver screen royalty.

As Lila made her way back, a hand wrapped around her waist, and with a cry of delight she was pulled into Freddie's lap.

"My hero," Freddie said, kissing her plum on the lips.

She grinned. "And you my heroine?"

"Oh my god, Lila, this party is too cute!"

She looked over at Kaylee, smiling painfully. The sweet thing seemed to be angling to take Freddie home tonight. And Lila, clearly, was the killjoy. It was too tempting.

"You know who's cute?" Lila said, and kissed Freddie again, long and slow.

"Excuse me, Miss, that's my boy toy you're groping," Kurt called from the far end of the table.

She threw back her head with a throaty laugh, and the rest of the table joined in, their eyes ping-ponging between the prized couple. At last, the crowning match had begun.

"And what, pray tell, does that make me, Mr. Royall?"

His mouth twitched into a smile. "Why, my muse, of course."

"Hear, hear!" someone cried sloppily.

"I'd like to make a toast," Kurt said, and pushed his chair back to stand. "Lila Crayne, my temptress, my beauty, my darling, my undoing.

My life was so very different before you, my love; and because of you, it will never be the same. This was the perfect birthday: a room full of the people I love and cherish most. As you all well know, in prepping for this next film of mine, I've been living and breathing Fitzgerald—and in my current F. Scott absorption, I can't help but feel tonight as though I've stumbled into my very own *Gatsby* soiree. Such a gorgeous crowd . . . so much style and celebrity and glamour . . ." He paused, winked. ". . . so much fucking alcohol—"

The proudly accused hooted, cheered.

"I like *large* parties, don't you?" Freddie whispered into her ear, and Lila grinned at the reference. "At small parties there isn't any privacy."

Kurt continued. "Thank you all for celebrating with me tonight. And thank you, baby, for bringing us together." He lifted his glass. "To Lila."

"To Lila!" the room echoed.

Lila stood and nodded at Freddie, who subtly pulled out his phone. She plucked up his glass, then turned to address the room. "Isn't it just like Mr. Royall to make a toast to someone else on his own goddamn birthday?" The room laughed. "But I'm not going to let him get away with it tonight. Kurt knows I don't let him get away with anything."

"She doesn't!" He shook his head ruefully.

Beside her Kaylee sniffed, and Lila made amends, reaching down to caress her tawny head. Despite herself, Kaylee beamed.

"Kurt, my love, don't you know that tonight should be all about you? In fact, I have one more surprise in store—well, one more that can happen in public." A woman whooped, a few men laughed wetly. She began to walk down the length of the table, her fingers touching the shoulders of the guests she passed.

"Kurt, the whole world knows you as a genius, a savant, ground-breaker, and earth-shatterer in the world of film. You've forever altered the landscape, created countless masterpieces; and with each film you make, your work only grows richer. You are a champion of projects you love, projects that really matter—projects like *Tender Is the Night*." She caught Starr's eye. "Thank you again, Bobby, for letting Kurt twist your arm a bit with this one."

Starr bowed his head, and the room chuckled in support.

"You are revered, and will continue to be recognized time and again for your incredible prowess. What the world doesn't necessarily know, however, is what a fucking man you are. And more than anyone else, I do."

"You bet she does," Zev intoned drunkenly.

"You've been so good to me," Lila said as she reached Kurt, and placed her hand in his. "You've cared for me, and loved me deeply; but as you know, nothing is more important to me than absolute, unequivocal respect." She squeezed his hand. "I can honestly say that Kurt Royall is the world's model for what it means to be a man today. And what a lucky girl am I to have captured him, am I right?"

The table cheered. Lila reached back to the nape of her neck, unclasped her gold necklace, her eyes never leaving Kurt's.

"But don't be fooled by this silly little dress: because tonight, I want to play the gentleman's part." She pulled the long chain from where it had dipped below her loosely scooped neckline, and suspended it, glimmering, in the candlelight. Slowly, she released one end into an upturned palm, revealing a thin gold band.

"When Fitzgerald described his love for Zelda, he said it was *the beginning and end of everything.* I've had that phrase inscribed here inside this ring, because no words could more accurately capture our love.

"Kurt Royall." She kicked off her heels, knelt down on both knees. "Will you marry me?"

She smiled up at him, and in the low glow of the candles, his blue eyes seemed black, the reflected flames dancing in their wetness.

The subjects fell hush.

At last, he spoke. "As if it were even a question. Lila, baby, of course I'll marry you."

The room screamed in celebration; and beyond the windows, the lightning flash of cameras: the press had arrived. Kurt scooped her into his arms, the musk of him warming her stomach, her loins. She ran her fingers through his hair, and when he leaned in to kiss her spreading smile, her teeth pressed into the soft plush of his lips. Still grinning, she bit.

```
PRIVATE NOTES OF: J. GABRIEL

Patient: L. Crayne
Date/Time: June 17, 10:30 a.m.
Session: 2
```

Unexpected development before session today. Received voicemail from L's mother:

Jonah, my name is Karen Wolfe. I hope you don't mind that I took it upon myself to get in touch. My daughter Lila mentioned she started seeing you last week, and told me she felt a strong connection with you. I understand, of course, that therapy is a private affair, and the last thing you need is a mother's nosy interference, but I just can't help myself: Jonah, I'm worried about my daughter. As you may know, she's in a relationship with Kurt Royall, and I have a pretty good idea it's an unhealthy one. Now, I've done my homework on you: I know that when it comes to therapists specializing in domestic abuse, you are the crème de la crème. So I'm hopeful you might be able to dig into their relationship in your sessions; and if I'm right, perhaps you can help my daughter extricate from her situation. I'd of course appreciate if you'd keep this communication between us. No need to call me back, but feel free if you want to discuss further. Alright, thanks in advance for your help, Jonah. Bye now.

Was taken aback by overbearing tone / blatant breach of privacy. Decided not to mention to L—at least not initially. Nevertheless, will probe L's relationship with Kurt, see if Karen's concerns legitimate.

Upon arrival, L announced she had news.

As I closed door, L asked if it'd been my girlfriend she'd just met.

Couldn't get pin code to work; had to knock. "A woman let me in. Brown hair, yellow top? Maggie, I think it was?"

Told L Maggie my fiancée. L congratulated me.

Noticed L's eyes markedly red; rash on neck/chest. L explained she'd had a bad reaction to makeup test for *Tender*.

Before I could offer, L flipped on kettle, thumbed through tea box— once again asserting presence in space.

"*Boil some water—lots of it.*" Looked at me. "Recognize that line?"

I did.

"I've been doing my Fitzgerald homework." Plucked up sachet. "Rosehip. I always thought that a rather saucy name for a tea." Flapped it between fingers, then walked length of bookcase, pausing at framed photo.

"Is this you?"

Knew hard to tell—photo dark, completely blurred—but yes, from a long time ago: me at Princeton.

L studied it in silence, then looked up. "Such a small world, isn't it? The universe works in amazing ways."

When I simply smiled in response, L returned photo to shelf, curled into seat. "Shall I tell you my news?"

Informed me she'd gotten engaged. Described surprise party she'd thrown Friday for Kurt's fiftieth (hadn't realized Kurt eighteen years older). And described how, towards end of dinner, Kurt made romantic toast, and L said to hell with convention. Timing and company perfect, and for once they'd evaded cameras. L had proposed.

Saw opportunity to explore relationship with Kurt. Curious if L's impulsive decision masked something more—perhaps deeper, anxious fear. I asked if he'd been married before.

"You mean because he's so much older? He's had a few serious relationships, but mostly he flew solo. Married to his career."

Asked if marriage important to her.

"Well, yes. Not that I had a strong model growing up. But isn't that a thing? When the parents have a bad marriage, the child either wants to chuck the institution altogether, or do it right and avoid her parents' pitfalls. Aren't those the two options?"

Said not quite so black and white. Believed person's relationship to love/marriage to be on spectrum. Forever in flux; can continue to change over lifetime.

Asked if she found this unsettling; she did. When I asked why:

"The thought that it isn't fixed. That anything, even somebody's love, might change or go away."

"Are you afraid of that with Kurt?"

Kettle started to boil. Switched it off, poured her cup. When I looked up, L forced smile.

"God, I guess I'm that woman. I'm scared that one day Kurt will realize I don't deserve him, and he'll up and run away."

Gently suggested marriage doesn't prevent someone from leaving.

"I know. But it does make it a bit more difficult, doesn't it?" Laughed suddenly. "I can't believe I'm telling you this. It's so embarrassing."

Asked why.

"Because! This isn't the image I want people to have of me. It's the opposite of who I'm supposed to be. I mean, I'm finally the lead in a film about female empowerment! My whole career, I've been cast as the ingenue. I would've killed for a role like this; and now, finally, I've gotten it. I want to deserve it. I don't want to be the helpless woman who needs saving; that feels so hypocritical. And yet, deep down? I've always had this strange fear that all men will eventually abandon me; and no matter what, I'll end up alone."

Wanted to examine root of anxiety: asked L about parents' relationship.

L remembers father as man born to fill doors. Had two sides: public, and then private, reserved for L and mother. Father hated that she and mother were close, hated she was a girl.

Mother opposite of father. Quiet, soft, warm. Feminine. (Intrigued by L's description; didn't match my impression from voicemail.) Played part of perfect housewife; if she didn't, paid the price.

Father could be calculating, cruel with words. Once in a while, if L fought back, would turn physical. He'd hit L hard. But mostly, L learned to hide.

Mother received brunt of abuse. In his eyes, she did everything wrong. Always belittling mother, finding ways to make her feel worthless, not enough. (Here L flushed, and I wondered if L heard echo in her own experience with men.) Father constantly threatening to abandon them both. But inevitably, L said, father would turn around and come after mother for sex.

Asked L what she knew about parents' sexual relationship.

L smiled sadly. "Mother and I were extremely close." Said mother divulged it all: dirty things he'd say, how he'd come onto her after having been horrible moments before. She'd describe sex in detail, how selfish he was, how she hated it, how much it hurt.

Acknowledged this must have been traumatic to witness. Said forcible sex without consent categorically defined as rape. Gently asked L if she felt father had raped mother.

"Of course," she said. "He forced her to have sex with him against her will; and he did it almost every day. If that's not rape, I don't know what is."

Thinking again of Karen's message, wondered if parental dynamic was repeating itself with Kurt. Moved conversation to L's own experience with men. Asked L to tell me about most important romantic/sexual relationships. At this L looked at me, mouth curving into smile I couldn't quite read.

"Does it make you uncomfortable to talk about this?"

"No, it's not that." Said she was "just about as damaged as they come." Had dated plenty before Kurt, but nothing meaningful/lasting. Asked why. Sensed L hiding something. L clearly resistant, but eventually admitted: years ago, another man forced her to have sex against her will.

Significant discovery that—by L's own definition—L a victim of rape. Will be critical to unpack in our work together.

Asked if L had sought treatment after this trauma.

"Maybe I should have. But it's in the past now."

Gently suggested L's experience might have more lasting repercussions. Recovering from sexual assault can take years; therapeutic work essential to healing. Important to have safe space with qualified professional to process experience / build coping strategies. Also important to develop self-care (physical and emotional) for mental health. Wanted to reaffirm L's decision to work with me, as my specific expertise can help L with past trauma. Asked L to continue.

Before Kurt, L wasn't interested in romantic relationships. Career full focus. And then five years ago, when L twenty-seven, met Kurt, and *Waiting Game* happened.

Asked what initially attracted L to Kurt.

"It's his energy more than anything. He's strong, in every sense of the word. You feel like you can throw anything his way, and he'll just catch it effortlessly."

"He makes you feel safe."

"Exactly! And I don't need taking care of; I've made sure of that. But having someone who can and will take care of me even so? It's wonderful."

Suspected L's rape trauma the catalyst for resulting desire for older, paternal, romantic protector. Asked how age difference manifested.

L shrugged. "Kurt doesn't feel old. He just feels grown-up. Whenever I dated men closer to my own age, I felt like I was with these little boys. They were so predictable, so weak. With Kurt, I was finally with a real man." Glanced at me. "No offense."

"None taken."

"Is Maggie our age?"

Unsurprised by L's deflection. Asked why she wanted to know.

"She's a bit younger, isn't she? You seem like Kurt that way, like you'd want to take care of a woman. Like you'd know how."

Was clear L was flirting. Perhaps to test whether I could be trusted as neutral third party, or if I harbored some secret desire. Or perhaps simply determining if L in control, with power to fluster me. Redirected dialogue back to L's relationship with K. Asked how it began.

L was attracted when she first met him at audition. "But I assumed he was off-limits. Kurt has always proudly called himself a feminist. He has this unmarred reputation—he's not a Weinstein. He's like this father figure of the film world." L laughed. "You probably think I've got some sort of daddy complex, don't you?"

"When did your relationship turn romantic?"

Happened early. Casting for *Waiting Game* about to be officially announced. In celebration, Kurt hosted gathering. Lot of alcohol/drugs at party; no one in right mind. Eventually, L and K alone. K told her he'd debated saying anything, didn't want to get in way of work, but couldn't stop thinking about her. Was attracted to her; and L confessed she enjoyed that power. (Clear L learned from parents' model to use sex as currency, measuring her worth in man's desire.) K told L if she wasn't interested, he'd never speak of it again. But had to ask.

"That's a pretty difficult position to put you in."

"Maybe if I didn't feel the same. But I did. We slept together, and the rest is history."

Sensed more to story than L letting on, but for today, let it go. Didn't want L to feel I was questioning reliability of narrative.

Instead, asked if we could further discuss incident of L's rape. But this clearly a misstep. L grew defensive, asked why. Said I was trying to understand full scope of experience to get better picture of relationship to men. Critical to unpack past trauma in order to fully heal, and approach present relationship with clear eyes.

"But why are we even talking about Kurt? I'm not here to talk about my relationship. *Tender* goes into production this week, and we've barely touched on my childhood. That's what's relevant to my work on the film. That's what I want to talk about."

"Okay," I said. "In this room, you're in the driver's seat. But you did come into this session wanting to talk about Kurt."

L hesitated. "No, I didn't."

"Lila, you did. It was the first thing you said. You even reminded me again to ask you about your news. It was on your mind. You wanted to talk about it."

Our time up, but I wanted L to leave on steady ground. Said next session we'd talk exclusively about whatever she'd like.

"I'm sorry," L said. "I shouldn't have questioned you. I hope you're not upset."

"No need to apologize."

L fell silent, wrestling something within herself. At last, she looked up.

"I want to feel when I come here each week that I'm entering a safe space. That our relationship is sacred."

"You're safe here. You can trust me."

L reached out suddenly, wrapped fingers around mine, gazed at our hands together. "I know," she said quietly.

Before I could respond, L pulled away. Opened door.

"Lila," I began.

But she was already gone.

26

IV

C elia Scott's car slipped along the satin thread of the Old Highway: a shining fish in downstream flight. Somewhere along the way, the trees had leveled, sand had crept to the sides of the road, and the great mouth of the sky had gone wide: the ocean was near. They streaked past knurled paths burrowing their way to the beach, water flashing through the scrub in brief, bright glimpses. Lining the road, imposing gates to Montauk's finest estates stood like sentinels, each protecting its own gilded, leafy grounds. The car made a sudden turn into one of these drives, jostling slightly as it crunched down the gravel path. From the back, Celia craned her neck, her breath catching as the palatial villa rolled into view.

"We're here, Miss Scott," the driver said, and Celia smoothed her skirt, checked her reflection one final time.

"Thank you," she said, then took a deep breath, opened the door, and dipped a toe to the ground.

"Cecelia Scott?" A woman in a trendy biker jacket—Bushwick chic: slick black bob, hips like pistols—regarded a clipboard wedged at her waist.

"Celia. Please." She extended a hand and smiled at the woman, who scratched a quick check mark, then regarded her with mild amusement.

"I'm Eden. 1st AD. My PA apparently 'slept through his alarm,' so

27

here I am, your illustrious welcoming committee." Grimace of a smile: jaw tight, lids low. "You can head straight through the main entryway. Most everyone's already out on the terrace." She jerked her head in the general direction, then looked over Celia's shoulder, smile widening unctuously as she spotted the next more important arrival.

Celia tiptoed through the vaulted foyer, her gaze drawn to the opulent chandelier dripping down from the keystone. She reached the glass doors yawning onto the terrace and hesitated, a single hand raised to shield her eyes from the sun.

To her right, a sudden salvo of shuttering. Celia turned, her mouth parting in a delicate O, and the shining black eye of a camera caught her expression in rapid-fire. She blinked at the intrusion, and the photographer tilted his head, offered a half-smile, then continued his work unfazed.

A hand palmed the small of her back. "Try to ignore him."

Kurt Royall, smiling down at her. Hand still affixed, his eyes traveled to the outfit she'd chosen, and she waited, smile wobbling. This morning in her new Upper East Side apartment (an enormous upgrade from her previous Harlem squalor, thanks to the first *Tender* paycheck), she'd laid her dress carefully onto her bed—a smooth, creamy silhouette—and stepped back, hands on hips, appraising the identity she'd soon adopt.

And now here she was, standing before the beau monde of film— before Kurt Royall himself!—on a warm sweep of terra-cotta terrace set upon the jawline of a cliff jutting over the Atlantic; but as a flicker of a frown crossed Kurt's face, it appeared she was already failing.

"You ready?" he asked.

"I've waited my whole life for this, Mr. Royall."

"Celia, please: Mr. Royall's my father, and he's an ass. Let's stick with Kurt, alright?"

"Kurt," she repeated, and the camera whirred again, catching them together.

Kurt held up a hand to block the shot, then stared the photographer down until he shifted away. Then he turned back to Celia, leaned in to whisper in her ear. "That dipshit's here at Lila's insistence, to document the whole day. I, on the other hand, prefer to keep my affairs private." He gazed at her. "Don't you?"

Before she could summon an answer, he turned as someone called his name. "Harry!" he answered, hand raised, then threw her a conspiratorial wink before walking away.

"Celia!"

Celia froze as Lila floated over and embraced her warmly. And again, the camera clacketed away.

"Don't worry, he's just a set photographer. None of the photos will leak till after we've wrapped." She leaned in. "Wouldn't want to spoil the press release introducing you in your breakout performance, now, would we?"

Celia ducked her chin, bit down on a smile.

She continued on. "Let's give him one good shot, and maybe then he'll leave us in peace."

She slipped her arm around Celia's waist, struck a charming pose. Celia did her best to mirror her, and the camera purred in response. But for the nine years between them, the two women could have been twins.

Lila turned to Celia, took her hands in both her own as the camera continued to capture them. "I can't tell you how happy I am to have you on board," she said, then whispered to the photographer, "She was my favorite."

"Thank you," Celia said, flushing.

Lila leaned in. "Listen. Don't let any of these fancy people get to you. They're all just as nervous, I promise. If you need anything—anything at all—please come to me." Lila looked at her meaningfully. "I'll be looking out for you."

"Good god, I'm seeing double!" A stately woman in a Chanel suit sashayed over with a steely grin, pinching a flute of champagne from the tray of a passing waiter.

Lila leaned into Celia. "Something tells me we're going to get that a lot." Then she turned to the woman, lifted her voice. "This is Celia Scott."

"I'm Karen Wolfe." The woman took Celia's hand in her cool, bony grip, teeth in a tight smile. "Executive producer and Lila's manager."

"Not to mention my mother," Lila added as Celia stuttered a response.

Karen took a healthy swig. "In another life, Celia, I, too, was an actress." She gestured to her daughter. "Lila will tell you I freely and unapologetically take all credit for my darling daughter's talent."

Lila threw her an amused grin. "It's true."

Karen lifted her glass. "Love that they added booze to loosen up our Russian investor friends. They should make a habit of it." She scanned the crowd, nose crinkling. "But Jesus, this circus is run by apes. Some of us would like to get back to the city before hell freezes over."

"I'm sure Kurt will start any minute now, Mother."

"Excuse me?" Celia blushed as the women turned. "I'm so sorry, but—is there a restroom I could use? It was such a long drive, and I'm about to burst."

Lila laughed and offered the directions; and Celia smiled before turning and tripping lightly inside.

"What do you think of her wide-eyed act?" Karen muttered.

"Oh give her a chance, Mother," Lila said. "She's just nervous, is all."

"Tough titty." But she considered a moment. "The resemblance *is* uncanny. If I didn't know my own vagina, I'd have sworn she was my long-lost prodigal child."

"Was that Celia Scott?"

The women tensed and turned to find Nancy Wright, the actress who'd play Rosemary's mother, scurrying up with a gossipy grin. "Hot damn, I just missed her, didn't I? I wanted that photographer to get a good shot of the two of us."

Lila smiled. "It's good to see you, Nancy. How are you?"

"Well just peachy now!" Nancy cried, clapping her hands together.

"Oh Lila, Lila, Lila: it's been too goddamn long. And Ms. Wolfe: the woman responsible for *making* this gorgeous creature. It's an honor."

"The pleasure's all mine," Karen said. "Especially after having been told my contributions begin and end with my birthing canal."

"Oh!" Nancy let out a terrified little laugh. "Oh gosh—I like you!"

Eventually she recovered herself and leaned in, lips pursed. "So tell me, ladies, what's *your* theory behind this provocative casting choice?"

Lila cocked her head. "What do you mean?"

Nancy let out a little whoop. "Well hon, in case you hadn't noticed, our young Rosemary is the spitting image of you! And that isn't in the book, now, is it?"

"That's a good point," Lila acknowledged. "I wonder what Kurt would have to say." She folded her arms. "I guess I saw it as further commentary on our country's systemic misogyny," she said slowly. "Men prey on women over and over through the generations, continually coveting the younger, shinier model; and as a result, women are stripped of individuality when viewed through the male gaze."

"Oh, that's good." Nancy nodded. "Very woke."

In the ensuing silence, the women all waited—and at last Nancy seemed to realize it was her cue. "If you'll excuse me, I think I see an old friend. We'll continue this later, yes? Ciao!"

"She looks god-awful," Karen said as they watched her scurry across the terrace. "And that wine face—Christ. Too liberal with the lunchtime chardonnay?"

"Now, Mother. Let's not be petty."

"Oh, throw me a bone." Karen's tongue glided over her perfect teeth, as though making sure they were all still in attendance. "We're playing eye for an eye, and the bitch who bore Rosemary ought to look worlds better than that midwestern heifer."

"God, I hate this forced mingling," Lila sighed. "When will it ever end?"

"Don't look now, darling," Karen said. "Methinks a false armistice is afoot."

The two women watched as Kurt and Dominic Reeves, who'd play Dick Diver, exchanged stiff thumps on the back.

"You two look like you're up to no good. What are we gossiping about?" Freddie came up from behind, then gave a little gasp as he discovered the object of their attention. "My god, I'd love to get those two in bed together. De-lish."

"If you like micropenises, sure," Karen said, and Freddie let out a devilish cackle.

"Karen, you and I are long overdue for a date. There's no one on earth I'd rather talk cock with."

"Anytime, doll. But for now: time to prance that tight little ass of yours back into the closet," Karen said, nodding towards her daughter.

He turned to Lila. Grinned. "We finally get our happy ending. Who would've known the two of us would wind up together?"

"Oh Freddie," Lila said, kissing his cheek. "I did. Don't you know I orchestrated the whole affair?"

"Alright party people, let's make some magic," Kurt boomed, and at the deep timbre of his voice, the collective bloomed and burst to cheering, then began to wade towards their prescribed seats on the terrace—the actors, to the tables at the center; the spectators (the film's private investors, all flown in direct from Russia, along with Starr and his Olympus team from LA, who'd sign on as *Tender*'s distributor, pending final cut), to the row of chairs ringing the perimeter. Zev Winters came running up and lifted Lila into the air before continuing to his place. The party, dizzied up like a snow globe, was settling.

Lila walked over to Kurt and folded her arms around him from behind. "Where do you want me?"

"Sweetheart." He turned. "I have you right here." He gestured to the seat next to Dominic.

Lila nodded. "I wonder. Should I maybe sit across the way instead— there, beside Rupert? That might open up the actors better for our audience, wouldn't it?" She cocked her head towards the investors hovering at the edges.

"Always thinking of everyone else." He kissed her temple, then called across the table. "Zev! Can I trouble you to play some musical chairs?"

"Anything for you, boss. Where do you want me?"

"Right here. I'll owe you a drink for indulging my mercurial mind."

"Oh, I don't know if you're so mercurial these days." Zev lifted his voice, pulling the attention of the terrace. "Yo peeps! Before our fearless leader gives one of those famously eloquent speeches of his . . ." Zev gestured to Kurt and Lila. "I believe some congratulations are in order!"

Whir of the camera as the assembled erupted. Then the scratch of patio chairs over tile as everyone settled into their seats, leaving Kurt the last man standing.

"Thanks, everyone. Lila and I are certainly very excited."

Lila looked up at him, beamed.

"You'll all have a chance to roast us at some point, I'm sure," Kurt said. "But today let's talk about this journey we're about to embark on together, shall we?"

Applause. The camera clacketing.

"Look, I know all too well that most of us secretly dread this first meet and greet. Right? I mean, how many times has each and every one of us exchanged that 'first day of school!' joke that isn't particularly clever or funny, but I'll be damned if we don't say it every time?"

The crowd leavening now, loosening. Smattering of chuckles, fanning smiles, eyes ever so slightly softening.

"But even despite all the bullshit, I have to tell you: I fucking love this day. And I know I'm a lucky man, in more ways than one"—quick smile to Lila—"but it's a true privilege to be in my position. I mean, look at where we are today. Look at this view!" Obediently, the crowd turned, squinting, to the shining stretch of ocean before them. "We've gathered you here today, the film industry's finest, because this gorgeous beach house will serve as the home of our main characters, Dick and

Nicole Diver. This very terrace you're enjoying will be the location of their notoriously magical dinner parties. Before the hard work begins, we wanted to offer our gratitude and give our esteemed investors a little taste of that Montauk magic. After all, look at this fucking crowd. Each of you is first-class, and every last one of you was my first choice. And I mean that! And now here I am, about to lead us all into one of the greatest projects of our lifetime."

He placed his hands on the shoulders of a jittery field mouse of a boy wearing enormous owl-eyed spectacles.

"Rupert fucking Bradshaw. Just your average twenty-four-year-old kid. No one had any idea who the hell this guy was. But one day, fresh out of college, Rupert decides to take his first whack at a screenplay. Didn't even have a goddamn agent. But I'm telling you all now: after the world sees our adaptation of *Tender Is the Night*, the press will be calling young Rupert here the writer of his generation."

Cheers. Rupert, the color of beetroot, half stood, bowed, then pushed his glasses up his nose and began to unfold some papers to speak. Seeing this, Kurt squeezed his shoulder, muttered in his ear—and Rupert, turning an even deeper shade of purple, zipped back down to his seat.

Kurt cleared his throat. "Don't ask me how he did it, but somehow this plucky, squeaky-clean kid was able to pull a few strings and get his script sent directly to Lila. Now, on any other day, Rupert's unsolicited email would've been immediate slush pile material. But lucky for us all, a couple of years ago, our Lila was battling a period of terrible insomnia. And on one of those sleepless nights, Lila's phone lit up with an email from a name she didn't recognize, and she thought, what the hell? She'd read *Gatsby* in high school like the rest of us and liked Fitzgerald well enough. So she opened the script he'd attached, and began to read.

"Well, by the end of the film's opening sequence, which we'll hear out loud in just a few moments, Lila was hooked. She kept reading. And reading. I woke as the morning sun was filling our bedroom, and I turned to my girl to give her a kiss. And I noticed she was crying.

34

"'What's wrong?' I said.

"And Lila wiped her eyes and said to me, 'We've just been offered a masterpiece.'

"For those of you who know Lila, you know: this woman is tough. Her standards are fucking high—I'm talking a whole other stratosphere. And don't get me wrong: I'm grateful for that! She makes me a better artist. Hell, she makes me a better man. But try to get Lila to say she loves something? Near impossible. But this—this goddamn script—she was consumed by it. So I knew: this was going to be big. I canceled my morning meetings and sat down with a cup of joe. I read it start to finish, without even stopping to take a piss.

"You know the feeling you get when you come upon greatness? The one that—pardon my French, ladies—you feel in your fucking balls? I'm not talking about an intellectual feat, something that begs dissection or debate, where you finish and say, 'yeah wow, that was really smart,' or, 'so interesting, what he did there.' I'm talking about the feeling you get once or twice in a lifetime—and that's if you're lucky.

"This script did it for me. And I'm willing to bet it did it for every single one of you here, didn't it?"

A sweep of zealous nods, some eyes already streaming. (Actors, after all.)

"Now I want to talk to you all about the genius of our adaptation; but first, in order to truly appreciate its excellence? Let's talk a bit about the original novel." Kurt folded his arms, grew pensive; the audience held its breath.

"F. Scott Fitzgerald. When most of the world hears that name, they think of . . . ?"

"*Gatsby*!" a voice cried.

"*Gatsby*." Kurt nodded. "Maybe the most widely read American novel of the twentieth century. Yet while *The Great Gatsby* is the most well-known of his canon, I'm going to argue that *Tender Is the Night* is Fitzgerald's true unsung masterpiece. *Tender*'s story begins in the Roaring

Twenties, just two months after *Gatsby* was published. While *Gatsby* represents the world a younger Fitzgerald hoped it to be, *Tender* shows the world as he actually experienced it. *Gatsby* is tidy, economic, compact; *Tender* is wild and unwieldy and exceptionally ambitious. But at its core, *Tender Is the Night* remains a dark and complicated love story. . . ."

Kurt looked to Dominic Reeves: his cue. Dom stood.

"Dick Diver," Dom said, introducing his character to the ring of investors. "Brilliant, charming psychiatrist—if I do say so, myself."

The investors chuckled indulgently.

Lila stood. "Nicole," she said with a smile. "A winsome young woman with a traumatic past, hospitalized for schizophrenia."

Kurt addressed the audience. "Despite the fact that Nicole is Dr. Diver's patient, Dick and Nicole fall in love and marry, absconding to their gorgeous new home." Kurt gestured to their surroundings. "But here, Dick's practice falls by the wayside in favor of a wildly opulent social life; and the Divers soon become famous for throwing the best parties in the Hamptons. Some of their frequent guests include . . ."

Zev stood, saluted. "Abe North, genius composer and wayward alcoholic."

Another actress joined him. "Mary North, his clever, loyal wife."

Freddie stood. "And what would any party be without Tommy Barban, devastatingly handsome and extremely hetero war hero?"

The crowd laughed. Once again, Freddie had stolen the show.

Kurt smiled. "But their jazz age rhythm is soon thrown into discord when newcomers enter the scene. . . ."

Nancy stood. "Elsie Speers."

Celia joined her. "And her daughter, Rosemary, a young movie starlet."

Kurt continued. "Rosemary's allure soon proves irresistible to Dick, and—without giving away anymore plot twists—his betrayal is the catalyst for the excruciating and inevitable collapse of Dick and Nicole's marriage. But let me explain how Fitzgerald got it wrong, and how our adaptation is going to get it right."

He scanned the crowd in solemn silence. "Fitzgerald was once quoted in an interview as saying, *Our American women are leeches. They simply dominate the American man.*" He paused for effect. "This was Fitzgerald's fundamental, misguided belief about women, a belief that colored and ultimately impaired his execution of *Tender.* But in our adaptation—a period piece with a contemporary twist—we'll tackle Fitzgerald's sexism head-on, transforming *Tender Is the Night* into a story of healing and liberation.

"Now, I think all of you know how important female empowerment stories are to me, personally—"

A flat cough: Karen.

"—and in our adaptation, it's Nicole, not Dick, who has our hearts. The importance of our story is rooted in the correction of Nicole's narrative perspective—in turning the spotlight to shine upon Nicole as our hero—as she overcomes the trauma she'd endured, and ultimately reclaims herself.

"Now, the genius of the film itself will be in its execution. I'm shooting in a style that might be deemed experimental"—and here Kurt winked—" but I prefer to call it visionary. We'll be shooting primarily in long takes to enhance the inherent theatricality of the piece and create an immersive experience for our audience, so that the camera feels like another character in the room. Our extended uninterrupted sequences will pay homage to classics such as Hitchcock's *Rope*, Anderson's *Boogie Nights*, Kubrick's *The Shining*, Welles's *Touch of Evil* . . . and, if you'll permit me—Kurt Royall's *Intruder.*" He turned to the Olympus team and grinned. "I've hit it out of the park before, Olympus, and I'll be damned if I'm not going to do it again!"

The crowd whooped in support.

"So here's the reason we're making this film. With this adaptation, we reclaim Fitzgerald's most ambitious novel and create a deeply important story of female exoneration. And in the world of film, we don't have enough of those by half. I consider it a privilege to work in an industry with such a vast, far-reaching audience; and I believe it our duty to take the responsibility that comes with that seriously. Change needs to happen, and it needs to happen now. And that begins by doing what we're doing right here: insisting that progressive adaptations like *Tender* are brought to light. Groundbreaking, boundary-pushing takes on stories that deserve to be heard. So let's choose to be cultural trailblazers. Let's shatter some glass. Let's be the change we want to see."

Impassioned applause, the party rising to its feet, swollen with its own importance.

"I want to thank all of you for joining me on this journey, and for having faith in young Rupert here. Thank you to our esteemed investors, who stood behind me in the making of this passion project; to Bobby Starr and all of Olympus Pictures for their enthusiastic interest in signing on as *Tender*'s distributor—"

Around the perimeter, the ironclad line of chiseled affluence: competing colognes, slick leather, shining jewels. Thin smiles, hard eyes.

"Thank you to our incredible production team, our brilliant department heads, and our amazing crew. You guys are the backbone of this beast. You're the ones who make shit happen."

Sprouting from the background: the practical, the lusterless, who'd always faded from focus. Even in their favorite tops, their nice jeans, their modest clothing rendered them invisible. Trained for the unglamorous, thankless grind, threadbare mornings and endless nights, these were the true workhorses.

"And of course, the face of this film: my brilliant actors—icons, all of you. I am truly humbled to have you grace us with your presence. Particularly my principals: Dominic Reeves, Freddie James, Zev Winters, Lila Crayne, and the budding star whose identity will be kept secret till after we've wrapped: the exquisite, enchanting Cecelia Scott. My god, what a lineup!"

Ardent applause. The camera unremitting. And the actors smiled their practiced smiles.

"So here we all are on this perfect day in Montauk, enjoying the scent of the salt breeze, the warmth of the sun on our backs, the magnificent ocean before us. We're gathered here together at the start of a remarkable journey. Let's celebrate our collective beginning. And what better way than to hear this glorious story aloud, all in one go? We won't have the opportunity again till after we've wrapped and the film is done. Join me now in reveling in the mastery of this genius creation. Are you with me?"

The terrace erupted in full-throated, rapacious cheering. He'd done it again: he'd won them all. Ten more minutes, and they might be renouncing their lives, ripping off their clothes and founding a cult, with him their chieftain. Whatever Kurt Royall wanted, he always received.

"We'll read straight through," Kurt said—a warning. "That means no breaks, and no disruption. If you need the restroom, go quietly. I'll read any necessary direction."

Light petaling of paper in the breeze, the sound of the sweetly squeaking birds, the distant wash of waves below. Shush of fabric: legs uncrossed, then crossed again. Quiet crack of knuckles, the spectators at the edges leaning in. The actors' spines stretching to attention. Pupils blooming, mouths set. Now the moment was theirs.

Kurt assumed his place at the head, regarded his company coolly. One by one, the actors met his gaze. Only Rupert's head hung forward, the back of his neck painfully exposed, his eyes locked to the page before him as he awaited the utterance of his magnum opus.

Kurt smiled. "Let's begin."

———

Two hours later, and the read was done. Chairs were scraped as Eden announced a fifteen-minute break before the table work began, her voice all but swallowed by the sudden surge of talk. Everywhere, bodies stretching and sighing in the late-afternoon sun, members of the cast wandering out to the property's edge to take in the stunning view.

The money folk were heading inside to retrieve their bags, their jackets from the coatracks, before wending their way to their cars for the long drive back to the city. In the ether: heady adrenaline, dizzying relief. The read had been a success. The script was solid; the actors well-cast. Now the real work could begin.

"How did I do?"

Kurt turned to find Dominic, a challenge in his eye.

"Inspired as ever." Kurt clapped him on the back. "Listen, I wanted to tell you: I'm so happy you came around in the end. I'm thrilled to be working together again. In my experience, I've always found it best to leave the past in the past."

Dominic nodded. "I'm sure that's served you well." He folded his arms. "And I've simply learned not to engage in a losing battle."

Kurt hesitated a moment, removed his hand. "Smart man," he said, smiling carefully. "I could learn a lesson or two from you."

Dominic looked at him, unblinking. "Perhaps you could."

"Yo, Royall!" Zev called from across the terrace, his arm slung flirtatiously over a pretty girl. "Is this film gonna rock, or is it gonna fucking rock?"

The girl rolled her eyes, skeptical of Zev already.

Kurt grinned at them both, lifted a fist in the air, then scanned the rest of the crowd. A cluster of Russian investors lingered nearby, clearly hoping to engage him. Everyone else milling distractedly; except, Kurt noticed, for Lila and Rupert, still in their seats, huddled in private talk.

He approached them quietly from behind. She was pointing to the page before her, speaking furtively, passionately. Rupert was fingering his glasses, staring at the script—listening hard.

Kurt placed a hand on each of their shoulders and they tensed, then turned and looked up. Rupert: anxious. Lila: smile already spreading.

"What did you think?" she asked.

"I think you two are brilliant," he said. "And Rupert here is the man of the hour."

Rupert blinked, eager smile wobbling onto his face.

Lila's brow knitted. "Well, I'm glad you approve."

"My little perfectionist." Kurt shook his head. "Tell me, did I catch you giving our budding writer some notes?"

"Of course not. If I had any thoughts, I'd bring them to you." She stood on tiptoe and looped her arms about his shoulders. "I was just picking his brain about the final scene. I wanted to understand what he was imagining for one of my lines." She kissed Kurt's chin.

He grinned. "Should've known. Couldn't even wait the fifteen-minute break before getting to work.

"Careful with this one, Rupert," he said, and Rupert started, his magnified eyes blinking in quick succession. "Give her an inch, and she'll go a mile. Before you know it, she'll have you wrapped around her little finger." He turned back to Lila, kissed her. Behind them: shiver of a shuttering camera.

"Celia," Kurt called, and Celia stopped and turned. "Great work today."

"Thank you." She smiled shyly at Lila, then ducked her chin. "Mr. Royall—I'm sorry, *Kurt*—I just wanted to say: I'm so excited to be a part of this adaptation. I know this film is going to do so much for women."

"That's sweet." He stroked Lila's hair. "Listen, Celia: do you have some time this weekend? I'd like to give you some more insight into what I'm looking for in Rosemary." He glanced at Lila. "You wouldn't mind, baby—would you?"

Lila threw him a bemused smile. "Why would I mind?"

"Excellent." He looked back to Celia. "I just want to make sure we're seeing eye to eye from the start. It's such a great role, with such potential, and I really want you to do it justice." He reached out, touched her arm. "Alright?"

"I like her," Lila said after Celia had flitted off, and Kurt had pulled her back into his arms. "She'll be star material in no time."

"And in the meantime: a pain in my ass," he murmured into her mouth. "She tanked in that table read. Remind me why I hired her over Kaylee?"

Lila clicked her tongue. "Because, according to your assessment, she nailed her screen test," she said. "She's just green, is all. Give me some time with her. I'll school her real good on how to succeed in Kurt Royall's world."

"She'd better be a damn quick learner," Kurt said, and nibbled her ear. "My patience is already wearing thin."

"It's Day One, darling," Lila said, and pulled back to look him straight in the eye. "You're embarking on a project you love, remember?"

"And all because of you."

"Save it for the acceptance speech," she said, and he swatted her lightly on the ass, then turned to the group of actors pretending not to watch.

"Alright, everyone," Kurt bellowed. "Recess is over. Time to make our masterpiece."

PRIVATE NOTES OF: J. GABRIEL

Patient: L. Crayne
Date/Time: June 24, 10:30 a.m.
Session: 3

Began today's session by addressing moment last week when L reached out, held my hand. Few instances now where L testing boundaries. Needed to be dealt with directly; wanted to better understand motive behind behavior.

Told L I had the impression her feelings towards me had become bit more complicated. Was quick to normalize; said transference process of assigning one's feelings for an important figure in her life to someone else (in this case, me). Happens often in therapy (though I'd never seen it develop this early on): patient in vulnerable state, and therapist, as sole receiver, begins to hold more meaning. But was my responsibility to ensure we preserve professional boundaries of patient-therapist relationship.

L's response fascinating. Understood concept of transference, but denied presence here. And that's when L said incident as I described it never happened.

While denial not altogether surprising (L could've been embarrassed, ashamed), L's behavior was. L spoke earnestly; seemed calm, at ease. Was evident L believed she was speaking truth.

L reminded me at session's end she was rattled, upset. Said I must've noticed, because I'd been the one to reach out, hold her hand. I repeated for clarification: did L think I'd initiated?

"I don't think it. I know it. I remember, clear as day. You took my hand and squeezed it gently. And you told me I could trust you."

Before I could respond, L said: "But don't worry! I didn't take it the wrong way at all! And I'm sorry if I somehow gave the impression I did. You were trying to comfort me. You knew exactly what I needed in that moment, and it worked. You shouldn't feel uncomfortable about it; there's certainly no need to apologize."

Knew definitively my own recollection correct—my notes detailing incident only further proof—but decided not to push. Didn't want L to feel I didn't trust her.

Instead, said fascinating we both believed other to be initiator. Acknowledged how difficult, perhaps impossible, it is to ever be completely objective. Asked how our discrepancy in perspectives made her feel. L's response remarkably perceptive:

"I think the mind has ways of shifting our memories without our even knowing it. Maybe it's a subconscious way of crafting our personal narrative to justify a sequence of events and let us make sense of our own story. Maybe it's our way of editing and shaping the story we want to tell ourselves."

I said perhaps truth of what happened lay somewhere in middle. While one of us had to have initiated, he/she likely responding to something perceived in other.

Asked if this affected her trust, if I seemed less reliable as therapist.

L said if anything, made her trust me more. Appreciated my addressing uncomfortable subject. Beginning to feel she could trust me more than anyone. While magnitude of L's words dangerous, also clear opportunity to better understand motive behind transference. Asked her to elaborate.

"It's just the way I've been feeling ever since we started seeing one another. We're only three sessions in, and we've already talked about things I've never discussed with anyone. It feels like you understand me in a way no one ever has. It scares me a little."

Said vulnerability can certainly feel frightening.

"But I feel safe with you. I could never talk with anyone else about some of the things we've discussed. Don't get me wrong: I have wonderful friends, friends I'd do anything for. But when you're at my level of exposure, you learn fast: you can never trust anyone completely. Because if, for whatever reason, something happens and the relationship falls apart, your secrets can become weapons against you."

Said must be exhausting having to self-protect all the time. Asked if she confided in mother.

"Oh, I'd never talk to Mother about any of this. I couldn't. After Daddy died, she changed. It happened almost overnight: she became a different person."

Thinking again of voicemail, I asked what it was about father's death that changed Karen so dramatically; L said she didn't know. Didn't remember anything from that night.

Told L I believed she'd repressed traumatic memory of crash; but memory could, in fact, be reconstructed. Believed confronting this memory directly could help L heal. Began to suggest we try EMDR; but before I could explain technique L cut me off, said it wouldn't be any use. Had tried countless times to remember. Memory was gone.

Could tell L shutting down, so returned to subject of mother. Had L describe Karen now.

"She's much harder than she used to be, much tougher. But inside? You'd never know it from meeting her, but she's really so fragile. It's made me protective of her.

"After Daddy died, Mother moved us to California, went back to her maiden name, and threw herself into creating her own career. She was one of the few women back then who was actually able to fight her way into the boys' club of the film world. She formed this kind of impenetrable shell, to self-protect after all she'd been through. But I think she overcompensated. She used to be so soft, so vulnerable. Now, though, she's got this mantra: *Never again*, she always says. *Never again will I try to find my worth in a man.*" Shook head. "It's been a long journey, but she's better now, I think; she seems stable."

"But it's thin ice," I suggested. "You're afraid if you confided in your mother now, if you tried to lean on her, the ice would break, and you—or she—would fall through."

"That's right."

"How about Kurt?"

"Kurt? Kurt would be the last person I'd confide in."

"But he's your fiancé. I'd think he'd be the first."

"What we talk about here—my parents, my history with men, all these secrets I've buried?—they're like these terrible, ugly scars I can never erase. I work so hard to keep them hidden all the time. Kurt doesn't know, and he can never find out. I don't want him to see how broken I am."

Said L wasn't broken; perhaps some of our work together should be to build L's self-esteem. Asked what Kurt thought of L starting therapy. L said he didn't know. Hadn't told him because afraid of his reaction— knew he'd be jealous. I clarified: jealous L discussing private matters with me, not him? Said yes; but also the fact I was a man.

Despite K's apparent feminist ideology, L explained K had always been possessive, uncomfortable with L's friendships with straight men. Said in a way, flattering. I asked if it ever felt controlling. L shrugged, said Kurt wants what he wants, when he wants it.

Treading lightly, suggested possessiveness/jealousy oftentimes reactionary to something internal. Could be projection of K's inner unrest, masking deeper fear. L cut me off quickly, said she'd always been faithful. Clarified: wasn't what I meant to imply. Asked if L ever sensed Kurt might be unfaithful to her.

At this L fell silent. "He's cheating on me right now."

L explained they'd had tough time finding actress to play Rosemary— no one quite right. But then L found young unknown, and knew instantly she was the one. (Here L apologized, explained NDA—couldn't say name.) But L knew K had to be the one to "discover" her, so arranged to have her audition for K. Night of screen test, K came home late announcing he'd found their Rosemary. L could smell perfume, saw hickey on neck. Had strong hunch something had happened, but tried to convince herself she was imagining it.

Then at *Tender*'s first read last week, suspicions confirmed. Actress clearly guilty/uncomfortable. K pretended he barely knew her, even complained about her to throw L off scent. But she could tell; K was never an actor.

Believes actress slept with K to get job. Commonplace in film world—just never thought K would do it. Made L feel K wasn't the man she'd thought he was.

Asked L how she felt about working with actress now.

"Oh, I don't blame her in the least. It wasn't right, what she did. But if you're a woman in this industry, you know: transactional sex happens all the time. And it works. I just wish I hadn't put her in such an awful position, where she felt she had to do it to get the job."

Told L hardly her fault. Would've been obligated to warn actress if she'd known, but she'd had no idea. Asked if L angry with K.

"Angry?" Shook head. "No, I don't feel angry at all."

This a red flag. L's inability to access anger likely rooted in parents. "Why not? I think you'd be more than justified."

"I just feel sad." Began to tear up. "From the beginning, I couldn't believe Kurt actually wanted to be with me. I always felt I had to be perfect to keep him from leaving. And now I know: I'm not enough."

Said K's infidelity wasn't about whether L enough. Had to do with him. Asked what L planned to do.

"I can't imagine losing Kurt. I don't know what I'd do without him. And there's so much riding on our professional relationship, on the brand we've built together."

I said plenty of movie star couples had survived dramatic breakups, but L said it wasn't the same. They'd built an empire together.

47

L's anxiety over being alone further indication her relationship with K is indeed unhealthy. Clearly L feels shame around own psychology, which is why only now, in crisis, this deeper fear revealed.

Asked if L planned on confronting K.

"If I do, he'll leave me. I can't."

Told L I had ample experience working through infidelity; couples can and do recover. But must be discussed—and needs to happen now, so that if/when they commit to marriage, it's with total transparency. If K is partner L deserves, he won't run. Said if L couldn't do it on own, could have couple's session; I could guide conversation.

L panicked. "He can't know I'm seeing you. He'd get too angry."

Taken aback by intensity of reaction. "It was only a suggestion. You don't have to do anything that makes you uncomfortable."

But this clearly didn't assuage her. "You have to promise me our relationship stays a secret."

"Of course. So long as you want it to, our work together will remain completely confidential. I'm here for you, Lila. I'm not going anywhere."

L looked at me. "Do you promise?"

I hesitated.

"Promise you'll never betray me," L said, so quiet I could barely hear. "Promise you'll never break this trust."

Despite my better judgment, I nodded. "I promise."

VI

She'd told them to meet her at Metropole, her favored neighborhood haunt. Karen liked it for its optics, though the steaks weren't shabby, either.

Lila had spotted her mother right away at the head of the glossed white bar, phone glued to her ear, stilettos kicked up at an inviting angle. Around her, the evening's offerings, pretty much par for the course: recycled smear of divorced men (telltale self-tanner, slack jowls, oily pomade, straining suit), and the lingering floaters (who hadn't yet left their wives, and likely never would), testing the waters, scouting the scene. And then of course: the women, alluringly poised on stools, the men hovered behind. Their features fossilized in the clay of their foundation, hair purposefully poufed to hide the scalp's steady deforestation, silk blouse softening the slow unfolds of baby belly. Mouths strained, eyes sharp and darting. Their desperation a zest, shimmering in the air.

Lila knew her mother loved this place—loved it for how it made her feel. The mod design—chartreuse, lavender, tangerine popping against shiny white; the clean, boxy cut and sleekly recessed lighting—all as predictable as its clientele. Karen loved eavesdropping on the tedious talk, a feeble veneer for their slow and lonely countdown. She usually arrived occupied with a work call, her phone her own razor-thin shield. Never again. Never again would her mother be one of those women, curdled by their hysteria to be chosen. She held herself above it all now. She'd learned the hard way the world was ruthlessly diametrically opposed; and for the rest of her life, Karen Wolfe would be the oppressor before allowing anyone ever to oppress her again.

Now Kurt came up behind Lila, palmed her back, muttered in her ear: "Let's get this over with."

The usual bristling to attention as the patrons noticed their presence. Karen, as always, was the last to acknowledge them. She lifted a finger as they approached, then finally interrupted the voice on the other end of the line.

"Frankly, Jerry, I don't give a shit. It's in her contract. Read it for yourself if you don't believe me. I want to see prototypes that show her face, where she doesn't get drowned out by the fucking billing block. I thought you guys were professionals. These samples are sophomoric—they're a waste of both our time. Don't call me again until you have something worthwhile."

Her mother hung up with a sigh, dabbed at her upper lip, then gave a cold, toothy smile. "Hello, Kurt."

"Sorry for the delay. Lila's ring fitting took longer than expected, and then we ran into a bit of a bottleneck." He cocked his head: sure enough, outside the restaurant the paparazzi were beginning to swarm, cameras flashing in the dusk, their bodyguards steadily edging them away.

Karen pursed her lips. "Lila, darling: you look stunning as ever."

Lila kissed her on the cheek. "How are you, Mother?"

"Don't ask. I was fine before I saw the new key art. Who hired those morons?"

"I did," Kurt said, leaning an elbow onto the bar. "As you may remember, I've worked with them on the past five projects, including both Oscars. Is there a problem?"

A tight-lipped smile. "Now Kurt, I shouldn't have to remind you of Lila's contract clause. Those halfwits currently have us looking at the back of her fucking head. I'm no expert, but how in the name of god could that possibly be marketing gold?"

"I'm not familiar with Lila's contract," Kurt said, "but I do trust our team. And I thought the shot was of both Lila and Dom in profile."

"Oh sure, if by seeing the tip of her nose you call that profile." Karen took an easy sip of her martini—seemed to be enjoying herself immensely. "I don't give a flying fuck about Dom, but as Lila's manager, I'll remind you it's stipulated in her contract that the subject of the key art must be my daughter's face. And as executive producer of an adaptation purportedly about female empowerment, I'll add my two cents that the current mockup, which has Lila demurely turning away, is a fucking travesty. But let's not mix business and pleasure, shall we? Especially in public." Her eyes snapped to the nearby oglers; Karen glared at them till they looked away. "God, they've packed us in like sardines. Shall we get our table?"

They were led to Karen's usual spot, a tucked-away corner setting; and for Lila and Kurt's benefit, the neighboring tables were kept empty, despite the cluster of patrons waiting to be seated.

"Now Lila," Karen said once they'd settled, "how are you? Tell me everything."

"I'm great." She smiled. "I'm thrilled we've started shooting."

"Dom's solo scenes, right? Were you there to watch?"

Kurt glanced at Lila. "She watched the dailies."

Karen's eyes snapped to her daughter. "I'm surprised you didn't want to be present."

"Of course Lila's welcome on set whenever she likes," Kurt said, setting down his menu. "But I think I can handle the directing, don't you, Karen?" He put a hand over Lila's. "We have a very unified vision."

Karen gave a hard smile. "I'm sure."

"Bobby Starr says hi, by the way. Said he didn't catch you at the industry read, and he owes you a drink." Kurt shook his head. "I fucking love that guy."

"Starr's an asshole," Karen said, and summoned a nearby waitress, who started violently, eyes glued to Lila.

"Good evening, folks," she said. "How are you tonight?"

"We're fine, sweetie," Karen said. "No need to be nervous. She doesn't bite."

The girl tomatoed. "Oh, I'm sorry. I didn't mean—"

In a blink, Lila snapped to attention, saving the girl from her mother's talons. She turned in her seat, rolled her eyes playfully. "I'm sorry, she's just giving you a hard time. How are you?"

"I'm . . . um . . ." The question had seemed to stump the poor girl. "Oh lord," she said finally. "Oh jesus. I am such a fan."

"You're new, aren't you," Karen said, eyes narrow.

The girl nodded. "It's my third day."

"Congratulations! Hey, I'll tell you what," Lila said, leaning in and touching her arm. "If you could do me a favor and keep everyone from snapping pictures, I'd be happy to take a photo with you before we go. Could you do that for me?"

"Really? That'd be amazing! Definitely. I'll watch like a hawk. I mean, I won't watch *you* like a hawk—oh god—"

"Fantastic," Lila cut in with a conspiratorial grin. "Man, I am dying for a drink. Would you mind making me a vodka soda with some muddled mint and extra lime? Mother, what'll you have?"

Karen slapped her menu onto the table. "Another martini. Tell Catalina when I say extra dirty, I mean *filthy*."

"Cocktails before wine?" Kurt said. "I'll have a Bulleit. Neat. And why don't you uncork this Carménère for us now, give it a bit of time to open up? I imagine it'll go quite well with our filets—rare, please."

"Excellent choice, Mr. Royall," the girl breathed. "I'll be right back with those drinks."

"I can't understand why you like this place," Kurt said once she'd gone, glancing around at the sea of gawking eyes. "Always the same boring Upper East Side crowd. It's such a depressing old watering hole."

"Perfect for putting a tired mare like me out to pasture. Right, Kurt?" Karen winked. "Oh, indulge me and my philistine tastes. It's my guilty pleasure. Following the mating rituals of this crowd is like watching the unfolding of a real-life soap opera. Plus, when you two are here, I feel like the center of small-town gossip." She pouted her lips, skin crinkling like papier-mâché. "Besides, I believe you owe me. Considering I wasn't invited to my own daughter's engagement dinner."

"Now Mother, you know that was Kurt's birthday dinner. The proposal was impulsive."

Karen honked. "Impulsive, my ass. I know you, Lila: if you are one thing, darling, you are deliberate. There isn't a spontaneous bone in that beautiful little body of yours."

Lila ignored the comment. "We just picked up my engagement ring. Don't you want to see it?"

Karen groaned. "I can't believe after all we went through with your father that you're still naïve enough to believe in marriage. And now there's a ring? What are you, chattel? Why don't we talk dowries while we're at it?"

Kurt let out an incredulous laugh.

"Mother," Lila said, eyes narrowing, "just because you don't believe in marriage anymore doesn't mean I have to renounce it, too, does it?"

"Oh, fine." Karen rolled her eyes, snatched her daughter's wrist from under the table. "Let's see the goddamn ring."

For a moment, the three of them fell silent and gazed at the ring: its striking marquise cut, the diamond a sharp, bladelike bolt against her skin.

Karen dropped her daughter's hand with a cursory pat. "Well, it's you, alright," she sighed. "It's definitely you."

Mother and daughter eyed one another in a silent standoff; and then at once they both cracked and broke into uncontrollable laughter. Karen threw back her head, her molars shining deep in the pit of her mouth.

Kurt looked between the two women, perplexed. "Come on, Karen," he said as the waitress returned with their drinks. "Aren't you going to congratulate us?"

"Oh my goodness." The waitress' eyes were riveted to Lila's hand. "Is that the ring?"

"No," Karen said, wiping away her tears. "It's my newly bleached anus." And when even this elicited no response, moaned, "For the love of god, *please* may I have my martini *now*?"

At this the girl seemed to stutter back to consciousness, and began to distribute the cocktails as the women tried to control themselves.

"How about a toast?" Kurt prompted.

"Oh for fuck's sake," Karen said. "Let me get some liquid courage first." She drained half her martini, then lifted the glass. "To my baby." And at last, Karen began to soften. "The most meticulous little architect of her own design—just like her mother." Then she lifted Lila's hand and kissed the diamond, smearing it red. "May every last one of your dreams come true."

———

"What a fucking cunt."

Lila turned. Kurt was flipping his phone aggressively in his palm, staring out the car window as the streets rolled slowly to cobblestone. The ropy silhouette of his neck pulsed in the darkness.

"Who?"

"Your mother, that's who." Kurt pressed a knuckle to his upper lip and blew out his breath, telltale signal he was descending into one of his moods.

Dinner had left them both the worse for wear. As always when the two of them shared a meal with Karen, they'd sozzled themselves silly in a desperate attempt to numb the nail-on-chalkboard tension; but two bottles of wine had only further lubricated Karen into reprising her outspoken opinions about marriage and her downright contempt for all straight males (her future son-in-law no exception). By evening's end, she'd drunkenly announced she'd rather be stabbed with her own steak knife than attend their wedding, then closed with a

54

final colorful threat to Kurt about fixing the fucking key art. Even for Karen, it was a lot.

"Jerry's work is amazing," Kurt said now. "Does it really say that in your contract? That we need to see your face?"

Lila twisted her ring. "I'm not sure."

Kurt slammed his phone onto the leather between them; picked it up, threw it down again. "I mean, seriously? We're supposed to go back to the drawing board, scrap his fantastic final draft, so that you can have your vanity shot? Who fucking does that?"

A tiny shrug. "Mother."

The car pulled to a stop in front of their home. Kurt opened his door and stepped out, then slammed it shut as Lila was scooting to his side. She blinked, then turned to the driver.

"Night, Daniel," she said, and reopened the door. Kurt was already at their building, punching in the passcode.

"Night, Miss Crayne," Daniel nodded, and Lila stepped out into the night and towards her fuming fiancé, who was propping the door with his foot.

They rode the elevator in silence; and as soon as its doors opened directly into their living room and the elevator had closed behind them, Kurt turned to her, eyes cold as scales.

"What did you tell her?"

Lila blinked, a single shoe hooked onto a finger as she balanced delicately on her remaining heel. "What are you talking about?"

"Don't play dumb, Lila."

"Did I do something to upset you?"

Kurt laced his hands on top of his head and turned to the Hudson, glimmering in the moonlight.

"Why don't I get you a nightcap? Tonight was tough on you." Lila tiptoed across the cool concrete floor to the bar, placed a king cube into crystal, then poured a few fingers of Japanese whiskey.

She met him at the sliding glass door, his hand braced on the metal frame.

"Want to go out on the balcony?" she asked, offering up the drink.

He took it from her, drained the glass. "Just give me a straight answer. How much have you told your mother about me? About us?"

"Kurt." Lila touched his shoulder, but he shrugged her hand away. She swallowed, then turned and sank into the couch. "She only knows what everyone knows; what's obvious to the whole world over."

"What the hell is that supposed to mean?" He took a step towards her; she shrank into the cushions.

"You're scaring me."

"God dammit, Lila!" Kurt turned and slammed the doorframe, the glass rattling in its bed. "What is it this time? We got the apartment, we're making the movie, we started our own production company—we're even getting married, for Christ's sake! What more could you possibly want?"

"Nothing!" Tears pricked the corners of her eyes. "I'm not asking for anything."

He cast his glass onto a table, the crystal sliding dangerously close to the edge. "Then why does it feel like no matter what I give you, it's never fucking enough?"

"Please—"

"No more mind games." He glared at her. "What does your mother have against me? It's abundantly clear she wishes I were dead. So you tell me: how much does Karen know?"

Lila drew her knees to her chest, spoke slowly. "She knows we're a franchise, that we've woven our careers together, and because of that, I'm dependent on you. As my manager, as a woman, as my mother: she hates that arrangement. None of this is about you. Mother simply blames you for being a man. You know it all goes back to my father."

"Ah yes. God forbid we go a day without mentioning your abusive father." Kurt rolled his eyes, but his anger had already begun to thaw. "So all that bullshit she pulled tonight was just because your mother's a feminist psycho. She hates me for having a dick, and hates you for wanting it."

She hesitated, then lifted herself from the couch with a timid smile. "How did you know I wanted it?"

Despite himself, he chuckled. "You're a dirty little bitch, aren't you?"

"Am I?" Her fingers reached for the lip of her dress. Slowly, she pulled it over her head, stood nearly naked in the center of the room but for a few bits of ribbon, small patch of lace. "Then why don't you give me what I deserve?"

Once more, this shadowy dance. They were finding their way back now, each pulling darkly into the other. Soon, very soon, they might be alright again.

The slightest smile across his lips, his eyes deepening with possibility. "Put your heels back on. Go to the balcony."

She slid open the glass door, stepped into the night. Far below, across the way: the woolly glow of streetlamps warming the boardwalk, slow sway of the water. A few wanderers in the distance. Inside, Kurt cut the lights, rendering them invisible.

He stepped behind her, watched as she leaned forward onto the rail. The deft flick of a belt unbuckled, muted rip of a zipper. She shivered as a single knuckle skipped down the bolt of her spine.

"Kurt?" She hesitated, deliberated. Then devised a different path.

"Pretend I'm someone else," she whispered. "Someone you hardly know. Someone you want."

He murmured his assent, throat thick with desire. Out here in the darkness, she could be anyone. The snaking lines of her back anonymous, her heels turning her taller. Her hair, spun into a knot, she now pulled loose and free—girlish (she knew he'd always liked them young). He reached for her hips.

And when he shoved himself inside her, the balcony rail shivering with the force of it, she looked out at the water, at the streetlights that blurred as her eyes grew wet, at the dull concrete, at the sleepless cars flying past unaware. She felt her insides warm as Kurt recast her as that younger, tender incarnation; and her thoughts folded back to the easy comfort of the past, when this had been enough, when this thrilling, all-consuming reverie was all she could ever wish for. He grunted deep, sound splitting to syllable at last when he climaxed, grabbing her throat and twisting her ear to his mouth, consummating the fantasy as he uttered the name of that enigmatic other woman—the name that Lila had already known.

PRIVATE NOTES OF: J. GABRIEL

Patient: L. Crayne
Date/Time: July 1, 10:30 a.m.
Session: 4

Malapropos start. L running late (missed almost entire session), which Maggie took as opportunity to discuss wedding planning. Unfortunately, L walked in on us mid-tiff. Mags starstruck by L—ignored protocol and allowed L to engage. M told L we live upstairs (L apparently our neighbor: home few blocks away), that she's an artist, studio in back. When L asked to see her work, M mentioned upcoming gallery launch. Eventually I had to ask M outright to leave.

L flung herself onto couch. "God, she seems amazing. She's so pretty! I would kill to look like that."

When I laughed politely: "I'm serious. She's so . . . soft. Sometimes I feel like this career has cleaved my womanhood right out of me."

Was curious about fascination with my fiancée; if Maggie (by extension) another manifestation of L's transference. And wondered at motives: hoping I'd protest, insist L beautiful? Was L jealous? And a veiled dig at M for not aligning with popular standards, against which L's appearance exalted?

L continued: sometimes wished she could be someone like M. Life so much easier. (Again—product of transference, as M my fiancée? Or masked insult to M's ordinariness?)

Steered conversation back to L's life. Asked how she was.

Panic attacks almost every night this past week. Textbook case: cold, dizzy, couldn't breathe, felt like suffocating/drowning. When young, thought it was heart attack. This new information. I asked about attacks in childhood.

Common when father alive. In recent years rare; but now suddenly more frequent.

Asked if L knew trigger. L said at times obvious; but sometimes she'll feel normal, even good, and attack will come suddenly.

Asked if she'd taken medication in past. Tried SSRIs (Prozac, Zoloft), but didn't help (nausea, insomnia). Asked me about benzodiazepines. Wanted something for emergencies.

Explained benzodiazepines tricky: highly addictive. Can't be used regularly or long-term. Drugs a quick fix; real cure therapy. Prescribed trial dosage of Klonopin for emergency use only.

At this, L relaxed visibly. Noticed L still wearing jacket—odd, as my AC broken, extremely humid. Asked if she wanted to take it off. L hesitated, then complied.

L had clearly concealed well with makeup and jewelry, but underneath, chest/arms covered in terrible bruises and scabs.

Asked if something L wanted to tell me. At first, L feigned confusion. When I asked more directly, L dismissed bruises, said she hurt herself.

"It was stupid. We have these concrete steps in our apartment that lead up to our bedroom. It was late at night. I was going down to the kitchen for some water, and I'd had a bit too much to drink. I missed a step and fell."

Asked if Kurt had anything to do with it.

L shook head, fear in eyes.

Said didn't think L being honest with me. Pointed to fingerprint marks on neck, asked where they came from.

L defensive. Said she'd told everything there was to tell, then fell silent, avoided my eyes. We'd reached impasse.

At this point, employed tactic that was perhaps questionable, but—given gravity of situation—knew it would be effective. Threatened to end our work together.

I stood, said we should end for the day. Wouldn't bill for session, but told L to give serious thought, decide whether to tell truth and move forward, or part ways.

L started to cry. Said she'd tell me everything; our relationship too important to her. Begged me not to drop her. I offered tissues, waited until she calmed. Then asked her to tell real story.

Happened last Thursday. Dinner with mother to celebrate engagement. L nervous beforehand: Kurt and Karen don't get along.

"After Daddy, Mother stopped trusting all men—Kurt included. And Kurt knows how much her opinion means to me, how much I value her approval. I think he feels threatened.

"Afterwards, he was in a terrible mood. He gets like that sometimes, when he's under a lot of pressure. But I thought I could maybe snap him out of it. So we . . . god, this is so embarrassing. Well, Kurt and I . . . . sometimes our sex life is a little . . . unorthodox?"

Asked L to elaborate.

"Oh god. I don't ever talk about this kind of stuff. But I guess . . . if you think it's important?" Inhaled. "Kurt likes to get aggressive. And he likes it when I'm, well . . . submissive. When I play the part."

This not surprising—maps directly into L's understanding of sex from parents' modeling.

"He gets pretty rough. He talks down to me. And he has me do things, demeaning things, in places we might be seen or even caught."

Asked if she enjoyed it.

"Of course!" This also unsurprising: likely in denial, convinced she enjoyed power imbalance—familiar echo of parent dynamic.

"It's just the way sex has always been with him. The first time we were together . . ." Shook head, forced smile. "The point is, on Thursday night he was really aggressive. And I went with it, like I always do—only this time, I couldn't stop thinking about you."

"About me?"

"I mean the conversation we'd had—about the actress he'd slept with. I kept thinking about how you'd told me I needed to confront him. And as it was happening, I began to feel like maybe this wasn't okay. Maybe I did want to talk to him about it. So I waited until he . . . you know . . . and I thought okay, now he's feeling better. Calmer. So afterwards as we were getting into bed, I asked if he'd slept with her. But he denied it."

"He lied to you."

Nodded.

"Then what happened?"

"He got really angry. Said he couldn't believe I'd accuse him of something like that."

"That often happens when someone is feeling guilty. He was gaslighting you."

"And I just stayed quiet, because all I could think was: but I know it's true. And: this isn't the Kurt I thought I knew. I guess I was hoping, in spite of everything, that if I confronted him he'd break down and apologize, beg my forgiveness. Promise it would never happen again. But lying to my face? And his rage . . .

"I guess he didn't like how quiet I'd gotten—it seemed like it made him even angrier. He started yelling about how ungrateful I am. That I'm this jealous, possessive woman who's imagining things. I don't really remember what happened next—I think maybe I blocked it out. I just remember suddenly his hands were on me. He started shaking me, trying to get me to respond. But I wasn't saying anything. Maybe I was crying? I just remember feeling numb. And then his hand grabbed my throat—right here—and that's when I got really frightened. I took a step back—I guess I didn't realize I was so near the edge. I stepped off the top stair, and I fell backwards.

"He didn't push me. He wasn't trying to hurt me. It was just a . . . a terrible mistake. I fell, and I guess I must've been knocked unconscious. When I woke up, Kurt had me in his arms. He was holding my head, saying how sorry he was. Acting exactly the way I'd hoped he would. Only now it was too late."

"Lila, you could've gotten seriously hurt."

"No, I was fine, really. I was bruised and a bit bloody, but I'm better now. Just sore." L put head in hands. "And humiliated."

"Lila, what Kurt did to you—the fact that he grabbed your neck, tried to choke you? That's a very dangerous sign. You know that what he did was abuse, right?"

L started to protest, then stopped. "I know."

She'd acknowledged Kurt as abuser: critical first step. Thanked L for trusting me, reaffirmed position as ally.

Wrapped arms around herself. "I keep telling myself this can't be happening. I thought I knew where my life was going. I thought I knew the man I was marrying. And now . . . I feel so trapped."

"I'll help you get out of this, Lila. I know you feel like you can't escape, but you can. You must."

L's eyes locked to mine. And for flicker of a moment, so brief I might've imagined it, thought I saw something new in L's expression: love.

VIII

"Alright, everyone, we're getting ready for the long take, starting with the Dick/Rosemary bedroom scene. That means closed set: skeleton crew only. Everyone else: thank you very much, you're wrapped for the day." Eden again: headphones as headband, glasses like goggles, bomber jacket zipped to chin. Ready for the big dive.

Lila wrapped her character's period dress around her body, the sash cinched tight as a garrote, then squeezed her way past exiting extraneous crew as she made her way down the paneled hallway of the Plaza Hotel and into the Fitzgerald Suite, where the final sequence of the day would begin.

The set was immaculate, a sharp deco design captured in black and white, with its kaleidoscopic rug and folded roman shades, its Charleston Pearl walls and studded, stretched leather, shining planetary chandeliers revolving overhead. At the mirrored minibar, Lila noticed a hidden homage: an ironed handkerchief with the embroidered initials *JG* looped within a daisy design. She fingered it delicately, then slipped it into her pocket.

As the crew buzzed around her, she moved into the sitting room, lingering at the corner that rounded into the bedroom. On the far side of the bed—the only bit of color in an otherwise achromatic world—Celia perched in a dropped-waist, light-pink dress, mouthing her lines to herself, fingers fiddling in her lap. Lila's heart sank as she watched Kurt approach, his palm sliding slowly down her back. Celia shivered, shoulders rising, then met his gaze with a nervous smile.

Behind her, someone studied and sprayed Lila's locks, fluffing and twisting the tendrils; then Eden squeezed past, clipboard clutched to her chest, and made her way to Kurt, said something under her breath. He muttered a response, then waved her away and sat down beside Celia, his hand swirling around the tiny knob of her shoulder.

"Let me look at you, lovey." Her makeup girl, Nadia: dark eyes, milk skin, big, fleshy fingers. She tilted Lila's chin, inspecting, and hummed a little with satisfaction. "Radiant—with just the slightest touch of trauma."

Kurt seemed suddenly to sense Lila's presence and turned, caught her eye. He clapped Celia on the shoulder, hoisted himself off the bed. "Sweetheart," he said, gesturing to the set. "What do you think?"

"It's perfect." She nodded to Celia, watching them quietly. "Celia looks gorgeous, doesn't she?"

His eyes flicked to Celia, then back to her. "Why don't you hang in the master suite? We won't need you for a while. Eden will cue you when it's time."

"I'd like to watch rehearsal, at least." She smiled. "If that's alright."

"But we got you a monitor in the master—"

"I know, but this scene is so important; and I want to watch your genius in action. I'll just tuck into that corner over there," she said when he began to object. "You won't even notice me."

He blinked, then gave a sharp nod. "Alright." He sighed as his eyes made their way down her body. "As usual, we're waiting on fucking Sound, so I'm going to have the actors run through the cuts once more."

Her eyes narrowed. "The cuts?"

"I made some cuts last night." He shook his head. "The scene wasn't working. Rupert's made Dick into too much of a predator."

"Does Rupert know?"

"We broke him for the day," he said, lifting a hand in dismissal. "And besides, it's a closed set."

She folded her arms, spoke softly. "Kurt, Rupert should be here."

A flash of annoyance across his face; but he quickly recovered. "I'll see if someone can get him back," he said, and glanced at Eden, who nodded, then headed out.

"Why hello, Miss Crayne." Dom wrapped Lila in a hug. "Will you be joining us? You know I love your company, but your addition to this scene might change the plot a bit."

"I'll make myself completely invisible, I promise," Lila said. "You won't even know I'm here." He followed her eyes to Celia, gazing anxiously after Kurt.

Dom sighed. "Don't worry, honey. She won't last."

Lila blinked, forced a smile, then moved to the farthest corner as Kurt lifted his voice to address the room.

"Alright, in case anyone missed the memo, this is a long take. That means no cutting until we're out of the bathroom scene at the end. Let's recap one final time, just to make sure we're all on the same page.

"We start with the Dick/Rosemary seduction scene, here in Rosemary's room. Then Abe and Peterson interrupt—can someone make sure Zev and Blake are ready by the time we get to them? We follow all four actors across the hall to the Divers' suite for their next scene. Afterwards, Peterson exits; then Abe follows. When Rosemary leaves, we follow her back here to her room, where she finds Peterson's murdered body—let's make sure to practice swapping these sheets out for the bloodied doubles so we nail the timing, alright? We continue on Rosemary as she runs back to Dick's suite, where Nicole has just come home; and then we shift focus to trail Dick for the rest of the scene—through hiding the evidence, removing the body, his exchange with the hotel manager—all the way until the end, when Dick returns to his suite and finds Nicole in the bathroom with the bloody sheets, schizophrenic, because she believes the blood came from Rosemary's stolen virginity."

Their DP Mike snickered, and Kurt's eyes snapped over to him.

"I love you, man," Mike said, shaking his head, "but this sequence sounds fucking insane. Are you really telling me that's all in the book?"

"It's all in the book," he said crisply, then looked around the room in challenge. "Any other questions?"

No response.

"Alright, then. While we're waiting, let's step through the new cuts once more. We'll keep moving forward with the scene until Sound is ready. Can we have quiet on set?"

Lila glanced at Celia and smiled. Celia blinked, then looked away.

"So we'll start on you, Dom, as you shut the door behind you. Celia, I want you in the center of the room, right at that mark there. Sure, use that armchair as a visual." He walked over and placed his hands on her shoulders, and Celia started at his touch. "We're going to hit you with that sidelight over there—see it?—so I really need your placement to be specific. Tilt your chin up this way." He took her face and lifted, his finger trailing the line of her jaw. A light cough: Lila turned to catch Nadia and Eden exchange a knowing glance.

"There," he said. "Remember that, alright? Now let's walk through the dialogue, shall we? Go ahead."

"*Take me*," Celia whispered.

Dom shook his head, amused. "*Take you where?*"

Celia hesitated.

"We blocked this yesterday, remember? Now you move into him." Kurt's hand at the small of her back, encouraging her forward. "And touch him. That's right. Rosemary's precocious, isn't she? So use these lines to really flirt. Continue with the scene."

"*Go on*," Celia said, her voice quivering. "*Oh, please go on, whatever they do. I don't care if I don't like it—I never expected to—I've always hated to think about it but now I don't. I want you to.*"

"Love that cross, Dom. Brilliant," Kurt said. "That mark on the floor is a good place to stop."

Lila tensed as she watched Kurt turn again to Celia. "Remember the new direction with these edits. Rosemary isn't afraid here—she's empowered. I want to see you take control. You want him, don't you? So really go after him." He nodded to Dom to continue with the scene.

"*Have you thought about how much it would hurt Nicole?*" Dom said.

"You don't give a shit about Nicole," Kurt whispered to Celia. "Seduce him into forgetting her and thinking only of you."

Celia's eyes flicked to Lila, then back to Dom. "*She won't know—this won't have anything to do with her.*"

Dom leaned against the desk chair. "*There's the fact that I love Nicole.*"

"I need you to work harder, Celia," Kurt said, his patience fraying. "I need you to make yourself irresistible to him." Again he took her by the shoulders and inched her forward—and again, she glanced at Lila.

"Jesus Christ," Kurt groaned. "Celia, honey, I know this is your first film, but you can't break character," he said, his expression incredulous. "You have to pretend there's no one else here except the two of you. The only person you're allowed to look at is . . . ?" He waited until Celia, humiliated, pointed to Dom. Lila closed her eyes.

"Good. Now keep going. And take another step towards him. Get good and close. Work that charm. I've seen you do it. I know you can . . ."

"*But you can love more than just one person, can't you?*" she said softly. "*Like I love Mother and I love you—more. I love you more now.*"

The hotel door banged open, and Rupert skittered in, panting. In his haste, he'd managed to misbutton his cardigan, so that one side bunched like a noose about his neck.

"I'm back!" he breathed, magnified eyes darting.

"Ah, just the man we were looking for," Kurt said with a tight smile.

"Um, Kurt?" Rupert lifted the wilted pages gripped in his fist. "Did I miss something? I didn't okay these cuts."

Kurt sighed, then threw an arm around Dom's shoulders. Dom tensed, then glanced at Kurt warily.

"It's just these lines, man," Kurt said. "We think they make Dick come off as manipulative, and, well . . . kind of a pedophile. He's pulling some serious reverse psychology on this vulnerable young girl to get her into bed with him."

Rupert blinked, pushed up his glasses. "But all those lines are taken straight from the book."

"Sure, but this is an adaptation, right? That grants *you* the freedom to change it. Zhuzh it up a bit," Kurt said, folding his arms. "The whole point of what we're doing here is to give the women of this story more agency, right? So your script needs to reflect that. Rosemary needs to take the reins. She needs to be the driver of this scene."

Rupert wavered, glanced at Lila.

Kurt raised his brow. "What?"

Lila inhaled. "I know this isn't my place . . ."

"No, it isn't," Kurt said.

". . . but I think the lines should remain as Rupert wrote them," she continued carefully. "The lines that were cut show our audience that Rosemary is in fact being taken advantage of here."

"You're making it out to be black and white, and it isn't," Kurt said. "The scene's genius is that it remains in the grey area. Those lines were working against us. They vilify Dick and flatten the narrative."

"They're also crucial to their dynamic," she insisted. "As a psychologist, Dick can't help but be drawn to the bird with a broken wing, to act both as lover and nurturer. Rosemary's innocence, her vulnerability, and Dick's need to be a savior of women—it's his Achilles' heel—his hamartia." She looked to Dom. "Right?"

Dom blinked, nodded.

"And the nature of the affair—the father-daughter undercurrent—is precisely what's so gutting for Nicole. It can't be swept under the rug."

Still Kurt shook his head. "But that version—the version you're advocating for—strips Rosemary of her power. It makes her into a voiceless victim. *She* should be pursuing *him*—"

SWEET FURY

"But Kurt: she's a *child*." Lila shook her head. "And because of that—not to mention the fact that he's married—Dick has to be held accountable."

"Look at the original text. Her first goddamn line. *Take me*, she says. Rosemary wants him, and it's only because she continues to pursue him that the affair comes to pass. Right?" He turned to Celia, eyes blazing, demanding a response.

Celia looked back and forth between Kurt and Lila, terrified. At last, she spoke.

"She might initially think she holds the power," Celia said slowly. "But she's so young. She doesn't fully understand her situation. And when she does . . . it's too late." She turned to Lila. "She realizes she never had any power at all."

The room was still, its collective breath suspended. Then, almost imperceptibly, Kurt nodded.

"Restore the lines," he said, then raised his voice to address the room. "We'll revert back to the script as it was. Let's continue to push forward. Actors, do you need to look at the pages to review?"

Dom glared at Kurt, then shook his head and reassumed his position at the leather desk; but for a moment Celia remained, watching as Rupert edged his way to Lila's side.

"From: *I'm afraid I'm in love with you*," Kurt prompted, planting himself next to Celia once more.

"*I'm afraid I'm in love with you*," Dom murmured, "*and that's not the best thing that could happen*."

"Kiss her neck, Dom," Kurt said, knuckle pressed to his upper lip.

Dom leaned in to kiss her, and Celia flinched involuntarily. He hesitated, glanced at Kurt, but Kurt motioned for him to continue. Lila folded her arms, sucked in her breath.

"*I'm in an extraordinary condition about you*," Dom said. "*When a child can disturb a middle-aged gent—things get difficult*."

"Now stroke his ego here, Celia. And reach out and touch his face,"

70

Kurt added. "I want to see your little hand on his cheek." Somewhere in the room, a crew member stifled a snicker.

"*You're not middle-aged, Dick,*" Celia whispered. "*You're the youngest person in the world.*"

"Take her by the hand and lead her to the bed."

"*Come and sit on my lap close to me,*" Dom said, "*and let me see about your lovely mouth.*"

"Move onto his lap, Celia. No, Jesus—not like that. Stop. Just stop. Dom, let me do it."

Dom blinked. "What?"

"Just move," Kurt said. "I'll show you exactly what I want."

The room was silent. Lila watched as Dom hesitated, brow furrowed, then stepped aside. Celia hugged herself, eyes wide.

"Watch carefully, Crayne." A tight, pointed smile. "And tell me if you think this is what our adaptation really *wants.*"

Kurt assumed Dom's place on the bed, then took Celia's hand and pulled, and she wobbled onto his lap.

Slowly, delicately, Kurt stroked Celia's lips with the tips of his fingers, her shoulders rising.

"Now reach up and play with my lapels," he murmured; reluctantly, she obeyed. "Good girl."

He smiled at her secretively, leaned in as though to kiss her—but Celia turned away with a sudden gasp, her eyes locking desperately onto Lila's.

"Christ, Celia!" Kurt leapt from the bed. "How many times do I have to tell you: do not look at Lila!"

Everyone froze as the two women turned to one another: Celia terrified, Lila's expression inscrutable.

"I'm sorry," Celia said in a tiny voice. "I can't—"

"I don't want to hear excuses. I just want you to do your job," Kurt said, jaw tight.

Celia's mouth opened. "But—"

"It's in Lila's contract to be on set at all times," Kurt said. "So you need to figure out how to handle it, or we'll find someone else who can."

"Please . . ." Celia begged, tears in her eyes, and Kurt turned away with an incredulous bark.

"I wonder if I could speak to Celia alone?" Lila asked.

Everyone turned to look at her.

"Just for a minute," she said quickly. "I don't mean to hold us up, but I think I might be able to help." Kurt looked from Lila to Celia, then shrugged.

"One minute," he said.

She smiled at Celia, and tilted her head to suggest they find someplace private, then walked out into the hallway littered with tangled black cords, folded tripods, stacks of reflectors, stagnant cups of half-drunk coffee. Celia followed, wiping at her eyes.

"Lila, I can't—"

Lila quickly turned to face her, then touched the microphone pinned into her costume: a warning. "First I just want to say: your performance is incredible."

Celia blinked.

"I mean it," she continued. "I know everyone's been giving you a hard time because it's your first film, and you're learning on the job; but really, the innocence you bring is exactly right. I can't take my eyes off you, Celia. Honestly, I feel like I'm learning so much from you."

She reached out and took Celia's hand in her own.

"I know my presence in there is a bit awkward. And I know Kurt can be tough . . ."

"He's a bully!" Celia blurted. "I don't think I can take it anymore—"

Lila shook her head. "I get it—I do. But that's just how he is," she said softly. "It's how he gets when he's working on something he cares about. And we all really care about this project. I know *I* do." She looked meaningfully at Celia. "And I think you do, too."

"Of course!" Celia whispered. "You know I do."

Lila smiled. "Just try not to let him get to you so much, alright? And listen to your instincts. Because I know you understand Rosemary better than any of us. All you have to do is react honestly in the moment, and trust that what you bring naturally to the role is exactly right."

Celia looked up, hesitated.

"And as far as my being there," Lila added. "Why don't you let it help you? Raise the stakes? Because Rosemary loves Nicole, too, right? And she feels terribly guilty for what she's doing to her." Lila tilted her head, smiled. "Doesn't she?"

Celia nodded, chin wobbling, and Lila opened her arms, hugged her tightly.

"Above all, remember why we're making this film—who it's for, in the end." Lila wiped a bit of smudged mascara from her cheek, and Celia met her gaze.

"Alright," Lila whispered, then squeezed her hand. "Let's go nail this scene."

————

Back in the Fitzgerald Suite, Kurt had coopted Mike's headphones, his arms folded as he listened intently. When he saw them reenter, he pulled them down around his neck and looked to Lila.

"We're ready," she said, then squeezed Celia's hand before returning to the corner.

He cleared his throat. "Alright, let's pick up from where we left off. You're on Dom's lap, Celia."

The actors took their places, and the room fell hush. Celia glanced at Lila, then ducked her chin and returned her focus to Dom.

Hesitantly, she touched Dom's lapels, then reached up to his face. Kurt turned and looked at Lila, nodded in approval, then returned his focus to the actors.

Dom kissed her suddenly, and Celia remained motionless, startled, as though she'd never been kissed before, as though she didn't know how. She was fresh and honest, instinctive and raw. She was perfect.

"*Oh, we're such actors—you and I,*" she breathed.

He kissed her again, more urgently; and this time Celia returned the kiss. Together, they relaxed back onto the bed, their kissing growing more passionate.

"Do we have Zev and Blake for their entrance?" Kurt called.

"Shit," Eden said, then pushed swiftly out the door to find them, muttering panicked orders through her headphones. The rest of the crew relaxed, the stillness broken as they resumed their prep.

Kurt walked over to Lila, who kissed him on the cheek. "You heard?" she whispered, subtly touching her mic.

"Every word," he murmured, his lips brushing her ear. "Impressive work, Crayne."

Lila shook her head. "I just told her what she needed to hear."

They looked at one another, smiled; and then Zev and Blake ran into the room. "I'll let you get back to it," she said. "I'm going to get ready for my entrance."

"Alright, we have our actors. Let's keep going," Kurt boomed.

On her way out, Lila caught Rupert's eye, nodded for him to follow. She walked down to the end of the hallway and rounded a corner, then pulled out her mic pack, switched it off. Moments later, Rupert appeared, looking sheepish.

"What happened back there?" she whispered. "Where were you?"

Rupert fingered his glasses, avoided her eyes. "It was a closed set. I was told to stay away."

"You're the *writer*," Lila insisted. "It's in your contract: you have a right to be there. And you always should be."

They fell silent as the rehearsed sequence moved out to the hall: actors, camera, and crew traveled slowly across the hallway to the room functioning as Dick and Nicole's suite.

"Zev and Blake, you guys follow behind Dom, and we'll follow you,"

Kurt said, his hand on Mike's shoulder. "Celia, you follow the camera, but—no! Don't shut the door—that's important. Leave it open. Let us lead—we're going to stay on you as you cross the hall. Follow us in, then shut the door behind you." The door to the Divers' suite closed, and the muffled sounds of dialogue continued.

"Listen," Lila said, turning back to Rupert. "Do you understand what happened back there? Kurt's convinced that a feminist adaptation means lending agency to the women—when all he's really doing is lifting blame from the men. Whether he's conscious of it or not, he's determined to preserve Dick as the hero of the story by any means necessary—even if it means ruining the film."

"I'm not sure I'm cut out for this," Rupert said, shaking his head. "Since when did being a writer mean being a punching bag?"

"Since the dawn of time. And it'll be well worth it when you get your Oscar," she added. "But you've got to stay strong and stand up to Kurt. We had it stipulated in writing: the only person allowed to make any edits whatsoever to the shooting script is you. But you've got to hold up your end of the bargain."

She fell silent again as the Divers' door opened and Blake exited, humming as he headed back to the Fitzgerald Suite for his murder.

"My entrance is coming up," she said. "Consider this a warning, Rupert. I need you to promise me you'll defend the script going forward, or else I don't know what you're doing here. Got it?"

His magnified eyes were distraught. "Got it."

She nodded, then began to head back down the hallway. The Divers' door opened once again, and this time Zev made his exit. He glanced behind Lila to where Rupert was hovering.

"Keeping our young writer in line, Crayne?"

Lila rolled her eyes, grinning, and Zev winked back, then headed to the holding room in search of a pretty extra to flirt with.

Lila threw Rupert a warning look. "No matter what anyone says, don't go anywhere."

Again, the door opened, and Kurt's voice lifted.

"Alright, now Celia, you're going to turn—yes, that way—and we're going to follow you out into the hallway. Will someone tape that fucking cord so she doesn't break her neck? We'll follow you back to your room—yes, the door will be open, just like you left it. And then close the door and go immediately to—"

The door closed, his direction muffling. Lila slipped into the Divers' Suite, where Dom was prepping for their upcoming scene. A crew member handed Lila her coat and purse as Dom unbuttoned his shirt.

He looked up at her, hesitated. "I'm sorry about earlier," he said, shaking his head. "I feel like a tool. I didn't realize Rupert hadn't approved those cuts."

"I know. It wasn't your fault." She reached around to the small of her back and flipped on her mic once more.

From across the hallway, Celia let out a blood-curdling scream, and Lila and Dom readied themselves—Dom hanging up his shirt, Lila sinking into the couch as Celia ran through the hall, then burst into the room, Kurt and crew following.

"*Dick, darling!*" she cried. "*Oh darling, come and see!*"

"Dom, you're going to push past her," Kurt said quickly. "The camera's coming in close on Lila to capture the moment she realizes they're having an affair." Silently, the heavy bulk of the camera approached until it hovered mere inches from her face, watching with its single unblinking eye; then suddenly it swerved, and Kurt and crew followed it out.

For a moment, Lila hung back, heart pounding, as she listened to his voice booming through the walls. Then she crept across the hall to the door, waited. Eden pointed: her cue.

She touched her hands to the door, spoke softly. "*Dick?*"

The door flew open: Dom, a wild, panicked expression. "*Bring the couverture and top blanket from one of our beds—don't let anyone see you.*"

Tears filled her eyes as he shut the door in her face.

Kurt's muffled voice: "Okay, Dom, I want you to drag the corpse by the ankles—awesome, just like that. Let him thud to the floor—Blake can take it. If you can, try to land him over here, closer to the camera so we can get a good look. Right. As soon as he's down, pull the duvet and blanket off the bed. It doesn't matter how—just strip it as quickly as possible. You don't want the blood to sink any deeper, right?"

A tap on Lila's shoulder: Eden, with a heap of fresh white bedding, motioning her silently back to the master suite to be cued.

Kurt continued, voice growing louder as they moved closer to the door: "Pile the bloody sheets up in your arms and step past the body. Open the door just a crack. A bit more so we can see what you're seeing. We'll have an extra rounding that corner down there with a room service cart. No, we're going to dub in their lines. Okay: go."

Eden received the cue through her headphones and pointed, and Lila opened the door, her arms filled with the clean covers.

"Lila, hand him yours first; then Dom, give her the bloody ones, then leave her there and head back in—careful of the camera. We'll tuck into the corner here so you can shut the door."

Lila stared at the heap of bloody covers in her arms, unnervingly wet and warm to the touch, and felt herself pull inward, the ambient sounds of the set fading away. She moved into the master suite, past the shifting blur of crew, the wide-eyed Rosemary, to her single place of refuge. Eden took the covers from her arms as Nadia helped her into the bloodied double of her dress, readying her for the final shot.

She closed the bathroom door: alone at last. The bath was already running, warm water fogging the mirrors, the air. She sank onto the wet, gummy tile, the bloodied coverlet blooming in her arms, and she pressed her face into it, heart thumping, the tender ripeness of the blood and the sharpness of Dick's cologne mingling and filling the steaming room. She closed her eyes, placed her palms to her ears, and her mind flew back to long ago, to that first bright betrayal—her entire life a reaction to that one unspeakable trauma that had haunted her through the years—made manifest now once more, before her very eyes. And deep within, a sweet fury began to burn.

Through the running water, voices approaching. Her eyes snapped open, and she saw her white dress drenched in blood, the fabric sticking to her skin. She screamed.

Hurried footsteps, then the door flew open. She moaned as she looked up and beheld him, looming above her. They locked eyes; and then Dick turned and shoved Rosemary away and slammed the door shut, trapping them both inside.

"*It's you!*" she cried. "*It's you come to intrude on the only privacy I have in the world—with your spread with red blood on it.*"

"*Control yourself!*"

She looked up, her vision blurred with tears. "*I never expected you to love me—it was too late—only don't come in the bathroom, the only place I can go for privacy, disposing of spreads with red blood on them and asking me to fix them.*"

Dick shook his head, lip curling in disgust. "*Get up!*"

The suffocating wet heat closing in on her now.

"*Nicole!*"

And the world began to grow dark.

"*Nicole!*"

"And—cut!"

Lila blinked, palms pressed against the moist floor.

A hand reached down to help her; she took it, attempting to slow her breath as she stood. But when she looked up, she was startled to see Kurt studying her closely, as though she were a stranger. He opened his mouth, about to say something; but then he shook his head, a grim smile on his face.

"Fucking brilliant," he murmured.

He opened the bathroom door, and a rush of chilled air filled the space. "Alright, people: Sound's finally ready, so let's reset, get hair and makeup for touch-ups, and get our first take."

SASH BISCHOFF

From across the room, Eden: "We're all set in the Fitzgerald Suite, Kurt. They're just taking final photos for continuity."

Behind Lila, Nadia began to spray and comb her hair, her original, unstained dress hanging limply in the crook of her arm, ready to be donned.

Rupert was perched before the monitor that had been set up in the master. Lila moved beside him, slipped on the spare headphones; he glanced at her, but she kept her eyes glued to the screen as Nadia dusted her skin with a fine powder.

"Let's have quiet on set," she heard Kurt say through her headphones. "Slate."

A click, clap, and then a soft whirr, the lights warming, shuttering down, focusing in. Movement stilled. An imperceptible hum of anticipation.

"And," Kurt, softly. "Action."

———

Three hours later, and they'd wrapped for the day. Lila had made sure to kiss the actors goodnight, thanking each of them for their hard work (except Celia, who'd somehow slipped out before Lila could find her). Kurt, on the other hand, had only deigned to give Dom a quick pat on the back, assuring him they'd gotten what they needed. One thing was certain: Rupert was on thin ice. He received only a cursory glance from Kurt, and a nod from Lila before she was whisked to her trailer to shower and change for their evening interview with Daya Patel, senior writer at *Vogue*.

They'd arranged to meet on the roof terrace of the Plaza's Grand Penthouse Suite. Earlier in the evening, Lila had texted Freddie to stop by for a quick cocktail. She'd slipped on an eyelet dress pulled just off the shoulder, with delicate crochet detailing and a full, flirty skirt. Oversized sunglasses, beige ankle-wrap sandals, hair blown loose and beachy—only

79

a few whisper-thin necklaces to better accent the ring. Kurt, meanwhile, was wearing a sky-blue linen shirt and light-cream khakis turned up at the cuff, his hair expertly tousled, his eyes bright.

Daya was waiting for them when they arrived, looking professional and chic in tangerine high-waisted shorts and pointy pumps, her black hair slicked into a low bun. They kissed and settled into sprawling loungers as ginger whiskey sours and lemony oysters on ice arrived. In the periphery, circling: the continual click of the photographer's camera. Far below, tourists in tees and cutoffs strolled along Central Park's edge, eyeing the posters for sale and pausing to rub the warm muzzles of horses, their coats shining with heat. Before them, the verdant park rolled forth in its shadowed, riotous glory, the bright coin of a pond a perfect mirror of the sky. Elegant uptown buildings neatly lined its borders, the east side bright with late-afternoon light. And to the west, through midtown's jagged teeth: the burst yolk of the sun, melting upon the horizon.

Daya smiled at the striking pair casually entwined before her—noted the fine lines of their clothes, their taut, tanned skin, the magnetic glow of their beauty. She glanced at her list of questions.

"It's easy to see why the two of you have been chosen as *Vogue*'s It Couple," she began. "Beyond being such a handsome, charismatic pair, you're at the apex of your careers, and are currently shooting one of the most highly anticipated films of the year, *Tender Is the Night*. How's it going?"

"It's going great." Kurt rested his arm on the back of Lila's chair. "Fitzgerald's story is exquisite; and as you know, we've got a dream cast. I love the energy on this set. With this group, it's all about collaboration. Take today, for example: we were shooting the Dick and Rosemary seduction scene—"

"Dick, of course, played by the brilliant Dominic Reeves," Daya cut in eagerly. "But I believe the actress playing Rosemary hasn't yet been publicly announced?"

"And I'm afraid, Daya, we're going to keep you in suspense for just a little bit longer," Lila said with a wink.

"Our audiences won't be disappointed, though—I can promise you that," Kurt said. "Our little starlet is a fucking knockout. But as I was saying, Daya: there we were, shooting that very intimate, very delicate scene . . . and it just wasn't quite working. We had to make a series of last-minute changes in the middle of a complicated long take, and everybody was totally game. My ask as director is that everyone leave his ego at the door. On my set, it's about getting it right, rather than being right." Kurt dipped a finger in the mignonette sauce, pulled it from his lips.

"God, that's refreshing," Daya said. "What I wouldn't give to meet more men who think like that, am I right?"

"I know." Lila shook her head. "Of course, that's not to say everything's perfect all the time. Kurt and I have our moments, just like any other couple. But at this point, we know one another so well. We always find a way to work it out, don't we, love? With us, the trust runs so deep." She skimmed a palm down his thigh; he placed a hand over hers.

"Okay, give me the meet-cute." Daya leaned in, cheeks rising like plums. "I want to hear all about your romantic beginnings."

For a moment, they hesitated. Lila glanced at Kurt. He coughed, laughed.

"Okay, I guess *I'll* tell the story. Well, this one came in and auditioned for a little indie film I was directing. . . ."

". . . which only turned out to be a cult phenomenon, and one of my all-time favorite films, *Waiting Game*," Daya said.

"That's very kind," Kurt said. "*Waiting Game* holds a special place in my heart. Anyway, Lila came in, and blew us out of the water. You've seen the film, Daya, so you know: her performance is extraordinary. And while I like to think I helped a little, Lila honestly gave an incredible first read. She was riveting. We couldn't take our eyes off her."

Daya nodded. "And that's when the attraction began?"

Kurt inhaled, rolled the cuff of his sleeve. "Well, I can't say I didn't notice her; she's obviously an attractive woman. But I've always had a strict rule: I don't mix business with pleasure. And I stuck to it; didn't waver a moment. Much later, once we'd gotten together, we learned we'd both had feelings for each other throughout the making of *Waiting Game*. But we never acted on it. We waited till after we were good and done, when there was no chance of anyone feeling pressured, or anything that might compromise the work. And then I asked her on a date. I'm old-fashioned at heart, Daya." He lifted a gleaming oyster, sucked the shell clean.

"A true gentleman." Lila propped her sunglasses on top of her head, squinted against the sun. "To be honest, I thought that type of man didn't exist."

"Come on, you two," Daya teased. "Give me the juicy details. Don't you remember your first date?"

Again, they hesitated.

Then Lila glanced at Kurt with a devilish grin. "How could I ever forget?" She leaned back, her eyes following the slow scud of cumulus clouds. "Kurt told me it was a 'destination date.' That's how you put it, right, love? He had me meet him at the private heliport on the west side of the island, and flew me directly to Montauk. We cracked lobsters right on the sand at Navy Beach, then headed to the Montauket for cocktails. We watched the sun set over Gardiner's Island and danced under the stars into the wee hours."

"How romantic," Daya said. "So is that why this adaptation of *Tender* is partially set there?"

Kurt hesitated. "There were a number of reasons behind that decision—"

"But it may have something to do with it." Lila smiled. "As I'm sure you know, the original novel was set on the French Riviera—and really, aren't the Hamptons our American equivalent?"

"And just a hop, skip, and a jump from Great Neck, where *Gatsby* was set," Daya pointed out.

"Exactly. The Hamptons all but scream Fitzgerald, don't they? The hedonistic, glamorous lifestyle, the irresistible beauty, the ostentatious wealth—"

Kurt jumped in. "And while in the book, the characters take a trip to Paris for the scenes we've just shot today, in our version, they travel to our American equivalent: New York City."

"I love it." Daya smiled. "I want to get back to the two of you. When did you both know that this was the one? Was it on that first date?"

Kurt cleared his throat. "Well, you have to remember, by that point we already knew one another so well. We were close friends, really. But up until then, I hadn't allowed myself to even dream that Lila would be interested in someone like me."

"Oh, what's that supposed to mean?" Daya teased.

Kurt leaned back, folded his hands behind his head. "Come on, Daya. I'm sure you've noticed I'm just a tad bit older than Lila? I figured she'd see me as, well, ancient. But that night, when we were dancing out on the deck of the Montauket—baby, you described it so beautifully. You took me right back. We'd had our fair share of drinks at this point, if you know what I mean. But I saw the way she looked at me, with such adoration. And I fell for her, right then and there."

"And did you tell her?"

Lila placed a hand on his knee, leaned in to Daya. "He did."

"So romantic. And how about you, Lila? When was the moment you knew?"

Lila picked up her drink, swirled the ice. "You know, I can't quite say there was one particular moment, the way there so clearly was for him. That was so sweet, Kurt. But my outlook on love is perhaps a bit nontraditional."

Daya cocked her head. "Tell me more."

She gazed at her ring, twisted it slowly. "I don't believe in unconditional love. I believe loving someone is a choice you make over and over again, every single day. I think the truest love happens when two people show up time and again for one another over the course of a lifetime; when, without fail, they continue to value and respect one another. Maybe that makes me less of a romantic than Kurt, but I have my moments.

"When I proposed to Kurt on his birthday, for example: it was me showing the world I was committing to him the way he'd committed himself to me." Lila smiled at Kurt, reached for his hand. Touched the gleaming ring on his finger. "It was my way of declaring to the world that, as Scott said of Zelda, Kurt was *the beginning and end of everything.*"

Kurt tilted his head, drained his glass.

"Which brings us to the wedding." Daya's eyes flashed gold in the dying light. "Have you set a date? Chosen a location? A 'destination wedding,' perhaps?"

"At the moment, the film is taking our full focus." Kurt reached out and ran his fingers through Lila's hair, then ruffled her scalp. "But I'm sure this one has some grand plan in store that I don't know about. Am I right?"

Lila licked her lips. "I've certainly got some ideas. But it's all going to be top-secret. That is"—Lila grinned—"unless *Vogue* wants to do an exclusive spread of the ceremony?"

"For America's Sweetheart?" Daya clapped her hands. "It would be an honor!"

"Then that settles it." Lila looked at Kurt, bit down on a smile.

"God, you two seem so down-to-earth," Daya said. "How do you do it? How do you, as you put it, keep work and play separate, and still give enough quality time to the relationship?"

"It's all in the details." Kurt squeezed a lemon over an oyster, offered it to Lila. "Old dog that I am, I wake up a little earlier than my Lila, so I always bring her a cappuccino in bed from our favorite café."

"What luxury."

Lila licked her oyster fork. "And I try to give to Kurt as much as he gives to me. Each night, I bring him a nightcap of his favorite whiskey I get specially imported from Japan. Our days are quite long, but we always take a moment to check in before sleep."

"And we try to get a date night in the calendar every now and then," Kurt said. "I've got to spoil my baby sometimes."

"You guys," Daya gushed. "Okay, before we wrap up, I've got a little game for you to play: a rapid-fire of sorts. Back in the Roaring Twenties, Scott and Zelda were New York's It Couple. Our *Vogue* readers want to know: a hundred years later, how would our modern-day flapper and her philosopher paint the town, Fitzgerald-style?"

"Oh, I love it!" Lila said, clapping her hands. "I've turned into quite the Fitzgerald fanatic, so this'll be loads of fun." She turned to Kurt. "Want to start us off?"

"Well, it's clear where our journey begins," Kurt said, opening his arms.

Lila smiled. "That's right. How could we not start right here with the Plaza? Scott once wrote it was his tradition *to climb to the Plaza Roof to take leave of the beautiful city, extending as far as eyes could reach.* The Plaza is a recurring character in so many of his stories and novels—he and Zelda were regulars here. We just shot one of our scenes in the Fitzgerald Suite, which the hotel created as a special tribute to the climactic scene in *Gatsby.* When you step in there, you feel as though you've gone back in time."

Kurt leaned forward. "Alright, from there, how about we head down a few blocks to St. Patrick's. Didn't you say that's where they were married, baby?"

"Well . . . not exactly." Lila grinned. "Our true Fitzgerald fans would admire the beauty of the cathedral . . . then head directly to the vestry where the ceremony *actually* happened—because Zelda wouldn't convert!"

Kurt gave a rueful shrug. "What can I say? Fitz and I share a weakness for headstrong women."

"Alright—then, celebrate the newlyweds by heading over to the

Waldorf," Lila continued. "Sneak into the kitchen, pluck up a chef's hat, and hop up onto the kitchen table to dance like Scott and Zelda did."

Daya laughed. "Where to next?"

Lila lifted a finger. "A pit stop at the Grand Hyatt."

Kurt looked skeptical. "The Hyatt?"

"The one at Grand Central Terminal—formerly known as the Commodore. In their partying days, Scott and Zelda lived in hotels, hopping from one swanky suite to the next. They celebrated their arrival at the Commodore by going round and round the hotel's revolving doors for half an hour!"

"Okay, I've got this next one," Kurt said. "From there, catch a cab, Fitzgerald-style: hop aboard the roof and ride it whizzing about town. Maybe snag tickets to the latest hit play on Broadway—"

"Or stroll down Fifth Avenue and splurge on a luxurious fur coat—hopefully faux, rather than Zelda's fur of choice: squirrel!"

Kurt leaned back, crossed his legs. "Then refuel at a speakeasy—Prohibition, after all. Find the secret entrance through the phone booth at Please Don't Tell, or head to my personal favorite, Death and Co . . ."

Lila slipped her hand into his. "And end the night in Union Square where, as Zelda did, you, too, can jump into the fountain, fully clothed!"

"So wild!" Daya laughed. "Okay: final question before I let you go. When it comes to *Tender Is the Night*, what should we be most excited about?"

"Lila, of course." Kurt wrapped a hand around the back of her head. "I can tell you already: this performance will be her best yet."

Lila smiled, flushing, then locked eyes with Daya, her expression intent. "I'm most excited about what this adaptation does for women. What I care about most, Daya—more than acting or film, or any of the flashy glamour it affords—is empowering victimized women. And in our version of *Tender Is the Night*, the *woman* is the hero."

———

"What the fuck was that?" Kurt snapped as soon as they'd said their goodbyes and were left alone.

Lila turned to him in the early twilight. "What, love?"

"'*What, love?*'" Kurt spat. "You know exactly what, *love*. The private heliport? Lobsters and dancing under the stars? You'd better fucking hope she doesn't decide to fact-check. What in god's name made you decide to spew that bullshit? Matt and Reena prepped us for that question. We had a story ready to go. A story that checked out."

"A story that was dull and uninspired." Lila sighed. "I was just trying to help. She clearly wanted something more romantic, so I gave it to her. Look at it this way: at least I didn't tell her the real story, right?"

He whipped around. "Not funny, Lila."

She shrugged. "It worked, though, didn't it? She ate it right up."

He fell silent, deliberating. "What if I don't want to do this anymore?"

Lila blinked. "Don't want to do what, exactly?"

"This. Us." Kurt gestured to the space between them. "What if I don't want to get married? What if I want out?"

Lila looked at her ring, gleaming in the shadows, and lowered her voice to almost a whisper. "You promised you wouldn't do this again."

"Well, too bad!" He threw his hands up. "What are you going to do about it?"

She looked at him, eyes shining. "Kurt, you can do whatever you want. I know I can't stop you. I just hope I don't have to remind you of all that we have, and all that stands to be lost. Do you really want to throw it all away?"

The doors to the terrace swung open. Freddie.

"Alright, you two, I've just spent the past hour getting trashed in Lila's trailer, which I sincerely hope makes me trailer trash. So if we're all done here, can we please go get fucking wasted?"

Freddie stopped short when he noticed the tears in Lila's eyes.

"God, I'm sorry," he said. "Lila, are you alright?"

"Kurt?" She turned to her fiancé, and a single tear slipped down her cheek. "Please?"

Kurt exhaled, nodded, and Lila ran into his arms, held on to him tight.

"Tell me you'll never leave me," she said into his chest. "Promise me you won't."

He buried his face in her hair, placed his lips to her ear. "You've caught me, Crayne," he murmured. "I couldn't leave you if I tried."

PRIVATE NOTES OF: J. GABRIEL

Patient: L. Crayne
Date/Time: July 8, 10:30 a.m.
Session: 5

A stounding breakthrough. Amazed at ground covered, as session had frustrating (if unsurprising) start: L initially seemed to have backpedaled in desire to change circumstances.

Entered office timidly, saying she had gift for me. I objected, said I couldn't receive gifts from patients, but L insisted. Pulled handkerchief from purse.

"It's from the Fitzgerald Suite at the Plaza, where we were shooting. It's pretty, isn't it? Daisies have always been my favorite flower. 'JG' stands for Gatsby, of course, but when I saw it, I realized you had the same initials."

Had sense L should be handled delicately today. Asked if Klonopin effective. L only used it once—worked well.

Happened last Friday. They'd been shooting all day: hotel scene when Nicole discovers Dick/Rosemary affair. Afterwards, *Vogue* interview. L said normally puff pieces fun, but that day felt jarring, false. L exhausted, off her game; inadvertently slipped and did something that upset K.

Happened when asked about first date, when relationship began. L said remarkably, had never had that question in formal interview. Gossip rags/websites assumed they'd met on set of *Waiting Game*. Before interview they'd prepped with PR team, but question hadn't come up. When asked, Kurt froze. So L stepped in, concocted romantic story of imagined first date. Had sworn never to tell true story.

I cited story L had told me previously (party before *Waiting Game*, when K came onto L), and asked if it had been true. At this L apologized—hadn't been full story.

K had indeed thrown party before *Waiting Game*, but L omitted fact that when she went, her contract hadn't been finalized. Her agent pushing for weeks to close deal, to no avail. Other side stalling—wasn't clear why.

When L arrived at party, felt nervous, out of place. Kurt's focus fixed on her. All night, kept L by his side. At first L assumed paternal protectiveness. But amidst drinking and drugs, explanation less and less plausible.

After a few drinks, K came onto her. When L hesitated, uncomfortable, K said there were plenty of other pretty, talented actresses who'd kill to be in her shoes. Everything came with a price; L had to play by rules. If L unwilling, K would tear up contract, offer role to someone else.

That night, L slept with him. Next morning, woke to finalized contract.

L numb, almost cold, recounting story. Was clear she'd taken great pains to distance self from trauma. I asked if she'd had sex with K against will; but this L rushed to deny. Decision had been hers. Wasn't willing to lose enormous opportunity.

Appalled by K's actions—completely contradictory to L's description of K as feminist—but given L's state, wanted to handle subject delicately. Asked how they'd transitioned to dating. Why was L with someone who'd made first encounter into contractual obligation? L said after first time, K acted like never happened, treated L like anyone else. His sudden apathy piqued L's interest. (Unsurprising, given father's avoidant tendencies.) So tables turned: L began to pursue. Began to date. Public loved them, careers thriving; eventually fell in love, and first encounter distant memory. But that was why beginnings tricky to navigate; without prepped answer, L panicked.

I suggested perhaps L told story she wished were true. Asked how K reacted.

Said he couldn't contradict during interview. But after, when alone, K threatened to call off engagement. And that's when episode triggered, turned into panic attack. When K saw how upset L was, backed down, promised he wasn't going anywhere.

Asked if they'd discussed since, but L said K out of town, shooting in Montauk.

Gave L homework assignment. Asked going forward that L keep journal, send me her entries. Interested in tracking L's thoughts about relationship with K. L agreed.

Asked how L feeling now, days after argument.

"It makes me wonder . . . Kurt needs me now for the movie, but once we've finished shooting, is he going to leave me for good?"

Asked L to consider: why be in relationship with someone who had foot out the door? Should be with someone who cares about her, is honest with her, makes her feel safe.

"You mean someone like you?"

Before I could respond, L shook head. "Jonah, that type of man— someone kind and thoughtful and caring—he would never go for someone like me. I'm too damaged. No, please just listen. I attract the predators of the world. The men who pursue me—while they might pretend to be otherwise, I know I can never really trust them. That's my lot in life. I've learned to accept it."

Said didn't have to accept. If we could understand reason behind pattern, could change it. Didn't have to be with someone like K. As long as L with him, never truly safe.

But this an overstep: L began to shut down. Too scared to leave. Reiterated fear she'll never be worthy of love, all men will eventually abandon her. Asked why L thought she felt that way.

L hesitated. "You think Kurt's similar to Daddy?"

"The way he demeans you. The way you never feel good enough. The power imbalance. The threats to leave. The physical violence."

"But that's only when he's angry. The rest of the time, he's wonderful."

"Right—just like your father. The quintessential alpha male: strong, confident, charismatic. But as his daughter, you saw more of your father's bad side than good. And it seems to me that the longer you stay with Kurt, the more his bad side will come out, too. It's in his private life with you that Kurt will show his true colors.

"I'd like to talk a little more about your father, what it was like to be around him when he was angry. Can we do that?"

L said she'd already told me what she remembered, couldn't recall specifics. I said often the case for people suffering from PTSD.

Was first time I'd presented diagnosis; L clearly taken aback.

Explained plenty of people have PTSD if they've experienced trauma. L's inability to recall specific memories around father likely brain's way of self-protecting from being flooded all over again. But ways to override, reconstruct memories. Reminded L of initial reason for therapy: to access and process own trauma as she navigates role in film. Our work here to help L better understand self, better navigate current crisis, help L to healthier future.

Told L I'd like to use treatment called EMDR. Conflicting opinions about effectiveness, but I'd had success with it before. Gave basic rundown: goal to locate source of trauma, diminish its potency to better work towards healing. L skeptical but willing to try.

Pulled together chairs so our knees almost touched. Instructed L to follow path of my finger with eyes. Said I'd guide as we went; would ask questions for L to answer, L should keep focused on finger, follow my lead. Considered attempting to access memory of L's rape, but realized doing so might shut her down completely. Instead, suggested we begin with car accident.

I held pointer finger between us, started to move it back and forth. Once L's eyes settled into rhythmic motion, asked L to take a breath, then exhale and close eyes. Paused, asked L to describe what she remembered. For a moment, L silent.

"I'm— I don't know how to do this. I guess . . . I'm in the back seat?"

Asked what time it was.

"I don't know, late? It's dark outside."

Asked her to go on.

"I really don't know what to say. . . ."

Asked what she noticed around her.

Inhaled. "It's raining. It's raining hard."

Asked L to continue.

"I can smell something. Maybe . . . I think maybe there's a bag from the restaurant? I remember . . . oh my god, I think I remember wanting to eat a cookie the waiter had given me." Shook head, smiling a little. "But Mother said I had to wait till we got home."

Asked L to open eyes, follow my finger, inhale with me, then breathe out, close eyes again. Asked what she noticed. L still, concentrating.

"There's a song on the radio. It's hard to make out—the rain is so loud. . . ."

"Go on."

Expression changed. "My parents are arguing. They're yelling, calling one another names. And I'm trying not to listen—to just focus on the rain."

"What else?"

Sudden flash of pain across L's face. Her eyes opened, refocused on mine, expression closed. "That's all I can remember."

Asked L for hands. L hesitated. Reassured L part of methodology. L placed hands in mine. I turned them to face upwards, put my thumbs in center of her palms.

"We'll do the same thing once more, only this time, look directly into my eyes. I'm going to press your palms like this. Okay?"

Began to press one palm, then other, over and over again, eyes locked. This time, a strong connectivity. Instructed L to inhale, then exhale, close eyes again. Asked what L noticed.

L's brow furrowed. Shook head.

"What is it?"

"Daddy's screaming at Mother. He says he's going to kill her. The car is moving faster and faster."

"What else?"

L squeezed eyes tighter. "He's telling her to slow down. He's screaming at her to slow down." L shook head. Eyes snapped open. "But . . . ?"

Knew breakthrough imminent. Told L to stay with it. L nodded, closed eyes again. Inhaled.

". . . That's right. He's not the one driving. Mother is. He's trying to grab hold of the wheel. And there are headlights coming towards us fast, growing brighter. And then Mother turns over her shoulder, screams at me to stay on our side of the car. Stay in my seatbelt. Cover my head. Daddy's screaming, 'What are you doing?' And then she swerves left, right into the opposite lane, and the oncoming truck slams on its horn, but it can't stop fast enough. It hits us—it goes right into the front passenger. Right into Daddy. Oh god."

Tears spilling from L's closed eyes.

"Lila? Are you alright?"

Her eyes opened, pupils dilating. L gripped my hands hard.

"She killed him. She killed my father. And she did it on purpose. She wanted him dead."

Act Two

A WILLINGNESS
OF THE HEART

If Jonah Gabriel had learned one thing from F. Scott Fitzgerald, it was this: every hero must have his heroine. Like most of us, Jonah liked to imagine himself as the hero of his own story—so this wisdom was not to be taken lightly.

Thirteen years ago, he'd found her. From the moment he'd first laid eyes on her, he'd known: for Jonah, Lila Crayne was the beginning and end of everything.

This morning he woke with a smile, insides lifting in anticipation. Blinked his eyes open to the warm rustle of the Siberian elm beyond their window, soft scratch of leaves against the wavy glass. Next to him: Maggie, in her familiar curl, fractal light flittering upon her skin. One hand woven into the tangled nest of her hair, the other tucked between chin and chest. Face swept clean of last night's tears.

He selected the first of many mineral-infused shirts, piled like bricks in stacks a dozen high—then a pair of lightweight wicking shorts (custom-made in London). Plucked up a pair of socks, adjusting the remaining buds in perfect rows to please the eye. Kissed the top of Mags's head—she stirred but wouldn't wake—then quick to the washroom to perform his ablutions, before slipping on his running shoes and stepping out of their brownstone and onto Horatio, the door closing with a quiet click behind.

The sun just beginning its upward tilt, though it was barely past six, the breezeless air already growing heavy with humidity. He began to move through his morning stretches, gliding from one pose to the next in a practiced dance. He hated this high summer heat, dreaded the inevitable sensation of clothes sticking clammily to skin, that insistent beading at the temple, the brow, the upper lip. When the AC in his office had broken a few weeks back he'd nearly lost his mind. Thank god for the new industrial unit, designed to chill to the bone.

He opened his tracking app, cued up his playlist, and set off on his morning run. First due west towards the Whitney, then a quick left onto Greenwich in its quiet amble, its soft blush of brick, windows like lakes reflecting Jonah back to himself, sidewalks lined with gated saplings and sleeping cars, all hush but for the occasional driver rumbling past. As he made his way south, his muscles began to unstarch themselves, loosening and warming in that way he craved, and Jonah steadied his breath, bore down. This was his morning meditation, calming in its consistency, its even predictability. He'd engaged his near-perfect memory by cultivating a mental checklist of the various points of interest, each architectural flourish a touchstone, each building a familiar face, and he anticipated every landmark he passed. And as he continued to follow his morning course, a phrase began to beat in his ears with a sort of heady excitement to the familiar clip of his stride: *There are only the pursued, the pursuing, the busy and the tired.*

If one were to credit Fitzgerald as the foremost model in Jonah's cultivation of a personage, one wouldn't be wrong. Every great lesson Jonah had ever learned, he'd gleaned from Fitzgerald's words.

He'd first discovered Fitzgerald as a teenager when, like the rest of America, he'd found *The Great Gatsby* on his tenth-grade syllabus. At the time, Jonah had approached it as he did every other book that had been prescribed: as an assignment, to be ingested, processed, regurgitated, forgotten.

But with *Gatsby*, Jonah's world cracked open. He felt as though he'd slept through all the years of his youth, and now—suddenly—he'd awoken, and life was pouring through, overwhelming the senses, every moment brimming with romantic potential. For the first time, he understood what it meant to be consumed, to feel the warm breath of a story's words in every living page. He felt distinctly that in Fitzgerald's characters he'd discovered himself. He *was* Nick—shared Nick's ability to see people for who they really are—and the world, in turn, would recognize him as a man who could be trusted with those privileged glimpses into the human heart. And yet, more than Nick, he was Gatsby incarnate, with his heightened sensitivity to the promises of life, his romantic readiness, his extraordinary gift for hope. He was not one, but *both*; or rather, Jonah hoped that nature had bestowed upon him the generous sum of both characters' finest qualities, while saving him from their fatal faults. Who was this writer, who had so perfectly captured the man he hoped to become?

He began his private education with *This Side of Paradise*, Fitzgerald's fictionalized autobiography and first published novel. And as he devoured, Jonah began to realize the sacredness of the affinity. Before this discovery, he'd been bumbling about lost and blind, with nothing more than an instinct towards his dreamed-up future glory. But in chancing upon the scripture of Fitzgerald's path, Jonah had miraculously discovered his own.

In Jonah's younger and more vulnerable years, his mother, Birdie, had been the dominant force of his childhood. Jonah had loved Birdie desperately, had held her aloft in his mind with a kind of terrified awe. His father had never been in the picture; he'd left before Jonah was born. Jonah's only memento, the only evidence he had that his father had ever existed, was the pocketknife he'd left behind. When his mother had discovered the knife, she'd immediately wanted to get rid of it, and Jonah had had to work hard to persuade her otherwise. He'd carried it with him every day since, feeling just a little bit safer for it—as though with this knife, his father was still looking out for him, protecting him in this small way.

More than a son, Jonah had occupied the role of his mother's companion; and from the time he could talk, she'd demanded he only ever call her by her first name. In him Birdie had confided all her secret hopes and fears, so that years before he'd even hit puberty, Jonah had become a sort of husband in miniature. She was an artist, a painter, who created wild, impassioned pieces as turbulent and volatile as their creator. Nervous breakdowns were frequent and commonplace, and when they happened, it was Jonah's job to soothe her.

Most nights were good nights. Most nights, his mother was the Birdie he adored, the charismatic, colorful woman with big hair and buoyant laugh, the woman who'd slide onto the piano bench during cocktail hour and fill their home with her soaring soprano, offering Jonah sips of her drink and delighting when he'd show signs of tipsiness. Then she'd sling him into her arms, and they'd dance around their living room together until he grew heavy with sleep. But even in those happiest moments there existed a quiet undercurrent of fear; for Jonah was never quite sure when his mother might leave—and in her place, the other woman would emerge.

One of his earliest memories: in the middle of mother and son's romantic nightly waltz, perhaps Birdie's drink had been made more potent, or perhaps Jonah had simply drunk a few extra sips; but in one of their wild and glorious spins, his body had grown unwieldy, and he'd knocked her martini glass from the piano, shattering it on the floor. He'd jumped down to pick up the pieces, world still whirling, and a sharp sliver had sliced clean through his finger. He'd looked up at his mother, tears in his eyes as his blood drip-dripped onto her prize rug, the moon of Birdie's face growing nearer and nearer, ruddying towards total eclipse. And before he knew what was happening, she'd reached out and slapped him, stunning him to silence as he clutched his stinging cheek. Then she'd taken his bleeding hand between her own, pressed the wound hard to her mouth. And she'd told him that all they had in the world was one another. She would take care of him; but in return, Jonah must promise always to take care of her.

Looking back on it now, he recognized this as the defining moment, the initial injury that had driven him to his eventual calling. Over the years, the memory had become inextricably linked to one of his favorite Fitzgerald passages, which had inspired his own raison d'être, so that he couldn't now summon the one without conjuring the other:

It isn't given to us to know those rare moments when people are wide open and the lightest touch can wither or heal. A moment too late and we can never reach them any more in this world. They will not be cured by our most efficacious drugs or slain with our sharpest swords.

He would devote his life to disproving this assertion, to showing one can in fact be cured. As a therapist, Jonah was certain it was never too late to heal; and with each and every case he accepted, he vowed to help his patient rediscover her own earliest wound; and then, against all odds, he would find a way to save her from herself.

He brushed these thoughts from his mind as he turned right onto Charles to run past Wilson's, a matchbook café of raw wood and glass designed, it seemed, to recall an old-fashioned general store, with its soaps and salves, its crates of crumpled coffee bags, neat stacks of mints and tea tins, its wicker baskets filled with flowers. Inside, the morning barista had just arrived and was sleepily setting up shop; a single industrial pendant lamp lit low cast the small space in shadow. He felt a haunting loneliness as he watched the poor young clerk reach across the counter, then knock into the lamp when he stood too abruptly, swearing and massaging his scalp as the disrupted light swung slow as a hanged man above. The clerk seemed suddenly to sense someone's presence; but as he turned to catch sight of his observer, Jonah had already run past—and the clerk saw only the quiet cobblestoned street, empty and undisturbed.

He'd kept his promise to his mother—had accepted his role as her caretaker; yet even as a child, Jonah had somehow subliminally known he could never rely on Birdie to take care of him. In reflecting upon it now, there was so clearly a hole in his life where the safe, steady presence of a parent figure should have been, a hole that had desperately needed filling. In discovering Fitzgerald, then, Jonah had found the father he'd never had.

In less than a year he'd devoured the entirety of Fitzgerald's body of work. And though he knew it might be déclassé, even gauche, to succumb to the plebeian vote—even then, even now, Jonah still considered *The Great Gatsby* Fitzgerald's masterpiece. With *Gatsby*, Fitzgerald had established himself as the Great American Dreamer—the voice of his country. And, of course, the fact remained that *Gatsby* had been Jonah's first—the one that had changed his life as he knew it—and he'd always been a romantic at heart. He'd vowed to himself to reread his new private bible every year—and every year since, he'd kept his promise.

As the self-appointed son of his chosen god, Jonah decided he would be about his father's business: the service of a vast, vulgar, and meretricious beauty. And so, at the age when a boy becomes a man, just as Gatsby had invented himself from Gatz, so Jonah followed the sacred doctrine of Fitzgerald's words to invent just the sort of Jonah Gabriel that a seventeen-year-old boy would be likely to invent—and to this conception he remained faithful to the end.

As Fitzgerald had attended Princeton, there was no question in Jonah's mind as to where he must go. He was accepted, as Fitzgerald had described it, into the pleasantest country club in America, where all who attended were lazy and good-looking and aristocratic. Jonah was enthralled. He spent countless days in the library, digging into the treasure trove of Fitzgerald's manuscripts, losing himself in his loopy scrawl; spent countless nights roaming his sequestered vale of star and spire, discovering the poetry of Princeton's architecture anew. At first Jonah hoped he, too, might become a writer; but this ambition was discarded after a single creative writing course his freshman year, where he was told in no uncertain terms that his style was derivative, sentimental, banal. He shrugged off the criticism; he didn't need to be a writer to be a hero.

He took great pains to transform himself into a veritable slicker, with his preppy, clean-cut look, his social cleverness, ambition, popularity, and—of course—his hair always slicked. He developed his own trademark smile that, when donned, possessed a quality of eternal reassurance. It beheld, or seemed to behold, the whole world for an instant—before turning and alighting upon his sujet du moment, with an irresistible prejudice in her favor.

As a result, women came effortlessly—a veritable kaleidoscope of girls. But no one individual would yet arrest his undivided attention, as his focus was still fixed, in that sweet, boyish way, entirely upon himself.

After freshman year, he successfully secured living quarters in Patton, Little, and Campbell Hall, the dorms where Fitzgerald had once roomed. When it came time to bicker (at Princeton, the equivalent of rush), he embraced the university's glittering caste system, and slid smoothly into Fitzgerald's eating club, Cottage. He was first to be tapped to join Princeton's secret society, St. A's, generally regarded as the university's intellectual royalty; and eventually, he was voted its president. By senior year, Jonah had secured his reputation as a romantic figure: someone slightly removed, yet highly revered. All that remained was choosing his heroine.

He turned onto Washington now, then continued south a few blocks more. And though he ran this path every morning without fail, even still his heart quickened as he drew closer to where Lila lay sleeping.

Jonah held tight to the memory of the first time he ever saw her, held it aloft as his brightest north star, guiding him through an endless sea of years. And even though he knew the reality of Lila Crayne today might tumble short of his dreams (not through her own fault, of course, but because of the colossal vitality of his illusion)—even still, he hoped.

The start of his senior year. Jonah had just returned to campus and was still recovering from a trying summer at home caring for Birdie. He'd spent June and July convinced his mother was merely having another of her dramatic, enduring spells; but in August, reality had proven him wrong. She was handed a terminal diagnosis: Stage IV ovarian cancer. She had a year at best.

A month later, and Jonah had all but fled back to Princeton and thrown himself into work on his senior thesis, an examination of the psychological underpinnings of Fitzgerald's prototypal *homme manqué*, and his tragic ruination due to the vampiric femme fatale in *Tender Is the Night*.

On this particular evening, he'd taken a break from his studies and was making his way across campus to Cottage for an early dinner with friends. He'd bypassed Woolworth, was headed towards the 1879 arch, when a corona of light caught his eye: there she was, in lemony dress, skirt splayed like a sunflower upon the lawn. Sandals abandoned, toes a bright bloody red. Though she'd hardly been there two weeks, she was already surrounded by a piping coterie of excitable girls: they mere constellations orbiting this new, incandescent sun. Brown boxes of tiny pastel cupcakes gaped open, the swirls of buttercream frosting slowly melting in the late-afternoon swelter. A birthday, perhaps, though they were still near strangers? Or simply a spontaneous celebration: of youth, beauty, of themselves? No matter; they were lost in this, their own easy bliss. Her laugh—the bright peal of a bell over the courtyard—seemed to Jonah a siren's call, hastening him home. He'd found her: his heroine, ne plus ultra.

If he'd perhaps paused a moment he might have seen what was happening, might have diagnosed his own pathology. He might've realized the sheer force of his immediate infatuation was reactionary; he was a double major in English and psychology, after all! He was well aware Birdie had abused him throughout his childhood, encouraging codependency and forcing him into a parenting role at too young an age. For the first twenty-one years of his life, his mother had been the only woman of significance; and now, with her unexpected death sentence, he found himself in freefall, scrambling madly in midair to secure some point of focus to replace his exploded supernova. And then, right as he was nearing the nadir: his panacea.

So instead of preparing for the imminent loss of his mother, instead of grieving the childhood he'd never had, Jonah became fixated, resolute. This perfect girl would be his Polaris, so blindingly bright he might never need to confront that crucial missing piece, that endlessly black chasm of pain.

It wasn't hard to discover who she was. His lab partner's little brother was an RA and had access to a directory of the entire freshman class. Jonah was prepared to go through all fifteen hundred photos himself, but the little cretin had already colluded with his buddies and typed up a vulgar list of Fuckable Frosh, organized numerically and in order of preference. There she was—number two—beneath some spray-tanned girl straight out of underage erotica: ropy muscle, buoyant breasts, shiny Lycra. Jonah was appalled: as if she could ever be anything other than number one. And while the list disgusted him—its denigration and blatant dehumanization of these poor women atrocious—he also couldn't help but be secretly pleased that so many other men desired her.

For six months he remained at a distance. In the interim, he occupied himself with the occasional passing fling—at Princeton, picking a pretty girl for a one-night stand was like shooting fish in a barrel. But with her, he was determined it would be different. She deserved so much more than a single drunken night, was so clearly a woman worthy of true love—and Jonah hoped more than anything that he might be the lucky man to give it to her. He knew she was it for him—for she was Rosalind, Gloria, Daisy most of all!—Lila Crayne, he'd decided, was all Fitzgerald's heroines, wrapped exquisitely into one.

It became a game, a fascinating hobby. He came to know her regular routes around campus, her favored spots to study or meet with friends, the eating clubs she'd frequent when she went out at night. When Lila was the lead in a fall play, Jonah went twice to see her in performance. He even, maddeningly, added Anthro 201 to his full course load, sitting in among the sludge of hungover freshmen who slept through every lecture, just so he could share the same room with Lila once a week. He witnessed the predictable unfoldings of her freshman year, the feverish all-nighters before exams, the drunken hookups on the dance floor, the late-night stumblings back to her dorm to bring those forgettable boys to bed. He remained her distant, faithful protector, making sure that Lila was safe. Did it ever make him jealous? Perhaps a little; perhaps Jonah now understood, as Fitzgerald had with Zelda, why they locked princesses in towers. But still he was unflappable in maintaining his controlled remove. He would wait until that single perfectly orchestrated night, when hero and heroine would meet at last. Then he would see her, know her, and devote himself entirely to Lila's happiness.

Jonah slowed as he reached the familiar large oak along the Hudson, gripped the trunk between his hands and began to stretch, his gaze gliding up to those windows' reflective eyes, now emerging, pale and enormous, from the dissolving night. He'd wait there in his own sacred vigil, would allow himself just a moment to glimpse Lila stepping out to the balcony before he'd continue on his way. It wouldn't be long now.

He thought back to that perfect spring evening when they'd finally met, all those years ago. They'd shared something special then, something extraordinary: a spark that happens only once in a lifetime. And then afterwards she'd vanished—and he found he'd committed himself to the following of a grail.

That Lila had forgotten the glory of their single romantic encounter was Jonah's own private tragedy. His only consolation, which sustained him even still, was the same blinding hope Gatsby had once felt: if he might only repeat the past, and fix it all as it was before, he might recover himself as he once was. Then she might recognize him, realizing just as he had that they were meant for each other—and one fine morning——

Lila Crayne would be his at last.

————

He placed the to-go cup onto the nightstand, and Maggie opened her eyes just enough to see Wilson's insignia, its thin lines a tasteful tattoo.

"Thanks, Jo." She hoisted herself up to sit, thick mop of chocolate curls cascading over her face as she took her first sip.

"New barista this morning," Jonah said as he peeled off his shirt. "My Americano tasted like fertilizer."

"Nothing like a fresh cup of morning mud." She blew through the sip hole. "Why don't you try someplace new? Kava is so much closer. And there's that place over on Hudson—"

"Wilson's is the perfect endpoint for my run. And you know I like my routine." He rolled his eyes playfully, slapped his wet clothes onto the rim of the hamper.

"Do I ever." She leaned back on her elbows in her tighty-whities, hint of her nipples just winking through the wifebeater.

"Looking good, Doryphoros," she said. "Hey, I'm in the mood to sculpt. How about a quick chisel?"

He grinned, shook his head. "I'd love to, Mags, but I don't have enough time. And I reek." He headed into the bathroom.

"Isn't that what showers are for?" she called after him.

"I don't want to get the sheets dirty." Jonah turned on the water and stepped into the jet stream. He closed his eyes, leaned his forehead against the spray, began to massage his shampoo to a frothy lather. Beside him: flip of the toilet lid, thin pling of a stream. He could feel her watching through the curtain.

"Jo?" She paused. "Can I join you?"

He knew what she was doing, knew she was trying to reconnect after last night's fight, but god, he just didn't have it in him. Not now. "Hold on a minute, okay?" he said gently. "I'm almost done."

Maggie murmured something in response, but he chose not to hear, focused instead on the drone of the spray against his skull, soap like a hockey puck gliding over skin, shampoo falling around him in great claps. And by the time he'd slicked his hair clean, cranked off the faucet, pushed back the curtain, Maggie was gone.

He found her in the kitchen, her back to him as she chopped. Mags

was an excellent cook, always whipping up her own fresh, original take—
something savory, whimsical, piquant. She pulled from her roots—Ital-
ian father, Mexican mother—braiding them into a delectable fusion. But
while her meals were always delicious, Jonah had observed a distinct
correlation between their excellence and her temperament. It seemed
to him that the angrier Maggie was, the more virtuosic the cuisine. And
lately, her food was off the charts.

He scraped back a chair and sat down at their multicolored mosaic table,
his heel already striking up its regular restless dance. Plucked up a kiwi from
the fruit bowl at the center, then flicked open his pocketknife, began to scalp
its bristly skin. He dropped the peels into Mags's abandoned cappuccino,
the deflated foam now curdled into a custardy film. She hadn't bothered to
change, he noticed; had merely slipped on a pair of old sweats stained with
paint and the odd bloom of bleach. And though they were ripped and ratty,
they still hugged her ample ass in a way that made him itch with desire. She'd
pulled the elastic cuffs halfway up her shins, the sinewy lines of her calves
flexing as she stood on tiptoe for a bowl just out of reach. He rotated the
glistening kiwi between his fingers, bit down. Their stout Maltese, Zelda,
wound her way into the room, mewling, then hopped onto the table and
sat on her haunches, staring at Jonah. Maggie began to whip Jonah's egg
whites just how he liked them, the delicate bones of her back fanning like
wings, full mane of her hair furious with movement.

He closed his eyes, felt a sharp pang of guilt. When they'd bought
this duplex four years ago, they'd dubbed it an investment in their relationship. And while the apartment was in Jonah's name (he'd used the
remainder of his sizeable inheritance from his mother's will on the
down payment and subsequent renovation), Maggie had been the one
to transform it into a home. The apartment had previously been owned
by a woman who'd lived there alone for sixty-five years before dying
right there in the kitchen; and when they'd purchased it, each and every
room had been filled floor to ceiling with her hoardings, derelict with
neglect. Jonah was so disgusted by the mouse droppings and crackly

carcasses of cockroaches, the rotting floorboards and rusted appliances, the woolly dust that caught him in a chokehold at the front door, the swollen splotches of water intrusion and feral, fuzzy mold, that he'd instantly wanted to walk. But Maggie, always the patient one, was able to look beyond the immediate wreckage to the building's bones; and in its foundation, she found possibility.

Jonah knew that for Maggie, acquiring this new home had been about a lot more than real estate. At that point they'd been five years in, and Maggie's patience was wearing thin. She'd been determined to secure their future together, once and for all; and with this home, she was sure she could do it.

It had come to a head the day they moved in. As the furniture was being hauled up the stairs, Jonah had found himself overwhelmed with a panic attack. He'd pushed past the movers, feeling the moldy spores of the place crawling deep into his throat, had toppled a column of boxes in his desperation to get out of their new brownstone, gulping at the air.

"Jo?" Mags had run after him onto the front walk. "What's wrong?"

"I can't breathe in there," he'd said, rubbing at his throat.

But of course, Maggie had known. Maggie had always possessed an uncanny ability for unearthing the truth at the root; then, its wet body cradled in her palm, she would expose it, gently, to the light.

"Look," she'd said quietly, "I can take care of the dirt and the dust. I can make all that go away. But this is going to be our home, Jonah. We're going to build a life here."

She paused, waiting for a response; and the longer the silence held, the more perilous it began to feel.

At last she sighed, looked down at her shoes. And when she spoke, her voice was so soft he could barely make out the words. "I've always been sure about you," she began. "But for some reason, I can't shake the feeling you've never been entirely sure about me. So if this is about more than dust—if this is about us—I need you to tell me now."

He'd looked at her standing there, framed in the entrance of their brownstone. And he'd done the only thing he could do: he'd pulled her in, wrapped his fingers in her hair, and told Maggie she was all he'd ever wanted. And at this she'd beamed and said something he couldn't now recall—and they'd slipped their arms around one another and headed back inside.

Mags had worked tirelessly to please him; and within a year, she'd transformed their new house into a home she hoped he'd never want to leave. She'd pulled up the warped floors, patched the leaks, pushed steel wool into holes, and painstakingly shaved every last layer of waxy paint from the mottled walls. On the ground floor, she knocked down every non-load-bearing wall that had made the rooms so cramped and dark, and split the whole level so that the front half became Jonah's cozy, wood-paneled practice, filled with plush rugs, rich leather, books the colors of jewels. The back half—power-washed, blasted to its concrete foundation, and opening directly onto the garden—would be Maggie's sun-filled studio, stacked with giant canvases, all wildly colored and full of motion, each as vibrant as Mags herself.

Early one morning during their renovation, Maggie had heard a light mewling emanating from the crawl space beneath her studio. She'd shone a flashlight into its depths and discovered a filthy, petrified, blue-grey kitten, blinking into the light. For Mags, there was no question: they had to adopt her. After much discussion, Jonah had acquiesced, on the condition he could choose the cat's name. And Maggie, of course, had rolled her eyes and agreed, laughing good-naturedly as she always did about his Fitzgerald fixation. Thus, Zelda entered into their lives.

Before they'd moved in, the backyard had been a patch of dirt, a burial ground for waste. In it Maggie discovered inbred weeds, terra-cotta shards, small, unidentifiable carcasses, and jagged bits of bone. Whenever she hit a block in her painting, she'd pull on her gloves and take to the dirt, stripping, raking, aerating the soil to its new beginnings. She'd sown the seeds that had, in time, grown into their garden: curling twine of tomato vines, A-frame trellis sprouting cucumbers, clumps of peppers in their beds, lemon tree tucked in the corner, rosemary rampant, mint run amok. And the flowers: clumps of hydrangeas like cabbage heads, dahlias and daffodils, the pink phlox, and azaleas lining the length of their fence. She'd laid a brick pathway that twisted into a spiral beneath a cast-iron table for two. Now, four years in, the garden had grown to lushness. Seated at the center, one could be lost entirely to the foliage.

Their living quarters on the second floor was Maggie made manifest. As a child she'd spent her summers in San Miguel, and the pueblo's warmth and vibrant colors, its tangy spices, flaky salts and astringent lime, had all woven their way directly into their home. She'd set the floors with fat Spanish tile, una cocina mexicana: kaleidoscope bursts of ocean blue, tangerine, meyer lemon, coral red. The wood left unfinished, the rugs bright and braided, ceiling beams exposed, windows wide, furnishings staunch and resolute. Theirs was a friendly house, one that begged for cooking, and invited company with open arms, no matter the hour.

In this new space Maggie had created a work of art, steadfast in her efforts to scrape away any lingering doubt and build a home where they could make a life together. She'd even kept a tiny second bedroom that, someday, might be converted into a nursery. It had all been thought through; and it was perfect. Jonah was convinced that Maggie was the other, better path—the path he wanted—where he might sink safely and sensuously out of sight. In choosing Maggie, he believed, Jonah had finally chosen right.

That is, until Lila came back into his life.

He thought he'd lost his only chance with her, all those years ago. After the stark, extraordinary miracle of that first night, fate had ripped them apart. Jonah's mother had collapsed, and he'd been forced to leave Princeton early to help Birdie to her slow, painful death, finishing his studies and completing his thesis remotely. Shortly after his graduation, Birdie had died. And for the first time in his life, Jonah had found himself completely alone.

He'd forced himself to move on, past the pain of his mother's death, tangled inextricably with the loss of his one chance with Lila. Adding insult to injury, at some indeterminate point in that period, Princeton's Mudd Library had called to inform Jonah that somehow, inexplicably, his thesis had been lost; but this news seemed minor in the brackish swirl of his present miserable existence. He'd boxed up his mother's paintings, put the rest of his inheritance in storage, and put his childhood home on the market. A week later, it had sold. And as Lila was returning to Princeton to begin her sophomore year, Jonah made his way to Harvard, where he might try to fill the exquisite tabula rasa of his mind.

In three and a half years' time, he received his master's, and moved to New Haven to pursue his doctorate at Yale—completing the Ivy trifecta, and fulfilling Fitzgerald's definition of a gentleman: *a man who comes from a good family, has money, dances well, and went to Yale or Harvard or Princeton.* (Ever the overachiever, Jonah had attended all three.) And then—a few months into his tenure at Yale, when he was least expecting it—Jonah met Maggie.

They met at a showcase exhibiting the artwork of Yale's grad students. At the time, Jonah's new friend Lee was moonlighting as a caterer, and he'd been staffed for the event. He kept nagging Jonah to come, promising free booze if Jonah would keep him company. In truth, he hadn't needed convincing. His recent move to a new city, and the accompanying sense of having to start his life all over again, without a home or family to return to, had Jonah missing his mother. He liked the idea of being around art again, and was curious to see how it would feel, four years after her death. So he'd shown up, thrown back a glass of cheap wine, and made the rounds. It was all vaguely depressing, the self-portraits displayed all derivative and disappointing, save one: a wild-looking oil of the artist, a woman, gazing into a shattered mirror. Her back was in the foreground, so that the viewer couldn't see the subject's face; but in each shard of glass, a different tiny detail was reflected back, the pieces all discordant and impossibly different, yet all stemming from the same single woman. It reminded Jonah, unequivocally, of his mother. The title: *Eco de Narciso.*

Feeling a bit lightheaded, a bit overwhelmed, he'd poured himself another drink and made his way to the open loading dock in the rear of the building. He'd pulled out a joint and laid on his back, gazed up at the dark sky. When he heard the click of footsteps approaching, he assumed it was Lee coming to take a quick break, and said, "If I see one more mediocre portrait of an artist, I think I might shoot myself."

"Tell me about it."

She sat down next to him, plucked the joint from his fingers, took a hit.

"They're so self-conscious, aren't they? You can almost smell the insecurity in the paint." She turned to him. "So why'd you come? No, let me guess." She leaned back, considering. "Supportive friend? Boyfriend? Stalker?"

"I'm here for the free booze." He turned to her. "You?"

She smiled. "I'm one of the artists."

Jonah choked on his spliff, began to cough uncontrollably. "Oh god," he managed. "I feel like such an ass."

She smirked. "You might be an ass, but you're also right. I'll forgive you if you can guess which one was mine."

Jonah deliberated. "The black-and-white pointillist piece with the artist's ear in red?"

She pulled out her phone, swiped through her photos, held it up: *Eco de Narciso*.

Jonah sucked in his breath. "Would you believe me if I told you that was the one painting I actually liked?"

She grinned. "I call bullshit."

"Well, I blew it," he said. "How can I redeem myself?"

"How about . . ." She tilted her head. ". . . you let me paint a portrait of you?"

He liked Maggie; he liked her very much. As they began to date, Jonah found her to be a perfect reflection of the wildly colorful, large-scale paintings she created: earthy and vibrant, visceral and warm. She possessed an uncanny ability to be the mirror of a mood within him, so that when he was with her, Jonah had the distinct sense that he was coming home. What's more, he liked the idea of her—the idea of associating himself with a revolutionary artist deep in the trenches, the way Fitzgerald had always kept company with the visionaries of his time. That narrative could work; it made sense. And he began to feel that Maggie was in fact infinitely rare, someone to be marveled at—an authentically radiant woman who, with that first moment of magical encounter, could blot out his years of unwavering devotion. During a sleepless night of deliberation, he'd looked Lila up and discovered she'd moved to LA to pursue a career in film. He took it as a sign. The circumstances, the timing—it simply wasn't meant to be. He had to accept that he no longer held the girl whose disembodied face floated along the dark cornices and blinding signs; he must instead draw up the girl beside him, tightening his arms.

The next day, he asked Maggie if she'd be his—to which she'd rolled her eyes at his pretentiousness, and said she already was. The following semester she moved in, and they began the grand experiment of building a life together. One Sunday morning as she lay naked on her stomach, sheets puddled about her, sketching the plummy curves of his toes, Jonah realized he'd fallen in love, and told her so. And at this she'd smiled, kissed the arch of his foot, whispered it was about damn time.

Five years later, his doctorate in hand, Jonah and Maggie moved to the city. They put in an offer on their "West Egg" brownstone, and Jonah began to set up his practice. By age thirty-one, he'd already attended the Big Three, bought a duplex apartment in the best neighborhood of the best city in the country, and was at the start of what was sure to be a successful career. He was handsome and healthy, with a great deal of charm; and he had a girlfriend he loved, and she loved him right back. In a couple months, he'd propose; and Mags, elated and relieved, would accept. Life was as vivid and satisfactory to Jonah Gabriel as in books and dreams.

But just as Jonah was getting used to referring to Mags as his fiancée, *Waiting Game* opened in theaters—an immediate box office hit. Suddenly Lila's name, her face, was everywhere, impossible to ignore. Lila of twenty-eight was still the same Lila of all those years ago—still just as fresh-faced and radiant, universally admired by the masculine eyes of the world—still a thing of exquisite and unbelievable beauty. As her fame grew, Jonah found he had to check his impulse to mention his own personal encounter with America's Sweetheart; he knew all too well that sharing the perfection of that memory might only tarnish it. Yet even despite her growing omnipresence, Jonah was determined. He'd worked so hard to put Lila out of his mind. He was devoted to Maggie now—he would not waver.

But then seven months ago, fate once again intervened, and this time, she made her intentions clear. Lila and Kurt were moving to New York to begin preproduction for their new project, a remake of Fitzgerald's *Tender Is the Night*. And with just a bit of internet sleuthing, Jonah discovered they'd bought an apartment in the Village, only a few blocks away from where he and Maggie lived—closer, even, than the sweet stretch of water separating Gatsby's estate from the green light at the end of Daisy's dock.

At first he'd told himself he was merely curious, as one might be about a childhood crush. He would simply check in on her—an innocent indulgence, a bit of heady escapism. Such behavior was, after all, quite common; and Jonah was nothing if not self-aware. He knew himself well enough to trust he would always keep his habits in close check.

And who hasn't had that single person who makes us just a little obsessed, a little bit crazy? How many of us haven't indulged in a little online perusal of that certain someone, a daily check-in of sorts—especially when that someone is an American icon, her name and face everywhere he turned, near impossible to avoid? It wasn't just Jonah; the whole world was in her thrall. Lila Crayne was the American Dream made manifest; no one could resist her exquisite appeal.

A few months ago, the opportunity was placed in his lap. During a session with one of his clients, a film executive named Brielle, she'd mentioned that her good friend Lila had just moved east and was in the market for a therapist. She'd asked if she could give Lila his name.

He could hardly believe the serendipity. He equivocated, heart racing—he really didn't have the capacity for new clients—but yes, alright, since she was her good friend, he'd see what he could do.

And so their sessions had begun.

He knew he was acting irrationally, his behavior self-destructive. He knew the risks, understood he was putting his career—his entire life, even—on the line. He'd fudged his process notes, of course, concealing the obvious conflict of interest and his own deeply personal investment. Though he'd indicated otherwise, he'd never actually recorded their sessions (to voluntarily create physical evidence of his own tampering would just be tempting fate). Still, he wasn't deluded enough to believe there weren't other ways to discover the truth. Only for Lila would Jonah be willing to risk everything.

The strength of their connection in her sessions had been immediate. And as Lila unfurled, so eager for his guidance in disentangling the knotty fabric of her life, Jonah began to wonder if the stars were finally aligning. It was all falling so effortlessly into place. Lila was in crisis, was desperate to escape the reality she'd built. And she'd progressed so quickly—after the breakthrough of her last session, when they'd unlocked the memory of her childhood trauma, Jonah felt certain it was only a matter of time now before he might save her from her situation. And then—would hero and heroine come together at last?

Jonah watched as Maggie nudged the whites with her spatula and flipped the fluffy moon of them, edges crackled with butter, then slid it, oozing with cheese, cilantro, pico de gallo, pancita, onto a cobalt-blue plate. Mags smiled at Jonah—a truce?—and licked her finger with pleasure. God, how was it possible to love two people at once? He was engaged to a wonderful woman, a talented artist, an incredible partner;

and someday, a beautiful mother. And yet: Jonah's fatal flaw had always been his hopeless romanticism. Deep within him rested the quiet knowledge that Lila Crayne was the one who got away. And if she became an option? He knew there was no contest. No amount of fire or freshness could challenge what man will store up in his ghostly heart.

In less than three hours, their next session would begin. He felt his pulse rousing as he wondered what perfume she'd spritz upon her skin, what clothing she'd choose to highlight her elegant form—what lingerie might be hidden just beneath. And he wondered if, perhaps, today might be the day she realized her feelings for him—and love, springing like the phoenix from its own ashes, would be born again in its mysterious and unfathomable haunts—

"Can we talk?"

Jonah blinked, resurfaced. Maggie was regarding him hopefully.

"I'm sorry about last night," she said. "I know you were only thinking of me—of us. And you're right: the launch *has* been all-consuming—and it's my fault we've fallen behind in the wedding planning.

"But Jonah, mi amor . . ." She touched his hair, and instinctively, he leaned back into her palm. "I know I can handle both. I *want* to. I've wanted to get married to you for so many years—and I don't want to put it off any longer. It's so important to me, and to my family. My grandmother won't be around forever. I want her to see me marry the man I love."

"I want that, too, Mags—I do." He sighed, rubbed his forehead—as though he might rub the lingering image of Lila from his mind. Then he took Maggie's hand, looked up into her eyes. "But more than that, I want what's best for you. Your career is about to explode, and when it does, I want you to be able to focus all your energy there. I don't want our wedding to distract you from what's most important. You'd regret it."

"That isn't fair," she said, color rising. "I'm telling you what's most important to me, Jonah—are you listening? Don't I get a say in this, too?"

"I didn't mean to upset you," he said, and dropped her hand. "Look, now isn't a good time. I've got a patient in five minutes. I'm sorry, Mags," he said when she opened her mouth to protest.

He took a final bite of her perfect omelet before pushing back his chair, leaving Zelda to the buttery remains. Kissed the top of Maggie's head, whispered he had to get to work, but they'd discuss it another time. Soon, he assured her. And as he headed towards the stairwell to the lower level, he felt Maggie watching in confusion, in dismay; yet even still, with the warm promise of Lila mere hours away, Jonah couldn't stop the smile spreading across his face.

Lila's Therapy Journal
for Jonah Gabriel

Entry #1
July 18

Dear Diary,

Confession number one: it brings me so much joy to keep a diary again, just like Gloria did in The Beautiful and Damned. (My private Fitzgerald education continues.)

In dubbing you "Diary," I instantly transport back to my preteen years. (I think that was probably the last time I kept a diary, complete with heart-shaped lock and tiny key. Note to self: must find childhood diary to rediscover childlike sense of wonder. Also: must find key.) If this were the movie version of my life, I'd be flopping belly-first onto a flower-patterned comforter, twirling my ponytail, blasting Britney, and kicking my legs, toes a-point.

In reality, however, this is simply me, the real Lila Crayne, the one the world never really sees. At your request, Jonah, these entries will be my best attempt to document the truth of my private life, and my complicated relationship with Kurt, in order to deepen our work together.

———

It's dead quiet, almost 2 a.m. After tonight's turn of events, I've curled up in my favorite velvety chair—the cozy one in the corner, walls of glass on either side with a view of the city's sparkling lights. It's times like these I wish I had a cat. Cats, I'm told, are nocturnal (much like myself), discerning in their affection, sparing with their trust. (Note to self: must be more catlike.) It would be nice to have one swirled up in my lap right now, with its pointy face, its soft, reassuring purr; but alas, I'm on my own, and having given up altogether on sleep, I decided now would be the right time to complete my first entry—which may, in fact, also be my last.

Today was one of those rare days that had initially appeared gloriously empty, a day where none of my scenes had been scheduled to be shot. I'd had grand dreams of desperately needed self-care (oh, to sleep in! To have a manicure! Even—gasp—to read a book!). But by morning, my freedom had been swiftly scheduled to within an inch of its life: three costume fittings and a makeup appointment, my daily two-hour physical training session, yet another interview with the press. By end of day, all I wanted was a nice stiff drink, and then off to bed.

Kurt, I knew, was scheduled on set till late, and I doubted he'd be home before eleven (. . . and likely much later, given his ongoing affair with our Rosemary). So there I was, dragging my sorry self into our elevator, ready to rip off my clothes and run with a bottle of something strong to burrow my way under the covers, when the doors ding open to reveal . . . Kurt (?!), in that soft cantaloupe tee I love—the one that clings just the slightest bit to the broad muscles of his chest.

"What are you doing home?" I ask.

"Surprising you," he says. "I wrapped early. I wanted to do something special for you. Remember this?"

He hands me a smoky blond cocktail, thick with fat ice cubes and a bright sprig of mint. I take a sip, savor the spicy bite of it.

"You didn't," I say.

"I did. Remember?"

How could I forget? The Pepper Smash. We'd discovered it years ago at a restaurant back in LA serving trendy gastronomic fare. It was, to date, the best cocktail I'd ever had—and somehow Kurt had re-created it for me.

"Take your drink and change into something comfy," Kurt says. "Dinner's almost ready."

"You cooked?"

He shakes his head. "I wouldn't subject you to such misery. No, much better: Pierre's been here all day, cooking up a storm."

Pierre! We'd first met dear Pierre in Paris a few years back when we'd taken the jet for a weekend getaway. We stayed right in the heart of the city at the Saint James Albany (which—you might know, Jonah—was where Scott and Zelda first stayed when they visited Paris!). Our first night there, Kurt's friend had recommended a newly opened restaurant on Île Saint-Louis rumored to be the next hot spot in town, Le Petit Perchoir (yes, *the* Petit Perchoir!). The chef was our sweet Pierre Dufrene, who—mere months later—would skyrocket to fame. That night, when Pierre came to our table to pay his regards, we found him so charming, we invited him to a glass. One glass became a bottle, which turned into two . . . and by the end of the night, we'd promised to invest in his next venture. The following year, we helped Pierre open L'Oeuf du Perchoir here in New York.

"You've just missed one another," Kurt tells me. "Pierre had to get back to the restaurant. I know, I know, baby. But I wanted to make sure this evening was just for us. I owe you some quality time."

This was quite sweet. Lord knows Kurt loves the limelight, whereas I am woefully the opposite. Though I'd never admit it out loud, I find the insistent cameras, the never-ending publicity, the constant recognition draining. (I just gagged a little: *poor little movie starlet me!*) But the truth, which I will only admit here, Jonah, is this: more than anything, I care about contributing something truly meaningful to the world—and I finally feel I'm doing it now. And all the baggage that comes with being who I am? Sometimes I think I'd give just about anything to start a new life and leave the title of America's Sweetheart behind.

I digress. So. I take my tasty little tumbler upstairs with me, change into a boho backless dress, then make my way out to the balcony.

The outdoor table has been pulled out and set, its center dancing with candles. Around the space: steel lanterns flickering. Kurt in his runner's stance, leaning against the rail, watching the water beyond. When I step out, he turns and opens his arms, and my stomach does a little flip. I allow myself to be folded into the safety of his chest. For just a moment: soft cotton, his musky cologne, my muffled breath, his heartbeat. I didn't realize how tightly I'd been wound, how hard I'd been trying to keep it all together. This, the first melt.

We enjoy Pierre's lavish meal, his staff working silently behind the soundproof glass, and split a bottle of red we'd saved—a Côtes du Rhône we'd discovered that same weekend in Paris. And it almost feels like it did back in the beginning. For once, work is off the table, which makes conversation slightly stilted, just a wee bit awkward. I feel nervy, in a good girlish way. It's quite lovely, actually.

By the end of our meal, the staff has cleaned and gone. We're silent in the dark, spirits softened by the wash of moonlit water before us. Both of us have early mornings, yet we stay as we are, humbled by the simplicity of the moment.

I'm leaning against Kurt's chest when I feel him inhale, his breath catching.

"Lila baby." He slips his finger beneath the angel hair strap of my dress. "I know I've been an ass lately. It's the pressure of the film. You know how I get."

I nod, though inside, my heart starts to hammer.

"But still, that's no excuse," he continues. "I've been taking my frustration out on you, and you're the last person I'd want to hurt. Will you forgive me?"

Heart like a military drum now, preparing once more for its own private never-ending battle. Jonah, I just can't help it: I've always been a romantic at heart. But I'm beginning to understand from our work together that this hopeless romanticism has exposed me to getting hurt, over and over again. So even though habit tells me to say *yes, of course, all is forgiven!*—this time, something holds me back.

"I need to tell you something." Why do I feel so nervous? "I've been seeing a therapist. I have been for a while now."

His face starts to close up, darkening in the way that makes my skin prickle.

"Who?" he asks quietly.

I hesitate. "He came recommended by a friend."

Kurt shoves back his chair and walks to the rail, his back to me.

"Kurt? What's wrong?"

"Why are you telling me this?"

I hug myself to keep from shivering. "I've been talking to him about us."

"You what?"

Still I push on. "He's concerned about our dynamic. He thinks it's unhealthy."

He slams the balcony rail. "What the fuck were you thinking?" He whips around. "You know what this could do to me if it gets out."

"Kurt, it won't. He would never. There's client confidentiality. . . ."

". . . which goes up in smoke if he thinks you're at risk. Jesus, Lila."

"I'm sorry," I whisper.

"How much does he know?"

"What do you mean?"

"Every story has two sides. Have you told him mine?"

"Kurt, if anything, I've been defending you to him."

"Bullshit." He sneers. "I know you, Crayne. For all the feminist dogma you spout, you love to capitalize on playing the innocent, victimized woman. That's how you lure people in. Case in point."

He knows how much this will hurt, yet still he smiles as he says it. I open the glass door, head inside. But he follows right behind, grabs my wrist.

123

"Listen to me." Reluctantly, I turn to look at him. "You want to make this work? You want our film to happen without a hitch? Then all our business stays between you and me. Got it?"

I nod, barely able to speak. "I won't talk to him about us anymore."

"Not good enough. You need to end it."

I try to pull my hand away, but he holds my wrist tight, bruising me. "Kurt, please . . ."

He cocks his head. "Or is there something more between the two of you?"

I hesitate. And in the moment I do, Kurt pushes me against the newel post at the foot of the stairs. And I know what's going to happen, know it long before he pulls up my dress, knees open my legs. There's no point in fighting now; I learned long ago it's better to pretend it's normal, pretend it's alright. He wraps an arm around my waist, and I hold tight to the iron balusters clanging in their beds. And I close my eyes and think, *What did I do to deserve this? Why is he taking away the only person I can really trust? How will I ever survive without Jonah?*

As he gets close, he demands an answer, and so I tell him what he wants to hear. Yes, I will end it. Yes, I promise. He finishes, then pulls me gently to the floor. And once again, he is tender, he is kind. Soon he stumbles up to our bedroom; and though I, too, am exhausted, now sleep evades me.

So I've crept back down to this chair to record this entry, even if it'll be my only one. I need to get it all down before sunrise, before I have the chance to cover it up, pretend it's alright. Because it isn't. I've got to escape this, once and for all.

Help me.

III

Jonah had begun to make mistakes.

All day long, he hadn't been able to think straight. He'd come back from his run that morning and almost dropped Maggie's cappuccino when he'd unclipped his phone to find Lila's name lit right at the top. He'd already suspected something was amiss: though he'd waited nearly half an hour, Lila hadn't come out to the balcony as she so often did. Instead, she'd eventually appeared at the window, and simply stood there a moment, her expression hidden behind the glass; and then, to Jonah's bewilderment, she'd turned and retreated inside.

When her name appeared on his screen, he'd had the absurd thought that she'd seen him watching. But he shook this worry away, fingers tripping over themselves as he'd unlocked his phone to find Lila's first journal entry.

A cyclical pattern had revealed itself in Kurt and Lila's abusive sexual dynamic, and it needed to be broken. God, he loathed Kurt: at his core, a narcissist, chauvinist, and chronic philanderer. How could Lila have ever believed that brute to be a feminist?

Lost in his thoughts, he'd sleepwalked his way through his shower, through a distracted breakfast with Maggie, and hastened to his office. As soon as he'd shut the door, too impatient to wait for his computer to fire up, he'd tapped out a response on his cell:

Lila,

Thank you for sending this entry. Let's plan to discuss at our ap-
pointment tomorrow—but if you need to talk sooner, please do let
me know. Stay safe and take care.

My best,
Jonah

His appointments that day had been a blur. His infallible focus was
slipping, and he'd catch himself only half-present as each patient swept
in with her own intimate revelations. He couldn't stop his restless heel
from vibrating—couldn't keep from eyeing the tiny clock propped on
the console behind the patient's head, desperate for the mere moments
between sessions when he might quickly check his phone.

In the early afternoon, when he'd finally convinced himself she wasn't
going to respond, Jonah nonetheless checked his cell once more to find
a text from an unknown number:

Thanks for your email. May need to talk sooner.

Had Jonah unwittingly given her his personal number? He never
did. His entire life, he'd always taken extreme measures to protect his
own privacy. But for Lila? He couldn't remember. Pulse quickening, he
responded:

Of course. When?

And then he'd suffered through his interminable afternoon sessions;
and with each hour that passed, Jonah felt an increasing desperation
when he received no reply.

By end of day, he'd forced himself to shift his outlook. Tomorrow's session was still on the horizon, and the hours in between steadily waning. In no time at all, he'd see Lila again.

He closed the day with a session with Lila's friend, Brielle. After years of work together, Brielle had finally extracted herself from her long-term abusive relationship. Two weeks ago, she'd secretly signed a lease on a studio of her own, then took a sick day and moved out of her boyfriend's apartment while he was still at work. In last week's session, Jonah had been worried she'd relapse—they'd broken up multiple times before, and each time, the boyfriend had begged her to come back, swearing he'd change, and each time she'd caved. But this time, Brielle had promised Jonah—this time was different.

"I can't stop thinking about that saying you'd told me," she said now. "*Hurt people hurt people.*"

He nodded, spoke gently. "And staying with him was only enabling him, reinforcing that behavior."

"I feel like such an idiot," she said. "I kept going back for more, over and over again."

"Because you loved him," he said. "Of course you did. And he loved you. *Love* is what makes abusive relationships so different from any other offense." He shook his head in sympathy. "I get it, Brielle—I do. It's incredibly difficult to reconcile the fact that the person you love—maybe more than anyone else in your life—is also the person who'd want to hurt you the most."

Jonah walked her through his standard protective measures: showed Brielle how to change the settings on her phone so that her ex wouldn't be able to trace her, made sure she'd canceled her credit cards, changed all her usernames and passwords so he couldn't hack into her accounts. "If you have regular routes and routines, switch them up," he told her. "Change any future appointments he knows about. Find new places to go for groceries, new coffee shops to try." Her eyes widened. "I know it sounds drastic," he continued, "but believe me, I know men like this. I've seen it happen again and again. It can get really ugly. Better safe than sorry."

Later that week, she'd take the train upstate to her family's country home, escape the city and her ex, let herself be taken care of by her parents for a little while. But she promised Jonah that if she felt herself backsliding, she'd reach out. And when she returned to the city, they'd resume their work together.

"Above all, remember this," Jonah said. "None of this was ever your fault. If at any point you find yourself thinking about contacting him, remember: you deserve to be safe. You deserve to be treated with respect. And you deserve to be happy."

"I never would've been able to leave him without you," she said. "I mean it. I can't imagine where I'd be, if not for you. Well, I can; but I don't want to." She wiped her eyes and stood. "Lila's in good hands."

He walked Brielle to the front door, where she gave him a heartfelt hug goodbye; and Jonah watched as she walked down the block and rounded the corner. He looked up as the leaves shivered in the air. The clouds had turned plummy and thick—a storm was coming. He suddenly had the odd sense he was being watched. He glanced to his right—

And saw Kurt Royall standing across the street, one arm resting against a tree. Looking right at him.

He blinked, mouth parting. Tried rapidly to formulate the best plan of action.

But Kurt was already crossing the street towards him in his alert, aggressive way, his hands out a little from his body as if to fight off interference.

"Dr. Gabriel?" Kurt said, extending his hand.

"Jonah," he corrected automatically, and folded his arms across his chest. But Kurt responded smoothly, slipping his hand into his pocket as he crossed past the gate to his front steps.

"I'm Kurt Royall—"

"I know who you are," he said simultaneously.

Kurt smiled—assuming, Jonah thought, that he must be a fan of his work.

"I'm sorry to disturb you like this. I just need a few minutes." He gestured to the door. "May I?"

"I'm afraid not," he said. "I really don't have the time. If you'd like, I can give you my email –"

"Please," Kurt insisted. "I wanted to talk to you in person. It's about Lila."

At this, he hesitated. "Is she alright?"

He frowned. "As far as I know, she's *physically* fine. But something's happened that's made me concerned."

Jonah inhaled. "What?"

Kurt lowered his chin in thought. Around them, the cool breeze swirled, and the looming clouds bore down. "I came across Lila's journal entry this morning. . . ."

"I'm sorry, what?" he said. "Those entries are private. They're meant to be shared only between Lila and me."

"I know that," he said, shaking his head. "And I get it, I do. But I read it, and I have to tell you: she's lying."

Jonah closed his eyes. "This conversation isn't appropriate. Lila is my patient, and this is violating our confidentiality—"

"I understand that, but what I'm telling you trumps any confidentiality agreement you might have. She's blatantly misconstruing what happened between us, clearly insinuating I—"

"This conversation is over."

"Will you just fucking listen to me?" For a moment, only the quivering leaves. Then Kurt clenched his jaw, pressed a knuckle to his lip. "I'm sorry. I didn't mean to yell. I'm just . . ." He exhaled. ". . . very angry. She's clearly up to something—I don't know what." He paused. "Look, the nature of our relationship, and everything going on with us now . . . let's just say it's an unusual situation. I really don't think you want to get tangled up in it."

Jonah blinked. "Is that a threat?"

"A threat? No, man." He laughed sadly. "It's just fucking absurd that now she's trying to involve some random therapist. . . ."

"I would hardly say I'm random," he cut in. "This is my area of expertise."

"Alright, fine. If you want to help her, then maybe you can. She's lying. She might even be pathologically lying. I'm telling you: Lila's unstable, and she needs serious help. So would you and your 'expertise' be able to get her a psychiatric hold?"

"Excuse me?"

"I'm not fucking with you, man," Kurt said. "I truly think that's the level of help she needs."

In the distance, thunder rumbled. "I need you to leave. Now," Jonah said. "Or I'll call the police."

Kurt fell silent, a puzzled expression on his face. Then he shook his head. "You don't know what you're dealing with."

He'd had it. "Believe me, I'm a highly accredited professional; and I have plenty of experience when it comes to situations like Lila's. I really don't think I'm out over my skis here. And I'm certainly not going to be bullied into submission by you."

And with that, Jonah turned and strode inside.

The fucking gall! In under twenty-four hours the bastard had forced himself on Lila, trespassed upon the sanctity of her private journal, had the nerve to show up at her therapist's home to save his own hide—and had even gone so far as to recommend Lila be institutionalized! There was no subtlety about it: Kurt was trying to take away her only ally, her only means of escape, so that he might keep Lila prisoner, and his own reputation intact.

He headed upstairs in a distracted, feverish excitement. Mags, her back to him, was busy chopping vegetables, something rootlike and tough. As always, she asked about his day, and he nimbly dodged discussion of the drama that had unfolded moments before, launching instead into a diatribe about a patient from earlier in the day.

If he'd been paying more attention, he would've seen the warning signs. Maggie was preparing her mother's signature Caldo de Pollo, a recipe Jonah loved, but which took many hours to cook. Mags only made it when she was muscling through something truly tough; and she certainly never made it in summer, when the kitchen was sure to be sweltering. Stray cilantro stalks and squeezed up limes were strewn about the kitchen; Maggie's chops steadily accelerating, cleaver banging violently against the wood.

"My agent called today," Maggie was saying now. "Apparently there's so much buzz around the launch that a gallery in DC has offered to feature my work this fall."

"Wow—that's amazing." He pulled an IPA from the fridge, flipped open his pocketknife, flicked off the bottle cap, turned and surveyed the room. At some point, Maggie's stretched canvases, her brushes and palettes and paints, had migrated from her studio and into the kitchen. Dirty scrapers, moist rags, and crumpled paper towels littered the floor, he noticed now, and thick smears of red paint oozed upon the table's skin. He pulled out his seat with a sigh, carefully shifting a wet canvas to lean against the adjacent chair.

"Word of mouth is so hot they're contemplating listing my pieces preemptively," she continued. "They think they might sell before the launch even happens."

"Huh." The mess was driving him crazy. He closed his eyes. Breathed. A little mess didn't matter, he told himself. What matters most right now is the launch, and that Maggie feels fully supported.

He folded his hands behind his head, leaned back on the chair's creaky legs and inhaled, focused on the pullet's salty simmer. He tilted the bottle to his lips, and as the bitter foam slid down his throat, Maggie turned to face him.

"Are you having an affair?"

He banged forward onto the front legs a little too sharply. "What?"

"You promised me—remember?" She folded her arms, jaw clenched; she was trying so hard, he knew, to steel herself, to stay strong. "All those years ago—after that girl at Yale—you promised it would never happen again."

"And I've kept that promise," he said. "I'm not having an affair, Mags. Where is this coming from?"

Tears of relief sprang to her eyes. She threw up her arms in a whole-body exhale. "You've been so distant all summer. You're not affectionate anymore. You don't even want to have sex."

"I do—"

"Not like we used to. I barely see you, and when I do, you're so distracted. It's like your mind is always somewhere else." She shrugged. "With someone else."

He listened, heart pounding, trying to decide what to do.

"Jo." Maggie wiped her hands on her jean shorts, then walked over and placed them on his shoulders, straddled his lap. Searched his eyes.

"Come on," she said quietly. "I know you. You're not here with me. Where are you, mi amor? Where have you gone?"

Outside, the low metal rippling of thunder. Jonah closed his eyes. This wasn't how it was supposed to go; he wasn't ready, wasn't yet sure what he wanted. And yet here it was, happening now, when he least expected it. She'd always been unfailingly honest with him; he knew she deserved to know.

But to tell her the truth; to risk losing Maggie, his future wife, his love? The two of them were good together; they made sense. His analytical mind and steadfast ambition had kept Mags grounded, tethered to reality; and she, likewise, had given him levity, had taught Jonah to laugh at himself. She loved his insatiable curiosity, his romantic, intellectual musings; and he loved her fiery spirit, the freedom of her dreams. Together, they satisfied every penchant of the palate: long explorations of the psyche, existential debates over art, dancing and cooking and laughter, wild, delicious sex. They could work, *would* work, for the long haul.

And yet.

Jonah inhaled, placed his hands on her hips. "I am struggling with something," he said, and he felt Maggie stiffen. "I'm having feelings for a patient."

She turned away. Listening hard.

Gently, he rubbed his thumbs along the waistline of her jeans. "I hadn't felt the need to discuss it because this sort of thing is quite common in therapy."

"Don't shrink me right now, Jonah," she said, lifting herself from his lap. "I don't give a shit whether or not it's common. That doesn't make it okay."

"I can understand why you're angry."

"Oh, thank you!" she cried, throwing up her hands. "Thank you for validating my feelings. I feel so much better now."

"What *would* make you feel better?"

"I want to know everything." She gripped the counter behind her, knuckles splotching white. "How long?"

Here, he hesitated. "About as long as you said. A couple months, maybe?"

She nodded. "Who is it?"

He shook his head. "It doesn't matter."

"Of course it matters. It matters to me, Jonah. Who is she?"

He rotated his bottle slowly, its sweat beading into a ring on the table. "You know I can't tell you that."

"I don't care!" she yelped. "Fuck confidentiality. I want to know who it is!"

He tapped his fingers together, crossed his legs. Waited.

"Are you in love with her?" she whispered.

"I love *you*, Mags."

She shook her head, looked at him hard. "Are you in love with her?"

He sighed. "I don't know."

"God dammit, Jonah," she said, tears in her eyes. "How could you?"

He leaned forward. "I never meant to hurt you."

"Well? You did." She shook her head. "Damage done."

He struggled to find the right words, wanted so badly to take away her pain. "Mags, I'm so sorry."

"Have you told her how you feel?"

"No, of course not," he said. "It wouldn't be professional."

Maggie laughed. "Right, but jacking off in the shower, imagining her? That's professional?"

"What are you talking about?"

"You think I never noticed?" She paused a moment. "So does this woman have feelings for you?"

Jonah hesitated.

"Oh god." Maggie turned her back to him, leaned onto the counter.

"I'm not sure," he said.

"But you think she might." She hung her head, curls falling over her face. "This is so fucked up."

"Mags," he said. "I swear I haven't done anything."

"But you're thinking about it." She turned to face him. "Right? So what are you going to do?"

Thunder again, louder now. "What do you mean?"

"You know exactly what I mean. What do you want?"

"I don't know."

She laughed in disbelief, watching him. "Were you just not going to tell me? Just start having an affair behind my back?"

"That's not fair."

"Jonah. Be honest with me. Do you want this? Do you want to work this out? Or do you want to be with her?"

Outside, the sudden whitewash of summer rain. The trees like guards beyond their window. Then:

A knock at the door.

"Who is that?" she asked.

He shook his head. "I have no idea."

Zelda wound her way into the room, curling her tail around Maggie's calves as she passed. The knocking resumed, and the cat stiffened, eyes wide, the silver hairs of her chin gleaming in the light.

Mags scooped her up, buried her face in Zelda's fur. "Aren't you going to see who it is?"

Jonah put down the bottle and went to her, cupped her arms in his hands as Zelda watched him, emerald eyes unblinking. He leaned in to kiss Maggie on her forehead.

"Don't," she said softly, and turned away.

"Mags." He waited, but she wouldn't look at him. "We can keep talking, alright?" he said gently. "I'll be right back."

She shrugged, then nodded.

Jonah made his way down the stairwell to the front door, where the insistent knocking continued. "Coming!" he shouted. He fumbled with the latch, swung it open.

"Lila."

She hugged herself, drenched and shivering in a hooded jacket—glanced nervously behind her. "I'm so sorry to bother you. But I had to see you—"

"Come in." He ushered her past him into the hallway, then peered outside, where the rain was shushing down in steady, silvery sheets. He shut the door, muting the rain, the hallway's sudden stillness startling.

"Are you alright?"

She shook her head. "Can we talk?"

Jonah glanced up the stairs. He knew Maggie was waiting, listening. "Unfortunately, now isn't the best time. I wish you'd called. . . ."

"I know. I'm sorry. I didn't mean to barge in on you and Maggie like this. But it was an emergency. I didn't know where else to go. I ran here." She pushed back her hood, revealing the beginnings of a black eye.

He sucked in his breath. "Okay. Alright. I can't talk long, but let's go to my office."

She lowered her eyes. "Thank you."

He followed her down the dim hallway lined with his diplomas, then stepped past her to unlock the door, their shoulders brushing. Felt her eyes on him as he struggled with the finicky lock. The floor must have warped with water intrusion, he realized, and the door had likewise expanded and jammed with the evening's humidity; when at last the door gave way, its base dragged along the floorboards with a terrible scraping groan. He cringed. He'd grown to accept this home as a world complete in itself. But looking at it now through Lila's eyes, he found himself invariably saddened.

He flicked on the lights, stepped back to let her in. "Just give me one moment." He sent Maggie a quick text:

Patient emergency. In office. Will make it quick. Sorry, Mags.

He pocketed his phone and looked up to find Lila hovering at the window's edge, looking outside.

"Do you want to sit?"

She shook her head. "Did you read my entry?"

"I did." He perched on the arm of the couch. "Did you get my response?"

Her eyes stayed trained to the street. "I just thought if you'd actually read it, you'd have realized the urgency."

He inhaled. "I hope you understood from my message that you can always reach out in an emergency if you need to meet sooner."

"Well, it got a lot worse." She touched the skin around her eye. Flinched.

Jonah leaned forward. "What happened?"

"What does it look like?" Her breath caught in her throat, and she shook her head. "I'm sorry. I'm just so scared. I saw Kurt on the street on my way to you—I don't know whether he saw me too. I don't know if he followed me here."

Jonah swallowed, debating whether to tell her that Kurt had shown up uninvited not half an hour prior. Now wasn't the time, he decided. Lila was in too fragile a state; telling her now would only frighten her further.

"How about if I close the blinds?" He glanced down the street, then lowered them, and guided Lila gently to the couch. "You're safe here. Try to breathe."

"We have to end this. I can't see you anymore." Lila raked wet strands of hair back from her face.

Jonah sat down across from her. "Lila, listen to me. It's very clear to me you're in danger. We need to get you away from him."

She shook her head. "If I leave him now, the film will fall apart. I won't risk it."

"But you'll risk your own safety instead?"

She closed her eyes, sank back into the couch. "Everyone would lose their jobs. Millions of dollars down the drain. My reputation would be ruined. No one would finance a film I'm in ever again." She sighed. "*Tender* is everything to me, Jonah. I have to see it through."

He watched her. "How much longer until you wrap?"

She shrugged. "Three weeks, I think?"

"Alright." He moved beside her onto the couch, and Lila opened her eyes. Watched him.

"Here's what I think we should do," he said. "For the next three weeks, we meet in secret. If you want to meet somewhere else, we can; whatever will make you feel safe. But we use this time to prepare you to get out of this abusive relationship. Leaving isn't an event; it's a process. This is going to be really tough, and you shouldn't have to do it alone. Let me help you."

She hesitated. "I can't come tomorrow. He knows that's when we meet. He's rescheduled my call time so he can keep track of me."

"Then we'll find another time. Another way." Gently, he placed his hand on her shoulder. "And going forward, if there's a way to make sure he doesn't read your entries . . ."

She looked up, eyes narrowing. "You mean . . . you think he . . . ?"

He hesitated. He couldn't tell her now, couldn't risk her fear of Kurt getting in the way of them working together. "I just want you to be extra careful," he said, and Lila blinked, nodded. "You'll need to cover all your tracks to make sure he doesn't discover we're still working together."

"I'm so scared," she whispered.

"I know." Carefully, he put his arm around her. "But we'll get you through this. This might be the hardest thing you'll ever do. But it'll also be the most courageous."

She curled into him, her nose against his collarbone, then the base of his neck, and drew a jagged inhale. "Thank you, Jonah."

Slowly, she looked up, and in the moment she met his gaze, his mind flashed back to that night so long ago: those same haunting eyes, shining up at him in the dark. She was so close to him now. Ever so slightly, he leaned in—

But she had already pulled away, was wrapping her jacket around herself, mercifully oblivious to the line that, in one reckless moment, he'd nearly irrevocably crossed.

"I should go," she said. "He'll get suspicious if I'm gone too long."

Jonah stood. "Isn't there somewhere else you can stay tonight? Somewhere safe?"

She hugged herself. "I'll be alright. That would just make him angrier, make it worse."

"Lila, I really don't—"

"It's just a few more weeks, right? I can survive that." She forced a smile.

"Do you promise you'll find a way for us to continue?"

She nodded. "I'm sorry I'm such a mess."

"It's not your fault." He touched her arm. "None of this is your fault."

Lila looked up at him, and once again he found he had to fight every urge to take her in his arms and tell her he loved her, promise he'd always protect her. He let his arm fall. "If you're sure you're alright, I should . . ." He gestured upstairs.

She nodded. "Of course."

He walked her back to the front door, opened it. Outside, the rain had faded to a warm drizzle. "Can I call you a car?"

"No, I'll be fine. It's not far." She stepped past him onto the stoop. "You know where I live."

His breath caught. "What?"

She turned back to him. "I think I told you, didn't I? I'm only a few blocks away. We're practically neighbors." Her gaze traveled beyond his shoulder, and she gave a light wave. "Hi, Maggie. I'm sorry I disturbed you."

"It's alright," Maggie said, and from the even tone of her voice, Jonah knew she'd realized that the woman in question was Lila Crayne.

"Well." Lila's eyes flicked between the two of them. "Goodnight. Thank you again, Jonah." She gave a tiny smile, then turned and started down the stone steps.

Jonah closed the door, gathering himself, then turned to face his fiancée.

Outside, a sudden gust of wind, then a swift downpour: storm of needles against the door. The lights faltered.

"End it, Jonah," Maggie said softly. "End it now, or I swear I'll leave you."

He inhaled, found he couldn't respond. Silently, Maggie started up the stairs, leaving Jonah stranded in the flickering hallway, alone.

Lila's Therapy Journal
for Jonah Gabriel

Entry #2
July 25

Dearest Diary,

Picture me now: crouched in hall closet with magnifying glass, dressed in a sensible herringbone tweed, lit from above by a single bulb pulled on with a bit of string. I write furtively, scratchy scrawl wild with inspiration, hold my breath when I hear the click of passing footsteps, threatening to discover me—and you—at last.

Of course, this is not the case. I have no such hall closet, no magnifying glass (alas, no sensible tweed! Note to self: must correct shameful oversight). But in the movie version of my life, this is how I'd draw it: a detective story, shadowy and sepia-toned.

In reality, I'm recording whispered voice memos into my phone whenever I can manage (though—fear not, Jonah—per your guidance, all passwords have been changed), then transcribing and editing these rambling thoughts into (hopefully) a more cohesive narrative.

Before you say anything: I know this is all a bit melodramatic. But if I can't write the truth about how I feel here, where can I? My thoughts turn to Mother so often now. I think of the nightmare she lived through with Daddy, and I wonder how she coped for so long. She was effectively his prisoner, living her life in fear. As long as Daddy was alive, she could never feel safe. I'm beginning, I think, to understand why she did what she did that terrible night.

In sunnier news, I feel fairly confident Kurt is convinced I've stopped therapy. Our schedules are so hellish now with the race to wrap that we've hardly had a moment alone together. And when we do find ourselves in the same room, he treats me with a sort of cold apathy, focusing all his attention instead on his young actress, whom he doggedly continues to pursue. Two months ago—hell, two weeks ago—I might've been delusional enough to believe our relationship might still restore itself. But now, thanks to your help, Jonah, I have more insight into Kurt's actions, and I see the pattern. And I am resolved:

I must get out.

———

Today we shoot the penultimate scene of the film, when Nicole decides she wants to be with Tommy, and ends her marriage with Dick. (Since you're the true Fitzgerald scholar, Jonah, you'd of course note it's actually a mashup of a few scenes from the book, piled one on top of the other to heighten the stakes.) I feel grateful Kurt waited till late in production to shoot this one. It's a real beast of a scene, and I needed to lay as much groundwork as possible to be able to do it justice.

But there's one crucial aspect that continues to gnaw at me (and which never felt quite right in the book): when Tommy and Nicole confront Dick, asking for a divorce, why does Tommy do almost all the talking? Why does he insist on speaking on Nicole's behalf? What do you think, Jonah? If by now, Nicole is healed, wouldn't it be much more satisfying if she were the one to confront her abuser at last and end the marriage herself? If this climactic scene is effectively two men bartering for her freedom, with Nicole standing silently by, I worry it throws the film's entire thesis into question. But I'm getting ahead of myself.

I arrive an hour early at the Montauk villa to allow myself time to wander about set. It's the first time we've had a scene in Dick and Nicole's master bedroom, and I need time to familiarize myself. The room is perfect—exactly as Nicole describes the place where she and Tommy first sleep together (*like the bare tables in so many Cézannes and Picassos*). The whole space is airy, warm, stippled with light. The thickly painted, undulating walls and arched doorways, the messy bloom of bedspread and tangle of sheets beneath, the lazy swirl of a plantation fan above, single wooden chair angled in the corner, bright Zapotec rug spread over terra cotta. The place makes me want to curl up like a cat for a deliciously long siesta.

I slip beneath the sheets, take it all in. And bit by bit, I fill the room with memories, pulling from my own past to ground Nicole's story in specific truths. I trace the light stitching of the bedspread, memorize the cracks of the ceiling, gaze beyond the glass door to the ocean rolling in the distance. I make it all mine.

At a quarter to the hour, some of the crew start tiptoeing about, trying their best not to disturb the insane lady in the bed (cut to me: eyes closed, arms crossed upon chest, silently weeping. LOON, I tell you.). Ten minutes later and the set is beginning to bustle, so I slip from bed and head to my trailer for hair and makeup.

Nadia makes me look dewy and flush with a post-coital glow, my hair made wind-swept and wavy with the salty breeze. I stick on those terribly annoying pasties, untwist that godawful strapless thong, then throw on a plush Turkish robe to make myself relatively decent and head back to set. Kurt, I'm told, has been held up in a last-minute meeting; but happily, my scene partner is already there, waiting for me.

"Lila." Freddie stands in the center of the bedroom, smooth, golden chest exposed beneath a matching robe. He opens his arms and I fall in, inhale his familiar blend of sunblock and cologne: a true Fitzgerald slicker, absconded to brighter, wilder shores.

"How you holding up?"

"Oh, surviving." I try to smile, but he knows me too well.

"Talk to me. What's going on?"

And for just a moment, I think about confessing all the dark secrets locked deep within me; Freddie, more than anyone, would understand, given the nightmare he just went through with his ex. *Surely I can trust Freddie*, I tell myself. *Surely Freddie would never betray me.*

"Crayne," Kurt calls from the doorway. "Come here a minute."

My silent deliberations evanesce as I walk over to my (soon to be ex) fiancé.

"Want to know where I was?" he says, his smile dangerously tight. "I was in a meeting with the entire AD team where I was scolded like a fucking child. Apparently, you were gallivanting about set unauthorized this morning."

One look at his expression, and I know what's coming, Jonah. "I just wanted to get used to the space."

"Well, you also created extra work for the set dressers, who had to fix everything you fucked up."

"I'm sorry," I say. "I thought I restored everything to the way it was."

"You thought wrong. So now we're behind schedule, which means more money down the drain." Freddie's eyes snap to me, his expression questioning; but I bite my lip, shake my head. Saying anything would only further provoke him.

"Morning, everyone," Kurt says to the room. "As I think you all know, we're a little delayed this morning thanks to Miss Crayne, but hopefully we'll be up and running shortly. In the meantime—Lila? Freddie?—let's step through the scene."

As the room falls silent, I try to slow the thrumming in my veins, tune out Kurt's seething presence. Freddie rubs his face and cracks back his shoulders, then turns to the opposite wall to gather himself.

And as always, I go inward. I slide my hands over my ears, close my eyes, and let the outside world fade away. Focus instead on the world within, the sounds of the sea like the slippery innards of a conch, breath like sand swept in water, warm thump of the distant heart. I tell myself I am all the secrets inside me. Tell myself: I contain multitudes.

My bones realign, muscles stretching to Nicole's physicality—a dancer's stance: spine like a string of pearls, shoulders pulled long down the back, hips petaled open, belly as fist, arms like water at my sides. This carefully crafted grace a map of her trauma, atlas of the turmoil within.

Freddie and I smile at one another from opposite sides of the bed, then untie our robes, let them puddle to the floor as we slip beneath the sheets. He extends his arm, and I curl into the familiar nook there. He touches my chin, and I look up, catch his tender gaze.

"*I'm going to look at you a great deal from now on.*" His fingers trace my cheek, and a curious smile spreads across his mouth. "*I thought I knew your face, but it seems there are some things I didn't know about it. When did you begin to have white crooks' eyes?*"

I blink, pull away. "*If my eyes have changed, it's because I'm well again.*" I sit up. "*And being well perhaps I've gone back to my true self—I suppose my grandfather was a crook and I'm a crook by heritage, so there we are.*"

He props himself up on one elbow, admiring me. "*Why didn't they leave you in your natural state? All this taming of women!*"

He pulls me into him, then kisses slowly down my body. I stretch my limbs deliciously long as he holds my feet with reverence. And as he begins his upward climb I reach out, touch his face. "*Kiss me on the lips, Tommy.*"

He looks at me, full of love, then draws himself up. We sit on our shins, smiling shyly at one another—and in that moment I feel brand new, as though anything might be possible.

"The door slams. Dick's home," Kurt says, and we jolt apart, look to the door, to one another. Swiftly, silently, we begin to dress.

Kurt continues. "Dick's presence should already be sending you back to the broken version of yourself. Freddie, notice it happening. Grab her hand to stop her."

"*Tell me you love me*," he whispers, and I hesitate, glance again to the door.

"*Oh, I do*," I say, shaking my head. "*But there's nothing to be done right now.*" I start to pull away; but he holds fast.

"*Of course there is*," he says.

And then I realize: the time has come. I inhale, nod, and begin to move to the door.

"Alright, people: we're moving into the second half of the scene," Kurt shouts. "Do we have Dom ready?"

"I'm here, Kurt!" Dom calls from down the hall.

"Excellent. Walk the path, Lila. You're going to follow the camera down the hall into the living room—we'll stay tight to your face. Good—that's good. Once you pass through the archway, stop right there at the back of that chair. Yeah: use it to anchor yourself. Dom, you're at the piano? Great—start playing "Thank Your Father." Go ahead—we've muted the keys. Your whiskey's set for you there on top—take a swig whenever you want."

Kurt moves behind me, whispers into my ear. "Really take him in—that black mood he's in. You can already tell this is going to be a losing battle."

"*I thought from your note that you'd be several days.*"

"Even more submissive, Crayne. I want you drowning already."

I grip the back of the chair, watch as he continues to play the silent piano. "*Did you have fun?*"

"*Just as much fun as anybody has running away from things*," he says.

"Good, Dom. Now twist the knife with this next one."

He glances at me, eyes glinting. "*I drove Rosemary as far as Southampton and put her on her train there.*"

Then he flips the page of sheet music and continues to play. And I find I'm unable to breathe, my heart cacophonous against the mellow roundness of the muted keys, soft click of his nails against ivory.

I swallow. "*I went dancing last night—with Tommy Barban. We went—*"

He slams on the keys. "*Don't tell me about it.*" He lifts his glass, drains it dry; then he sets it down and begins once more to play.

Oh, Dick. I move to him, touch his shoulder; but he flinches, jerks away.

"*Don't touch me!*"

"That's right, Crayne," Kurt whispers. "You know exactly where this is heading—what he's about to do to you, all over again."

He turns to me, gaze clinical. "*I was just thinking what I thought of you—*"

"Take her down, Dom. No holding back."

And once again I begin to shrink into myself, smiling sadly as I shut my eyes. "*Why not add the new classification to your book?*"

"*I have thought of it,*" he says coldly. "'*Furthermore and beyond the psychoses and the neuroses—*'"

"You should be backpedaling faster," Kurt whispers to me. "You don't stand a chance. You should be crumbling."

Yet still I clench my teeth. "*I didn't come over here to be disagreeable.*"

"*Then why* did *you come, Nicole?*"

"Attack her harder. She's the real enemy, isn't she?"

He shakes his head wildly. "*I can't do anything for you anymore. I'm trying to save myself.*"

I smile, the tears falling freely now. "*From my contamination?*"

"Fucking nail her, Dom!"

He looks at me, his eyes filled with hate. "*Profession throws me in contact with questionable company sometimes.*"

A pause.

"Do we have Tommy?" Kurt booms.

Silence.

"Will someone get Freddie? He missed his fucking entrance!"

"Um. Actually, Kurt?"

Eden: rubber soles of her combat boots squeaking against the tile, a ream of papers in her hand.

"Yes, Eden?" Kurt says, eyes blazing.

She offers the papers apologetically, and he throws up his hands.

"What?" he snaps. "What is it?"

Eden winces. "It's Rupert."

"Rupert?" Kurt scoffs. "What about Rupert? I thought old Owl Eyes couldn't handle being on set with the big boys and hightailed it home to LA." He looks around the room, eyebrows raised in challenge.

"Well, he just emailed a new ending for your approval," Eden says. When Kurt remains silent, she continues. "In his email, he says he's taken one of Tommy's lines from the book, as well as a passage from Dick's perspective, and he's given them to Nicole. He says the reassignment of those lines is critical to the adaptation. You might want to take a look." She glances through the papers. "It cuts Tommy's entrance entirely."

"This is ludicrous," Kurt says. "We're already behind schedule, and now our dearly departed is emailing last-minute changes for my approval, cutting a principal from the scene we're about to film? It's absurd; it's fucking unheard of. So no, Eden: as a matter of fact, I *don't* want to take a fucking look."

"Well I do," I say. "The ending doesn't work, Kurt—you know that. Nicole can't remain his victim for this final confrontation. She has to stand up to him, once and for all. Maybe these edits will fix it."

He clenches his jaw, temple pulsing; but he knows I'm right. He gives a sharp nod, and Eden quickly distributes the pages around the room. I glance at the new lines in red, then look to Dom, to Kurt. "Should we just hear it aloud?"

"Be my guest, Crayne," he says with a wide sweep of his arm. "From where we left off."

I begin to read. "*Do you remember what you wrote about me, Dick, in your studies of my malady? Here—I'll read your own words to you, right from your book: 'One writes of scars healed, a loose parallel to the pathology of the skin, but there is no such thing in the life of an individual. There are open wounds, shrunk sometimes to the size of a pin-prick but*

147

wounds still. The marks of suffering are more comparable to the loss of a finger, or of the sight of an eye. We may not miss them, either, for one minute in a year, but if we should there is nothing to be done about it.'"

I look up at Dom. "*You have always treated me like a patient because I used to be sick. According to you, these wounds of mine would always remain—I should harbor no hope of healing.*

"*But you are wrong, Dick: my wounds are gone. I'm not sick anymore—I'm healed. And I can finally stand alone, without you.*"

I glance to Kurt, then back to the page. "*When you gave me this ring, you told me I was 'the beginning and end of everything.' At the time, I thought the notion romantic. But now —when I hear those words?—now I hear our damnation.*"

I swallow loud in the silence. "*Isn't it true you're not happy with me anymore? And I'm not happy, either.*" I extend the ring. "*So I release you.*"

"Is this some kind of fucking joke?"

I hesitate, then dare to look at Kurt. He's glaring at me, furious.

"Outside. Now."

He opens the door to the terrace; reluctantly, I follow, and slide the door shut behind me. Kurt's eyes are fixed to the horizon, his arms folded tight. A breeze whips in from the ocean; and even in the blazing heat, a shiver runs down my spine.

"What did you tell him?"

I shake my head, heart racing. "What do you mean?"

"You obviously told him about us," he says. "Why else would your little pet put in that line about the ring?"

My mind is spinning as I scramble for an excuse. "It's a famous quote, Kurt—about Fitzgerald's love for Zelda. It makes perfect sense—"

"You're lying." He pulls the ring off his finger, holds it inches from my face. "I'm asking you one last time: how did Rupert know about the inscription on this fucking ring you gave me? Why would he write that?"

And before I can stop myself, I blurt out the truth, which—I'm so ashamed to admit, Jonah—I'd concealed even from you:

"He didn't write it."

Kurt shakes his head. "What?"

I steel myself. "I wrote it."

"What do you mean, you wrote it?" Kurt says. "You wrote the new ending?"

"Kurt, I wrote all of it." I force myself to meet his eyes. "I wrote the whole film."

He jerks back, looking at me in bewilderment; then he lets out a shocked cough of a laugh.

"You must think I'm really stupid, don't you? You must think I'm a fucking fool. Concocting that discovery story: the voice of his generation. What did you do, hire that mindless idiot behind my back as some sort of figurehead?"

I struggle to respond—and Kurt slams his hand against the wall right next to my face.

"We're all just pawns in that fucked-up mind of yours, aren't we?" He presses his finger to my temple, his eyes wild. "It's Lila Crayne's world, and the rest of us just live in it. So who needs a director, right, baby? Hell, you can write, direct, and produce it all yourself. Enjoy making your own fucking film. I quit."

———

I take a moment to gather myself, willing the tears back from my eyes, then head back inside and, divulging as little as possible, let Eden know that Kurt had left. She makes the announcement to cast and crew: we're wrapping for the day. As we head to our trailers, Dom asks Freddie and me if we want to grab a drink.

We choose the Montauket—far enough from set that we're less likely to cross paths with anyone we know. The sun is low on the horizon, and the place is beginning to get good and crowded; yet mercifully no one approaches, asking for a photo or autograph.

We order a round of beers at the bar, then head out to the cliff's edge. Select a stretch of wooden rail at the very end to lean against, then turn to the glittering bay before us; and I think of that line Fitzgerald wrote about Montauk—do you know the one, Jonah? He wrote, *I like it here where everything's rugged and harsh and rude, like the end of the world.*

At first Dom attempts to talk shop, but the conversation quickly dwindles to an exhausted, brooding silence. We drain our beers, and Freddie offers to buy us another round. As he heads back inside to push his way through the growing crowd, I hear Dom say:

"Want to tell me about that bruise?"

Fuck, I think. In my haste to escape, I'd covered the lingering bruise around my eye, but I'd forgotten about the one on my wrist, where Kurt had grabbed me last week when he'd . . .

Well. I don't have to tell you. You know.

"He did that to you," Dom says. "Didn't he?"

And all I can do is stare into my drink, hold my breath. Because while I could deny it, make up something—anything!—then change the subject the way I have so many times before . . . right now, for the first time, I just don't have it in me.

For a moment, we simply stand there in silence. Then Dom says, "Do you know why I almost didn't take this job?"

I shake my head.

"When Kurt and I worked together on *Intruder* about a hundred years ago, he did something terrible. Unforgivable. A certain pretty young actress starred in that film—I think you know who I mean. It was the role that would launch her career; but back then, she was still a nobody. She had no leverage, no power; so what do you think Kurt did?"

"He blackmailed her," I whisper.

"Damn straight. He forced her to sleep with him before he gave her the part. She was an incredible young woman, a real talent. And on a night not unlike this one, Kurt had gotten upset about god knows what, and the girl broke down and told me what he'd done to her. I tried to convince her to say something, but back then, things were different. Weinstein hadn't happened; #metoo hadn't had its heyday. Kurt had threatened that if she ever told anyone, he'd see to it she never worked again. She made me promise to keep her secret safe.

"I've felt so guilty all these years, not speaking up on her behalf. I tried to tell myself I was doing the right thing by respecting her wishes; but I knew it was bullshit. Because by staying silent, he'd keep getting away with it, over and over again."

Over Dom's shoulder, I see Freddie approach, and I shake my head to warn him away.

"There are rumors, you know, rumors that the two of you aren't the only ones. But Kurt's a real pro at keeping his affairs private, and he's made damn sure that everyone he corners is too terrified to go up against him. But that needs to change."

Dom places his hand over mine. At last, I dare to look at him.

"You say the word, and I'll leak something anonymously. And it can all come tumbling out. He'll be eviscerated, and you can escape."

I feel tears prick my eyes. "Thank you, Dom," I say. "But I don't need you to do that."

He shakes his head. "Don't you want to be done with this bullshit?"

I swallow. "I have to finish the film."

"How can you stay with that asshole?" he asks. "How can you possibly love him?"

"I don't." And relief floods through me as I realize it's true. "Not anymore. But I need to see this through. And then . . . I have an escape plan."

He locks eyes with me, lowers his voice. "If you need any help—anything at all—I'll stand by you. You have my word."

As the sun sets before us, Dom wraps an arm around my shoulders, and I allow myself to relax into his embrace.

"You guys are too adorable," Freddie says from behind. I turn, and smile when I realize he's just taken a photo of us. I lean in impulsively, kiss Dom on the cheek, and Freddie snaps another.

"We've got to protect our girl here, Freddie," Dom says as Freddie distributes the beer. Freddie throws me a quick glance, and I try to smile.

"Oh, I wouldn't worry about this one," Freddie says, ruffling my hair affectionately. "She may look fragile as a flower, but Lila Crayne is the strongest woman I know."

The sun slips all the way to the horizon; and even though I should feel comforted by their support, still I can't help but hesitate. Freddie loves me, I know; but he has no awareness of all the dark horrors of my life. As much as I want to trust him, it would be foolish to risk it. And even with Dom's promise to help me, I'm not sure I can trust him, either. He talks a big game, but back then on *Intruder*, he took the easy way out. And despite everything, he still agreed to work with Kurt again, didn't he?

My only comfort, really, is the secret knowledge that I have someone I'm certain I can trust, a man who means more to me than even he knows. I have you.

V

wilight: the city's outline backlit against the sky, streets smudged with evening rouge.

It was Thursday—and happy hour still—when, for a few precious hours, the Chelsea neighborhood slowed its pulse and unwound, became its own idiosyncratic village. Directly overhead, verdant flora exploded through the iron rails of the Highline, great shocks of firetail mountain fleece, blackberry lily, smooth sumac peeking over the edge like the electrified tresses of trolls, ablaze against the sky's burnished glow. And below, spread over a few long blocks in the West Twenties, the galleries of Chelsea opened their doors, offering cups of cool chardonnay to lure the public in. Scattered pedestrians wandered the length of the dusky streets, ambling from one gallery to the next. Here, unlike the rest of the city, strangers actually met, even socialized; and with wine, time slowed, became somehow more significant. And it might seem, if only for that brief hour or two, that there was nothing more important, more sacred, than art.

As Jonah and Maggie strolled down one of these streets, they glimpsed their destination: a glowing white cube of a space at the far end of the block. Out front, the beginnings of a crowd had already started to congregate. Beside him Maggie tensed, her spine stretching in anticipation.

He turned to her. "How do you feel?"

153

She licked her lips and rubbed them together, her focus locked ahead. "I feel good." She nodded as though to convince herself.

Jonah took her hand, kissed it, and her eyes narrowed with his touch. "I'm proud of you, Mags," he said. "Enjoy this night. You deserve it."

For a moment she hesitated, then swallowed her response. Said instead, "How do I look?"

Jonah took her in: the bloodred bandeau looped luxuriously over her breasts, the matching high-waisted skirt, the skinny heels, earrings flashing within her curls, Maggie's mouth a bold, bright wound.

"You're perfect," he said. "I'm a lucky man."

But it seemed he'd somehow gotten it wrong. Maggie raised a single brow, said nothing.

He tried again. "Thank you for letting me be your date tonight," he said. "I'm so happy to be here with you."

Of course, the fact that she almost hadn't wasn't exactly a surprise. He'd had to work hard to convince Maggie he wanted to be there for her on this very important night.

Tonight was the grand opening of the new gallery ExE, and Maggie had been selected as one of its featured artists. ExE was the passion project of two of Maggie's classmates from Yale, identical twins Emmy and Elle. The twins were gorgeous, waifish girls, born and bred Manhattanites who came from buckets of money and featured prominently in the socialite scene; and while Maggie had confided to Jonah that the twins themselves were lacking in artistic talent, they'd certainly made up for it in taste. After grad school, they'd promptly made the switch to a career in curation, as though attempting the life of a starving artist had never actually been in the cards. They'd each already climbed the ladder at Christie's and Sotheby's, respectively. Privately, they'd become collectors of some noteworthy up-and-comers.

And now with ExE, the twins were making their first public foray. A year ago, they'd purchased a warehouse space lying vacant amidst the galleries and poured money into a chic redesign that had put them on the map. Last November, the twins invited Maggie to drinks and asked her to feature as one of five artists in their launch. While it wasn't the debut she'd dreamed for herself—Mags was worried Emmy and Elle's socialite status might precede them, and the gallery wouldn't be taken seriously by those that mattered—Jonah had convinced her to accept. ExE's opening was certain to get a lot of attention, he'd pointed out, and the optics would only help her career. And besides: the quality of Maggie's work would speak for itself.

In the weeks leading up to the launch, the gallery had gotten more buzz than they'd anticipated. A number of heavy lifters in the industry were rumored to attend, and almost as soon as invitations had been sent, the RSVP list had been filled to capacity. This was going to be big.

So when Maggie had announced that morning that she wanted to go on her own, Jonah, though unsurprised, was more than a little upset.

"Mags," he'd said. "Come on. I know things have been a bit rocky lately—"

"A bit *rocky*?" she'd repeated. "As far as I'm concerned, the engagement is off until you figure out what the hell you want. In fact," she said, pulling the ring from her finger, "it's silly for me to even wear this right now. It doesn't mean anything."

"Don't say that," he said, catching hold of her hand. "Of course it does. I want you to wear it."

Gently, she pulled herself free. "I'll wear it when you choose me for good. But Jonah, that hasn't happened yet." She placed the ring into his palm.

"Maggie, please." He touched her shoulder. "I'm here, aren't I? I'm with you because I choose to be."

She hesitated, grew quiet. "What are you saying?"

"I'm saying I'm sorry." Jonah closed his eyes. "She's only a patient, Mags; nothing more. I know I have to deal with it, and I'm going to. She's just in a very difficult situation."

Maggie scoffed.

"I'm serious. It's awful. You know I'd tell you if I could. She's in crisis—that's why she showed up here that night—and I can't abandon her now."

"You don't have to be every woman's savior, Jonah," Maggie said. "Every woman is not your mother."

"I know that—I do," he said quickly. "I just need to get her through the next few weeks, and then I'll recommend she start with someone else—Lee, maybe; or Kenneth. I know I can't in good conscience keep her on. And I don't want to," he added when he saw her reaction. "I just need you to stick with me for a few more weeks. And then it'll all be over, and we can move on to the life we're building together. I choose you, Mags, alright? I love you."

"I don't feel good about this," Maggie said softly; but even so, she'd let him slip the ring back onto her finger.

"Maggie, love!" Elle threw open her arms as they climbed the steps to the entrance. Or was it Emmy? He could never quite tell. Whoever she was, she was wearing what looked like a giant yellow tarp that could easily have fit both twins inside, and bangles stacked all the way up her skinny arms. They clanged loudly against one another as she folded Mags into a bony embrace.

"We've got a few photographers already circling, so look sharp. You know the drill, right?" She smiled flirtatiously at Jonah. "And fuck me, do we have some big swingers tonight. The *New Yorker* has RSVP'd, as has *New York Mag*. The *Journal's* a maybe? No word from the *Times*, but our fingers are crossed! Here." She tap-tapped her phone. "I just forwarded the list with a face page so you have all the deets."

"Oh, Em, you're always so on top of it," Maggie said. (Emmy, after all.) "The place looks gorgeous."

"Jonah, let me take your coat. It's summer, for god's sake! We don't need that weighing you down in the photos." She pulled the jacket from his arm and blithely tossed it to the intern hovering behind her.

"And look!" She grabbed hold of Maggie's elbow and pulled her around the partition and into the main room. "Guess who we decided to feature!"

Jonah sucked in his breath. There, front and center, was Maggie's work. He knew this painting, knew it well: it was the portrait of Jonah that Maggie had begun the very first night they'd met. And while he knew the piece was spectacular, perhaps even her best, just looking at it filled him with dread.

It was an oversized landscape, twelve feet in length; a thickly painted combination of acrylic and oil. The subject was abstract, meant to be interpreted by the viewer; but he knew the painting had been heavily inspired by the framed picture in his office, the dark, blurry photo of Jonah at a masquerade ball at Princeton.

In the painting, the vibrant colors Maggie had chosen contrasted sharply with one another to create the hazy lines of Jonah's silhouette. The sharp contours of the mask; an arm midway to extension; the wavy frame of hair; and a collar, wrapped tight about the neck. The painting seemed full of motion, the smudges of color shifting and pulsing with life. But for all the wild blur, the focus seemed to angle towards the painting's brightest point, about a third from the left—a blinding swirl of movement, a silhouette of golden-white light. Mags had employed trompe l'oeil to provide the illusion that the right most portion of the canvas, where her rendering of Jonah stood, was saturated in a thick bloodred, and felt nearest the viewer; while the furthest was that glowing golden point of focus to which Jonah's likeness irresistibly turned.

He'd been rereading *The Last Tycoon* when she'd painted it—Fitzgerald's last unfinished novel—and now, framing the painting in a tiny, delicate scrawl, was the passage he'd read aloud to her as she'd worked, which had eventually inspired the painting's title:

He had flown up very high to see, on strong wings when he was young. And while he was up there he had looked on all the kingdoms, with the kind of eyes that can stare straight into the sun. Beating his wings tenaciously—finally frantically—and keeping on beating them

*he had stayed up there longer than most of us, and then, remembering
all he had seen from his great height of how things were, he had settled
gradually to earth.*

The title: *Ícaro.*

"Oh, Em," Maggie said, eyes shining. "I can't believe it."

"Well, start believing," she quipped. "You deserve it. This painting is
a fucking masterpiece. Right, Jonah?"

"A masterpiece, indeed," he said. "I find it the most haunting of her
work."

He felt Maggie watching him and turned. She was looking at him
intently—as though she'd just recognized him as someone she knew a
long time ago.

A sudden clamoring behind them—the quick, clicking stampede of
heels against concrete, then a bustle of echoing voices, the clacketing
of cameras.

"Emmy!" Elle's face popped from around the corner, attempting
subtlety as she gestured frantically for her twin.

"Duty calls!" Emmy winked. "I'll catch up with you in a bit. Happy
roaming!"

"Someone important must have arrived," Maggie murmured, eyes
flicking nervously back to her work.

Jonah scoffed. "Who could be more important than the artist of the
evening? God, those two are a caricature of themselves." He touched
the strip of skin on her back.

She flinched. "They're doing me a huge favor," she said. "And they
mean well. I wish you wouldn't be so condescending. They've clearly
done an amazing job."

"I'm sorry," he said. "I only meant—we always used to laugh at them
together."

"Well, maybe we were wrong." She sighed, closed her eyes. "Can you
please just be happy for me tonight? Can you treat this as something
important, instead of poking fun?"

"You're right," he said. "Of course you're right. It sounds like they've done well with the industry list . . . ?"

"Oh just stop, Jonah." She pulled away.

"Mags—"

She sighed. "Just—let me have this night. Alright?"

He nodded, still confused, but took her hand in his. "Come on. Let's go find the rest of your work."

But just as they started to move, the clamor erupted into a deafening din as a surge of people came from around the partition and into the room where they stood. The crowd of bodies angled inward—Emmy and Elle's tinkling voices ringing above the rest—and at the periphery, cameras flashed.

"What's going on?" he asked; and then a sudden fissure, a window in, and Jonah sucked in his breath.

Lila.

"Maggie!" she called.

Jonah watched, unable to breathe, as Lila crossed to his speechless fiancée and wrapped her in a hug. She didn't even glance his way, didn't even acknowledge Jonah's presence, as she slid her hands down Maggie's arms and whispered into her ear. Jonah watched, heart battering, as Maggie's expression began to morph from indignation to confusion to—*was it possible?*—a reluctant, blushing smile. But though he strained with all his might to hear the exchange, the room's booming acoustics overwhelmed their conversation.

A whiff of bold cologne. "Friend of the artist?"

Jonah turned to discover Freddie James, his chin raised a little jauntily, gazing coolly at the women in the center of the room. Around them, Jonah noticed, men and women alike were watching Freddie, desperate to catch a bit of his elusive glow.

Jonah cleared his throat. "She's my fiancée, actually."

Freddie looked him up and down with a certain hardy skepticism; finally he raised his brow in approval. "Lucky devil." He offered a conspiratorial smile. "I'm a total ignoramus when it comes to art; my handsome plus-one over there practically had to drag me here. She couldn't stop talking about your fiancée's work." A rueful grin. "And when Lila gets invested, god knows she loves to create a bit of a stir."

Jonah turned back to the two women, still deep in muted conversation. As the cameras flashed, Lila gestured to the painting, her face radiant with admiration, and the smile on Maggie's face grew brighter.

"It's all very . . . dramatic. Isn't it."

Jonah turned back to him. "What?"

But Freddie merely cocked his head, smiled. "The painting?"

"Oh." He shook his head. "I suppose so."

He wondered then just how much Lila had told Freddie. Did Freddie know about him—and was he teasing him? Or was Jonah simply being paranoid?

Then—so briefly he almost missed it—Lila glanced at Freddie and nodded, her eyes never once alighting upon Jonah. It was as though he didn't even exist.

"That's my cue." Freddie lifted his glass, winked. "Here's to the happy couple." He downed his wine in a single swallow, and waved his hand in a jaunty salute as he melted past his adoring oglers to Lila. She bid a final farewell to Maggie, and Freddie whisked her deeper into the gallery; and with them, their security team and the persistent cameras followed.

The crowd began to disperse. Jonah made his way over to Maggie, reminding himself to breathe.

"Maggie, you slut! You didn't tell me you knew Lila Crayne!" Elle exclaimed with a wicked grin. (Yes, this was Elle, he noted; while the twins were wearing matching yellow trash bags that evening, Elle was in leather boots, while Emmy had chosen stilettos.)

"I don't," Maggie said, bewildered. Her eyes flicked to Jonah. "I mean—I hardly do."

"Well then, who invited her and Freddie James? I'm *obsessed* with those two."

"Elle, darling!" someone called.

Elle turned back to Maggie. "Come with me, babe. You've got droves of admirers dying to meet you. High time to make some introductions, hm?" She smiled mischievously and began to drag Maggie off. Mags, still dazed, threw an indecipherable look to Jonah before disappearing.

What was Lila doing, showing up here? After she'd sent yesterday's entry, Lila had texted she'd be in touch soon with a way to have their next session in secret. And then: nothing. So what was this chance encounter? A way to bait Jonah, or worse: to hurt Maggie? Was Lila actually trying to push their relationship to its breaking point?

"It's thrilling, don't you think?"

He started at the sound of her voice, having just witnessed her exit. He turned to face her, took her in. She was wearing a man's white button-down rolled at the cuffs over a tight leather skirt, fingers thick with gold rings. This Lila—hair slicked back, eyes rimmed with liner—this wasn't the Lila he'd grown accustomed to. This Lila looked edgy, almost androgynous.

"There's something so inscrutable about it," she continued, studying the painting. "I told Maggie I might buy it." Then she turned to him with a smile. "What do you think?"

He glanced around the room. "What are you doing here?" he whispered.

She blinked. "I'm here to support Maggie," she said. "I felt terrible for intruding on the two of you last week. I wanted to make it up to her, draw some attention to her work." She shrugged. "It's one of the few ways being famous can do something worthwhile. She seemed to appreciate it."

Of course: Lila was simply being thoughtful. Why was he jumping to such inane, irrational conclusions?

Lila glanced at Freddie, who'd been tolerating Emmy's fangirl chatter a few feet away. "I need to go; we shouldn't be seen together. But I wanted to let you know I've gotten myself a getaway, a little pied-à-terre. Can you meet me there next Friday at eight?"

"Next Friday?" His head was spinning; he tried to think. Lila looked to Freddie again, who caught her eye, raised a single inquiring brow. "I think so. But how will I . . . ?"

Lila bit her lip, smiled. "Check your coat."

Then she walked over to Freddie, kissed his cheek. Together, they rounded the corner; and then she was gone.

———

Two hours later, and they were saying their final goodbyes. Mags had been the star of the evening; everyone they'd met had gushed over her work. They eased their way through the remaining crowd and out into the summer night, tipsy from the free-flowing wine.

He'd felt he had no choice but to try to drink his way through the evening; yet even so, Jonah had felt jittery, distracted. He'd hovered at the fringes of conversation, engaging in small talk when necessary—trying to be a good partner on this most important of nights. And yet: he couldn't stop thinking about Lila.

Maggie's annoyance, however, had long since evaporated. As they made their way home to the West Village, she yawned, arms spreading wide. "Oh, this was the best night in a long time," she said, beaming. "I don't think it could've gone better, do you?"

"Everyone loved you—I couldn't believe the turnout." He hesitated. "Thoughtful of Lila to come show her support."

She flinched at the mention of her name. "The pieces were going to sell regardless." She shook her head. "My work speaks for itself, Jonah—with or without Lila Crayne's blessing."

"You're right," he said. "You deserved every bit of your success tonight."

She nodded, seemed chastened, and pulled Jonah's coat from his arm and draped it over her shoulders. His stomach flipped; he hadn't yet had a moment to check its pockets to discover what Lila had planted. But he swallowed his worry away as he helped Mags into the sleeves, then kissed the side of her head. "You were incredible. And you looked gorgeous. I couldn't take my eyes off you."

She grinned, looking like a little girl in his jacket, her hair falling over her face. "I'm quite the hot fox right now, am I not?"

"You are," he said, and felt the lust well.

Something was stirred in him—something not accounted for by the shimmering evening, the triumphant vividness of Maggie's red . . . And then at once he understood: it was the sudden, looming threat of their separation, the knowledge that he might soon lose her. Already it was happening: the air even now filling the space from his hand to hers, the dark patch of pavement between them stretching . . . and in the distance, always, the city's soft, beckoning blur. Yet in this moment, Jonah wanted to stop them, freeze them, just as they were. In this moment, he felt, perversely, that he loved Maggie *more*.

He grabbed her hand, pulled her around a corner, and Maggie cried out in surprise. "I think we should celebrate," he said, breathless. "Don't you?"

She giggled nervously but let him pull her off to the side of someone's private drive. They were just barely blocked by an ivy-covered wall; anyone passing might merely peer around the corner and discover them there.

"Jo," Maggie whispered, and he brushed back her hair, bit down hard upon the sweet drupe of her ear. She moaned softly, and he thought, *Oh Mags, what am I doing? What have I done?* In this moment, he wanted only to merge himself back with her, to the way they were before. In this moment, he wished Lila had never come into his life.

He lifted her up against the wall, and she wrapped her legs around his waist, her fingers fumbling with the button of his pants. She inhaled as his hand found her throat, pressed upon the warm delicate cords

163

there. And when he pulled into her, Jonah felt as if there was nothing else, could never be anything else, if only they would stay conjoined, burrowed deep in each other forever. If only the world was just the two of them, with nothing to come between them.

A sudden sharpness jolted him back to surface, a bright pinprick of pain just below the hip. He flinched; and again, it dug in. Maggie's fingers roamed his hair, her mouth soft against his neck, unaware. Still holding her, Jonah reached a hand down, trying to discover the source. His fingers landed upon his jacket, traced the lip of the outer pocket. Blindly, he reached inside, felt the bit of metal, warmed by Maggie's heat, its jagged form unmistakable:

A key.

Lila's Therapy Journal
for Jonah Gabriel

Entry #3
July 27

Dearest Diary,

Let me first begin with an apology. Jonah, I've been stewing miserably over our misunderstanding at the gallery last night. Of course I realize now how my behavior must have seemed: at best, tone-deaf, and at worst . . . insidious? I noticed Maggie was initially a bit frosty; I hope I didn't inadvertently offend her. I don't know her, of course, but the little I *do* know, I like very much. With your blessing, I would like to go ahead and support Maggie in buying *Ícaro*. Would that be alright? If one thing is true, Jonah, it's this: though my means may be terribly messy, my motives have always been pure.

Onto the headline story: my fiancé has disappeared.

He's done this before. When Kurt gets really angry, he vanishes. Not only is this behavior triggering, Kurt knows that in this given moment, his disappearance is precisely what will hurt me most. You see, Jonah, the film can't go on without him (more on this later); so until he resurfaces, production is at a complete standstill, and with every minute lost we are hemorrhaging money we simply don't have. Kurt is deliberately putting *Tender* in jeopardy.

It's been forty hours now since he walked from set, and still no word. So I go to the one person in the world who knows the whole messy truth of my situation, the only person with enough sway over Kurt Royall to persuade him to come back.

I go to Mother.

Cut to Mother in slippers, robe, and mud mask in the doorway of her Upper East Side apartment. I step out of the birdcage elevator; behind me, the operator closes the brass gate, and it begins its rattly descent. Mother has her phone held away from the wet goop on her face; and even from where I'm standing, I can hear the yelling on the other end of the line.

"Care to tell me what the hell happened?" she asks me with false sweetness.

I point to her phone, put a finger to my lips, but she waves away my concern. "Darling, please. We're on mute."

Still, I speak quietly (with Mother's technological ineptitude, one can never be too sure). "Who's on the call?"

"It's Bobby Starr and the whole Olympus crew, furiously swinging their mini gherkins," she says. "They've wrangled all *Tender*'s Russki investors, who've been dropping like flies over the past 24 hours. Olympus just made it official: they're threatening to cut ties with *Tender* altogether."

This hardly comes as a surprise; yet even still, my stomach drops. Olympus (frat house of the film world, comprised entirely of conservative, sexist men) hadn't even batted an eye before rejecting producing *Tender*'s feminist adaptation. Kurt had had to pull together his own team of private investors direct from Russia, all of whom would give their firstborn son to be associated with a Kurt Royall film. Once financing had been secured, after a few too many whiskeys, cigars, and other unnamable stimulants, Olympus had agreed to sign on as distributor – pending final cut. But now, with Kurt's unexplained departure, all our investors are refusing to send final installments until he resurfaces. Without their continued financing, the film will remain unfinished, and Olympus will drop distribution. In other words: without Kurt, *Tender* falls apart.

"Come in, come in. You're just in time for the grand finale: Starr's dramatic dressing-down. Now how do I put this on speakerphone?"

"*...with Kurt's reps, but they're either withholding information or they haven't heard from him, either. As everyone here is painfully aware, this film is already behind schedule and two million over budget; and now, due to Kurt's mysterious absence, production has lost an additional two and a half days and counting. Olympus has shown great patience with this project's amateurish process, but we're unwilling to forgive this behavior any longer. We've told Kurt's reps we need to hear from him by end of day, or we're cutting our losses and terminating the agreement. So if any of you has any idea where Kurt Royall is—if you have any special ties, any favors you want to call in—I suggest you do so now.*"

"Good god." Mother ends the call and pockets her phone. "Want a drink?" she calls as she shuffles her way to the bar.

"It's ten in the morning."

She throws me a pointed look. "Since when has that ever stopped either of us?"

I shrug. "What are you having?"

"Oh, have a little faith in Mother." She sweeps around the bar like Ginger Rogers, robe billowing behind, and begins to scoop ice into a cocktail shaker. She smiles, teeth shining, the clay on her face beginning to crack. "When have I ever steered you wrong?"

Mother swizzles and shakes up something tart and strong—and I have to admit: it's exactly what I need. We settle opposite one another on poufy couches before the wide swath of windows overlooking Fifth Avenue and the thicket of trees beyond.

"So," Mother says. "Want to tell me how you fucked everything up?"

I look into my drink, steady myself. "He knows I wrote it, Mother."

She grows still.

"I tried my best to keep up the charade—I really did," I say. "But it became so obvious. Honestly, by now everyone probably knows. Rupert was the wrong hire. I thought he'd be convincing as the young, ambitious writer, but he was too soft. He had no idea how to stand up to Kurt, even when I literally put the words in his mouth."

"I'm still waiting for the punch line." Mother spreads her arms along the back of the couch. "So he found out you're the ghostwriter. It's still a fucking great script. One little lie shouldn't change Kurt's desire to direct it."

"But it's *my* script, Mother," I say. "That's why I had to pull this ploy in the first place. To Kurt, I've only ever been sweet, helpless Lila. That's how he first saw me, and that's how he wants me to stay." (Jonah, I can't tell you how many times I've wanted to invoke Eleanor's line from *This Side of Paradise*: *Rotten, rotten old world, and the wretchedest thing of all is me—oh why am I a girl?*)

"Kurt's ego would never allow for the possibility that I might be capable of creating something smart and powerful, something game-changing," I continue. "I knew that the only writer who could get him excited about a feminist adaptation was someone young and spineless and *male*, who he could bully around in the name of mentorship. If Kurt had known that I'd written *Tender*, he never would've gone to bat for it. The film never would've been made."

(Jonah, here again I must apologize. Of all the people I kept this secret from, I feel most ashamed of not having been honest with you. But you see, I was so desperate to see this film through, I felt I couldn't risk telling anyone—not even you. Of course, now I know I should've been honest with you from the start. So if you'd indulge me, please allow me to correct my mistake now, and tell you the whole truth:

A few years ago, a young film major named Rupert Bradshaw watched *Waiting Game* for the first time in his life, and—to use his exact words—"*the movie totally rocked his celluloid world.*" He'd written Kurt a fan letter, enclosing his painfully bad screenplay, announcing to Kurt they

168

were destined collaborators. Well, of course Kurt never even opened Rupert's letter—but I did. This was nothing new—Kurt knew I'd often open his fan mail and personally respond to any sweet, impressionable kid in need of a little encouragement. But this time, when I read Rupert's letter, I got an idea.

I reached out to him, and asked if we could meet. And over coffee, I explained to him the important lesson I'd learned the hard way: oftentimes, the most difficult step to having a career in Hollywood is finding a way to break in. I suggested that—for the moment—Rupert set aside his quixotic dreams, and focus instead on finding his *in*. And then, with NDA in hand and an extremely generous pile of cash, I offered Rupert the job that would not only provide him entry—it would launch his career and give him the platform he needed to get the work he cared about greenlit. He accepted on the spot.)

Mother swipes a bit of mask from her cheek, puts the finger into her mouth. "Salty."

"Is that even edible?"

"Here's what I don't understand." She swirls her drink with her muddy finger, ice chattering like molars. "You're such a good actress. Why would you ever let him find out?"

"I just couldn't take the abuse anymore," I say, shaking my head. "I snapped. In the moment, my ego got the best of me."

(Jonah, what do *you* think? Maybe underneath it all, I *do* want the world to know that Lila Crayne—actress and woman!—can really write. I'm tired of men always getting the recognition. Perhaps Zelda felt the same way when she learned Fitzgerald had stolen the words right from her mouth at their daughter's birth, taking all credit for Daisy's famous line: *I hope she'll be a fool—that's the best thing a girl can be in this world, a beautiful little fool.*)

"I regretted it as soon as I told him, of course," I add quickly. "Kurt was furious. So he hurt me the way he knew it would hurt the most: he walked, knowing Olympus and all *Tender*'s investors would walk with him."

"So now you've come crawling to Mother, hoping I'll save the day." She drains the rest of her glass and heads to the bar, wets a washcloth, and begins wiping the mud from her face. "Tell me, darling. What is it you want?"

I swallow. "You're the only person who knows the full story, all that happened between Kurt and me. I need him back to see the film to completion. Without him, the film goes up in smoke. Kurt knows that. He knows I'm trapped."

"An offer Kurt Royall can't refuse." She begins to make a second drink. For a few moments, the only sound: the metallic whir of ice.

I can't stand it any longer. "What do you think?"

Mother tweezes a maraschino cherry on top of her drink, takes in my expression. "Darling, why the long face? No matter how many times you get yourself into some terrible mess with a man, Mother will always be there to bail you out.

"Now, where are my glasses," she murmurs, before plucking them from an armchair. "Alright now." She pulls out her phone and settles herself, flicking back her robe with a flourish to better showcase her legs. "This should be entertaining."

As Mother deliberates, I turn my focus to the shimmering rush of treetops, the leaves thrilling in the morning sun. And I realize: this is it. This is the end of my relationship with Kurt. In just two weeks' time, this nightmare will be over, and I can move on to a better life, a normal life; a life where I finally feel safe.

The low swooping sound. Mother tilts her glasses to the tip of her nose. "Sent."

My heart guns. "You texted him already? What did you say?"

"Oh darling, don't you trust me?" She reaches for her drink. "I wouldn't worry if I were you. I have a feeling this will all play out exactly as you want it to."

"But how?"

"Think, Lila. What does Kurt Royall want, more than anything? We both know the answer. Now think about your endgame. After all these years, you're so close to achieving everything you ever wanted. How can Kurt help put the final piece in place?"

Suddenly I realize: I know exactly what Mother has asked of Kurt, and what she's offered him in return. It's brilliant, and it's terrifying. Perhaps it's the sheer relief of knowing her plan will work; or maybe it's the utter exhaustion from struggling to keep myself together even as my life has completely fallen apart. Whatever the reason, I can't hold back any longer: I start to cry.

Mother moves beside me, her fingers gliding through my hair just like she used to do when I was little. I crumple into her lap, bury my face in the muted warmth of her robe, breathe in her familiar verbena scent. She says nothing, simply continues to stroke my hair down the length of my spine.

And suddenly a memory—the night of the crash—flashes to the fore— one I must've forgotten long ago . . .

Blood rilling down from my scalp, its sweet warmth finding my mouth—my tongue probing the soft pulp of my gums, fresh from the loss of a tooth. Rain from all sides like an all-swallowing roar—and Mother's hand, reaching slow through the dark to check Daddy's pulse. How *quiet* she'd been—and I'd known instinctively that I should be quiet, too. Eventually, her fingers had lifted from his neck, her face glistening—with blood? with tears?—a silent smile spreading through the wet. And then at last, she'd seemed to remember: her child—oh yes, I was there too, right behind her! Her *child* was there with her—but hadn't made a sound. Had I . . . ? Was I . . . ? And at last she'd turned and reached for me—

"Honey," Mother says softly now. "Your eye."

My hand flies up to hide it.

"That monster." She shakes her head, face flushing just as mine does when I'm upset. And I think: what must this be like for her, to have to watch her own child make the same terrible mistakes? For all her own suffering, all the risks Mother took to extricate us from our misery, I'd nevertheless managed to re-create the living nightmare of my childhood home.

I know that now is the time to ask her about that night in the car, about what really happened. Because, I realize, we're not that different, Mother and I. And the frightened desperation she must have felt to free herself is all too familiar to me now. I want so badly to ask her, so that I can finally face the trauma of that night and come to terms with the truth, as you've so patiently encouraged me to do. And also: so that I can meet my own crusade with clear eyes, and determine once and for all how to take control of my life.

I wipe the wet from my face, push myself upright. "Mother . . ."

And maybe I imagine it, but in that moment, I sense she knows what I'm about to ask; and I see fear in her eyes. And I realize: yes, I want to hear the truth—but at what cost? Don't I already know it, deep in my bones? Somehow, Mother was able to reframe the events of that night and convince the authorities of her innocence. She found a way to put her trauma behind her, to heal herself. Asking her to confess to it now would not only be selfish, it might also threaten the peaceful existence she'd so rightfully earned. Better to let the past remain in the past. Better to protect her, to keep her secret safe.

"Lila." She takes my hand in hers. "You know as well as I that being a woman in this world is tough. For most, it means suffering millions of tiny betrayals, swallowing it all in silence and bearing the pain alone. That life is nothing more than a long, slow death. But a lucky few find another path, a way to slice through the belly of the beast and carve their own way out. I was one of those women. And you're one of us, too.

"It's a man's world we're living in; and it always will be. But I know you can create your own path; you're doing it already. Only you can change your fate."

A light ding: through the pocket of her robe, the bluish glow of

Mother's phone. She adjusts her glasses, unlocks it, reads. At last she looks up at me.

"Congratulations," she says simply. "Kurt accepted the offer. He's on his way back. Now it's time you do your part. Finish what you started, Lila, and set yourself free."

VII

Jonah was running late. This never happened.

He'd arrived at 12 Charles Street with a couple minutes to spare, then attempted to jam Lila's key into the slot—only to find it didn't fit. He'd then stood outside for the next fifteen minutes like an idiot, waiting for a response to his text asking which apartment to buzz.

The sheer strangeness of the circumstance had him rattled. And even though he told himself this was purely another session, meant to prepare his patient for her imminent escape from a toxic relationship, he knew it was a lie, knew there was so much more to it now than that. The intimate gift of a key to Lila's getaway apartment—an apartment no one else knew existed—made this meeting illicit.

Because what they hadn't yet directly acknowledged—what they'd have to acknowledge tonight—was Lila's unexpressed feelings for Jonah. He'd tried to tell himself he was reading into her journal entries' careful, circuitous language, teasing out hoped-for implications rather than accepting a simpler, more plausible truth—yet every time, he drew the same conclusion: Lila wanted him to make the first move, to admit his very real feelings for her, so that she'd finally have permission to confess her own, as well.

He unlocked his phone, scrolled to the message she'd sent earlier that day with the apartment's address. His stomach dropped. 12 Charles *Lane*.

Not Charles Street, the classic West Village thoroughfare. 12 Charles *Lane*.

Swearing under his breath, he typed the correct address into his phone. It was a ten-minute walk away, five if he ran. He texted Lila a quick apology explaining his mistake, then clutched his phone in his palm and began to run west.

As he jogged along Charles, he watched as, one by one, all the pretty, lonely women wandering the leafy street heard the urgent tread of his gait and turned to watch him as he passed. In his restless mind, he entered now into each of their lives, pursuing them as they turned the dark corners of quiet streets, their curious smiles beckoning him to follow.

The light breeze he generated felt good against his skin, a momentary reprieve from the summer swelter; but Jonah knew as soon as he stopped, the sweat would begin its steady pour, and all his efforts to look his best would be undone.

Despite his attempts to normalize the situation, he'd changed an inordinate number of times before settling on a selection that felt timeless, soigné – nicer than his everyday wear, but still casual enough, not *too* nice: slim cut Brunello Cucinelli slacks, navy linen button-down from the Armoury, caramel woven venetian Fryes. It was a decent upgrade, a sound option for a date (*which it isn't*, he reminded himself).

He'd stood before his full-length mirror earlier that evening, appraising his own reflection—trying to tell himself he'd gained rather than lost in appearance in the years since their first romantic encounter; that perhaps his face had even taken on a certain tangible air of tragedy, romantically contrasted with his trim and immaculate person.

Mags had made plans with her group of girlfriends that night and would likely be out bar-hopping till the wee hours; but as she passed their bedroom on her way out, she paused to poke her head around the doorframe.

"All dressed up for dinner with Kenneth?"

He'd started at the sound of her voice. "You know Kenneth. Can't help but feel the need to impress."

And she'd smiled sadly and rested her head against the wooden frame. "You look good, Dr. Gabriel." Before he could summon a response, she'd disappeared down the hall.

At eighteen our convictions are hills from which we look, he'd recited to himself; *at forty-five they are caves in which we hide.* He was still only thirty-five; and yet, with each ensuing hour that passed, Jonah found himself sacrificing the tenets on which he'd built his estimation of himself, burrowing deeper and deeper into his own endless cave of hypocrisy. His guilty conscience over the blurred lines of his conflicting roles in Lila's life made the truth all too painfully clear: regardless of what would happen with Lila that night, he knew his intentions were not to be faithful to Maggie.

Lila, on the other hand, still represented just the opposite: in her, soul and spirit were one. The purity of her intentions, her genuine *goodness*, seemed to Jonah to radiate from within, shimmering upon the glory of her skin. All his life he'd felt an insatiable romantic hunger for beauty, conflating it in that Kantian way as the symbol of the morally good. But as he'd inspected his reflection one final time, hoping to perfect his image even as he tore into himself for the betrayal he might that same night commit, he'd realized that such congruency was misleading, even an outright lie. Even if beauty might be seen as morality's symbol, it in no way indicated the presence of morality, itself. All Jonah had to do was look in the mirror to see that it might, in fact, be just the opposite.

He shook off these obsessive ruminations and increased his pace, jogging past Wilson's, long since closed for the day. Behind the glass: a ghost town in miniature. The wooden chairs were upended onto tables, their pointed legs in rigor mortis. The overhead lights had been killed, the floor swept clean. The only evidence of life: the same single suspended bulb, lit low and swaying, as it always mysteriously did.

He hooked a right onto Washington, then slowed his stride as he turned left onto the tiny, tucked away lane. As he walked down its cobblestoned path, he wondered why Lila would pick an apartment here, mere steps from her place with Kurt. It didn't make sense; this close to one another, they'd surely cross paths, and it'd be no effort at all for Kurt to discover her asylum. But perhaps upending her life seemed only feasible in baby steps, her panic so overwhelming it had clouded her decision-making. . . .

This, truly, was one of the most difficult parts of his job; yet Jonah knew that as her therapist, he had a moral obligation to let Lila make her own mistakes—even one as misguided as this. And while of course it'd be painful for him to stand by and watch, reserving judgment was, he reminded himself, a matter of infinite hope. He'd comfort himself with the knowledge that he'd be there to support Lila now, when she came out on the other side.

He stopped when he reached the address, taking extra care this time to ensure he was correct. This wasn't an apartment; it was a *house*. A carriage house, in fact, complete with garage and—he strained, looking up—its own private balcony. A place like this surely cost a fortune; but then again, why should Lila Crayne consider anything less? It certainly made more aesthetic sense than the first drab destination—an apartment building, it seemed, for finance bros shot straight from undergrad who only cared about the status of the zip code. But this? This was romance made manifest, the sort of place you'd only dream of when you uttered the phrase, *pied-à-terre*.

He checked his phone. *Only twenty-two minutes late*, he thought to himself. *Way to make her feel at ease, Jonah—like she's in really trustworthy, capable hands.* A delicate constellation of sweat lifted from his skin. He pulled the key from his pocket, hesitated. Should he knock? He was already so late; and besides, Lila had given him the key because she wanted him to use it, hadn't she? He licked his lips, inserted the key, turned.

He stepped inside, then paused a moment, waiting for his eyes to adjust to the darkness within. "Lila?" he called. "It's Jonah."

His eyes beginning to sharpen now, the fuzzy unfolding into grey particulate matter. "Lila?"

A light vibration. He pulled his phone from his pocket, its sudden glow blinding. Text from Lila, sent three minutes ago.

Meet me out on the terrace.

Relax, Jonah, he told himself. This explained the silence, the darkness, right? The sun had only just set, and she was outside; she hadn't yet thought to turn on the lights. Right? He felt along the walls for a switch; but finding none, turned his phone into a makeshift flashlight and began to walk down what seemed to be a hallway. As he bypassed the gaping mouths of doors, he had the distinct uncanny feeling he was being watched. He willed himself not to squint into the thresholds' dark innards, to discover what might silently be hiding there. A few steps more, and to his left a staircase was revealed, pillar candles lit on every other step. The quivering glow they cast stirred in Jonah the memory of their night together, all those years ago. Heart pounding, he switched off his light, turned his phone to silent, and began to climb.

The top of the stairs opened onto a great room, the entire southern wall a sleek, modern kitchen, Scandinavian in design. The rest of the open space would serve as living and dining room, but for now it remained empty save for generous clusters of candles flickering in the corners, and an enormous suspended chandelier like a Catherine Wheel, casting spidery shadows over the room. To his right: a dark staircase, leading up to the bedrooms. The wall opposite was entirely glass; and beyond, the private terrace.

Jonah opened the door to the balcony, and his stomach swung slightly when he saw Lila balanced upon the stone ledge where it abutted the building, leaning against the exterior wall. He thought suddenly, absurdly, that he need only push her gently, and she would topple over the side. He could picture it now: her eyes stretching wide as she beheld him, her inconceivable betrayer. The silent pop of her lips, the final fall—too sudden for a scream. And then below, in the gloaming: the unthinkable.

He closed his eyes to compose himself, knew this voice all too well as his own ugly imp of the perverse; and as he breathed, the notion shuddered away. And yet, a certain coolness lingered in the quiet corners of his mind, and Jonah wondered: if he were to lose control, lose hold of himself in a single crucial moment, could he be capable of such horrors?

He opened his eyes to find Lila watching him, a curious smile on her face.

"It's *l'heure bleue. . . .*" she said, and he smiled, impressed at her reference to one of Fitzgerald's obscurest stories.

". . . *When everything is really blue,*" he finished. For a moment they simply looked at one another. Then he cleared his throat. "I'm sorry it took longer than expected," he began, but she waved the thought away.

"Please. I was grateful for the time. It's so peaceful here." She reached down, lifted a bottle of wine. "Care to join me?"

He hesitated a moment, and she grinned. "Come on, Jonah. Isn't this all a bit subversive? Surely one glass of wine couldn't hurt."

He inhaled. "One glass."

"I'm sorry about the lack of furniture," she said, glancing up as she poured. "I haven't had the chance to set the place up. It's my first time here, actually. You're helping me christen my new home."

His pulse quickened at the intimation, but Lila simply offered up his glass, then continued on. "One of the things I'm most looking forward to is shedding my past life, that whole identity, and starting from scratch."

"Well then. To new beginnings," he said, and they clinked, drank. And he allowed himself to take her in, noted once again how different she seemed now from the various versions of Lila he'd known: straight from the shower, and without makeup, her hair still slick and shiny.

She was barefoot, her toes a bright coral, wearing terrycloth shorts and a soft white tee; hadn't even bothered with a bra, he noted with an inner thrill, the tiny fig points of her nipples just barely showing through. She seemed to him impossibly clean—reminded him, in that moment, of Maggie.

He swallowed, took a few steps away to gather himself. Placed his glass on the stone ledge.

"It's nice, isn't it?" She gestured before them. "My own private slice of water. Not as dramatic as the view from my place with Kurt, of course."

"That's true," he agreed, then inhaled. "You'd mentioned you lived right on the highway, didn't you? Right on the water?"

"Did I?" A smile curled her voice. Was she teasing him?

"I think so, in one of your entries." He took a generous sip, enjoyed the crisp minerality of the wine. He drank again—felt suddenly parched—then set his glass back on the wall, willed himself to slow down.

Lila pulled her legs up onto the ledge and looped her arms loosely around the backs of her thighs, so that Jonah could just glimpse the slight curve of her ass. He cleared his throat, leaned against the wall.

"I have to admit, I've never done a home visit before."

She placed her chin onto her knees. "I'm sure this breaks all the rules," she said. "Thank you for humoring me. It just seemed like the safest way. Kurt doesn't know I've gotten this place. And I'm not sure Maggie would have liked me showing up again, either," she added.

"Please don't worry about that. She was very appreciative of what you did for her at her opening, and for so generously buying *Ícaro*. In fact," he said, shifting his seat on the ledge, "I wanted to apologize. My reaction was inappropriate; it wasn't fair to you."

She shook her head. "No, you had every right. I'm the one who should be apologizing. I assume you read my entry?"

"Yes, we have quite a lot to discuss." He cleared his throat. He was anxious to steer the conversation towards Karen, and the mysterious message she'd sent after Kurt's disappearing act.

"Congratulations on persuading Kurt to finish the film," he began. "I'm sure that was a big relief."

"It was." Lila sighed, reached down to refill her glass. "I mean, it certainly didn't help with his anger. He's been especially vicious since he's been back. But I can stomach anything for five more days if it means finishing the film."

"Five more days," he echoed. "That's it? Incredible."

She nodded and looked up at him. "And then I'm free."

He tried to ignore the flittering feeling in his chest, and debated simply asking his burning question outright.

"Tell me more about your conversation with your mother," he said instead. "I'm curious about your change of heart in wanting to confront her about the accident."

"Oh Jonah, I don't know." Lila picked up the bottle and walked over— and before he could protest, she'd refilled his glass to the rim. "It's all in the entry. I feel so grateful to you for helping me unlock that memory. I know it's true; I know she did it. And I guess I felt no good could come from saying it out loud. It's not her obligation to make it okay for me. I have to make peace with it on my own. And after all that I've been through with Kurt, I think I understand why she felt driven to do what she did. Why she felt she had no choice."

"Are you angry with her?"

Her brow furrowed. "You've asked me that before. I'm not an angry person. Why would I be angry with her?"

Why would she be angry? How could she possibly not be?

He could see it so clearly—he'd pictured it so many times—how, just as in *Gatsby*, it hadn't happened as the world had so readily assumed. It hadn't been the man who'd held the wheel steady, throttled the accelerator, and driven towards death in the cooling twilight. The man had been swiftly presumed guilty; but in truth, it had been the other unexamined witness who'd been the real murderer. In truth, it had been the woman.

"If your memory's correct," he began carefully, "then your mother was responsible for the death of your father. Even if he brought you both a lot of pain, he's still your father."

She shook her head. "But he abused her, Jonah. He raped her."

"I know he did." He touched his glass, turned it slowly on the ledge. "But what about you—that night, in the car?"

She hesitated.

"You were in the car, too, Lila," he said. "And you were just a child." He paused. "In addition to putting her own life in danger, your mother also chose to risk yours."

Her eyes widened, gone bright with pain. Then she blinked, looked away—struggled to gather herself in the dark.

At last she swallowed. Shook her head. Said, almost to herself, "She did what she felt she had to do to survive. Which is exactly what I'm doing now."

He nodded. "It does seem like she understands what you're going through."

And yet still the riddle remained: what was the offer that Lila and Karen had made, that Kurt had had no choice but to come back?

"I wanted to ask you something," he said. "Provided you feel comfortable discussing it, that is."

She sat down beside him. "I think I know what you're about to say."

He paused. "What am I going to say?"

She gazed at their hands side by side on the ledge, their fingers so close he could nearly feel her touch. "You're going to bring up my feelings for you. Aren't you."

He swallowed.

"Please don't tell me again it's transference," she said. "It's so much more than that. I've felt so childish dropping hints in my journal, hoping you might pick up on the clues. And I think you have—I know you have. That's why you reacted the way you did at Maggie's opening, wasn't it? Because you knew how I felt about you, and it wasn't fair to Maggie. Which, of course, god, I understand now."

She stood, began to pace. "I feel so guilty for feeling the way I do. You have Maggie, I know. And Maggie seems . . . well, she seems like the perfect woman. I keep telling myself you must be happily in love. And what right do I have to interfere? Except—I keep getting this feeling—" She stopped, looked him directly in the eye. "This sense that you feel the same way I do. If I'm wrong, then just say it, and I'll never ask again. But if I'm right . . ."

She took a step closer. "I'm laying my feelings bare. And maybe I'm about to get my heart broken; but it's a risk I'm willing to take. I know I have no right to make any more of a move than I already have. But if you feel the same—and god, I hope you do—please tell me now."

His heart was pounding in his chest. This was the moment he'd dreamed of, the opportunity he'd thought he'd lost forever. Lila Crayne had come right out and said it: she wanted Jonah, was giving herself to him!

His mind spun with all the swiftly whipping confutations: he was engaged to Maggie, had sworn he'd cut this off; Lila was his patient (though he'd lost count of all the boundaries they'd already breached); and she was in crisis, vulnerable, the victim of terrible trauma; to insert himself now would be unethical; to take advantage of her fragility might even jeopardize her ability to heal. And yet he and Lila loved one another—didn't they? And yet—

Lila hugged herself. "This is so humiliating."

"Lila," he pleaded. "I'm just trying to do the right thing. I'm trying to think—"

"Don't!" she cried. "Don't think! I know you, Jonah, and I know if you think this through, you're too moral, too *good* to ever let it happen. I know what's appropriate, what's right. But that's not what I *want*. Just for one night, will you stop your mind from turning? Just for tonight, please don't be my therapist. Just be you. What do you want?"

She stood before him—trembling, raw—and what he wanted tore through him with such ferocity that he knew he never really had a

183

choice. He knew that when he kissed her, an imperfect, mortal reality would replace the shining dream of Lila he'd upheld all these years. But he couldn't stop himself, couldn't wait a moment longer. He crossed the terrace, pulled her in by the small of her back, pressed his mouth hot upon hers—

—And the incarnation was complete.

It was just as he'd imagined, so exactly as he'd memorialized it in his mind. Countless times his thoughts had swept through that night so long ago, until every thread, every angle, every breath and momentary spark had spun itself into his own sacred waltz. He'd memorized it all perfectly, so that now he might recreate their connection; and Lila, feeling it once more, might wed herself completely. The girl he remembered was miraculously unchanged, so delicate, so hesitant. His hand slid around her neck, wrapped up about the base of her skull with certainty, and he pulled her firm against him, just as he'd done before. She reacted just the same, almost frightened, which only made him feel stronger, more certain in his desire as he tugged at the thick mane of her hair, kissed her curious and lovely mouth. She gasped a little, and his confidence swelled. He pulled her tighter against his hips, her beseeching palms against his chest. *God*—she was his, finally his! At last he would take her, knowing she wanted nothing more than to be taken by him. He'd give up Maggie, his practice, his freedom—he'd give anything at all—if it meant loving Lila Crayne for the rest of his life.

She shivered lightly, and so he grabbed her by the hand and took her inside, the crowds of candles like eyes, glowing from the corners. He turned to face her, and again she hesitated, seemed nervous, and so he pulled her roughly in. She stumbled a little, then fell to the floor, and he followed her down, down, so hungry to taste every last part of her, to consume her whole once more. First biting softly on the sweet grapes of her toes, then gliding his tongue along the length of her legs, his fingers pinching the edges of her shorts, teeth grazing ribs; then, her shoulders pinned, he began once more to discover the delicate puckering of her nipples beneath the thin cotton of her shirt, when Lila suddenly cried out.

He looked up, his hand tracing the rope of her neck.

"It's alright," he told her. "You can trust me."

She looked at him with those same haunting eyes from long ago. "I know," she whispered.

Slowly, her fingers interlaced with his upon her own neck.

"You like that?" he whispered.

And with sudden thrilling strength, she pushed his hand hard against her pulsing neck, watching him all the while.

"What do you want?" he asked, his lips hovering over her skin.

But then something changed, and she seemed to disappear into herself, seemed at once so far away. She closed her eyes, her voice lowered to a whisper, so soft he could barely hear. "I want to do this right," she said. "I need to leave Kurt, and you need to leave Maggie."

He groaned, pressed himself against her. How could he possibly stop now?

"Please, Jonah," she said, and he looked up at her, caught her eyes. "In so little time it'll all be over. And then we can truly be together. Will you promise me you'll end it with Maggie for good? Jonah?"

He closed his eyes. "I promise."

He leaned down to kiss her, and she bit him hard. He jerked back and touched his lip, then drew his fingers away. Blood.

"Go," she said, and pushed him off gently, then sat upright, hugging her knees. "We both have so much to do."

He stood, inhaled. She looked so vulnerable, so alone, there on the floor in the dark. "Are you going to be alright?"

Her eyes far away. "I know what I'm doing. I have it all worked out."

Still he hesitated. "Lila . . ."

At last she blinked, looked up at him. "Just go," she whispered.

He nodded, still not quite satisfied, but kissed the top of her head, then headed down the stairs and into the night.

The village was eerily quiet, the air suddenly cool. Something tugged within Jonah, a pinch of some fibrous cord, warning that something wasn't quite right; perhaps he should pause, think it over. But no, he'd told Lila he wouldn't do that. Thinking would only pull him away from the one thing he'd wanted all along.

A cloud slid over the moon, and the world grew dark. But Jonah didn't notice; or if he did, he'd just as happily have continued blind. His recent past had all but melted away—and in its wake, that fresh, green breast of a new world was just before him, was finally nearly his. She would be his destiny—deep down he'd always known this to be true. For Jonah Gabriel, it had always been—would always be—Lila.

Lila's Therapy Journal
for Jonah Gabriel

Entry #4
Aug 10

Dear Jonah,

Dear Jonah, Jonah, Jonah! It feels so delicious to write directly to you at last. Fitzgerald said in Gatsby that life begins all over again with the summer—and now I fully understand the truth of those words.

Before I dive in, something has happened that's left me a bit unsettled. I've been deliberating whether to tell you—you, who I trust more than anyone!—because I don't want you to think I'm questioning you. And yet . . . in the spirit of being honest, and showing you that I do trust you, I won't conceal the doubt that's been seeded in my mind. More on this later.

But first, some happy news: today we officially wrapped Tender! Of course, now begins the editing, the marketing, and all the publicity . . . but for me, the real meat of the work, the work that makes my blood sing, is bringing this story to life before the camera. And now that chapter is done, its ending bittersweet. My one consolation: wrapping this film means extinguishing my relationship with Kurt, and striking up a new life with you.

It's our last night in Montauk, and as always, the prospect of leaving fills me with longing. I'll miss this place: the beaches here like fat white cakes, sugary sand dusting the wind – the ocean's seething crash and pull. Days here are made of heat, salt, lust—marked only by the sun's slow rub across the sky, its bright, wet pour, its lingering, whole-body kiss.

Official wrap party tonight at Duryea's, the perfect setting for Tender's closing. Candlelit tables stretching down the length of the dock float like ghosts over the water's skin. Directly before us, the sun in its fiery descent. And the rest of the world, cleft in two. Dark, shimmering water, endless bleed of sky.

I arrive with my beloved Freddie: partner in crime, infallible bodyguard, and gorgeous eye candy to boot. And as we make our way through the clusters of cast and crew, I'm stunned: happiness, true happiness, is in the air. The last few weeks had been such a slog, Kurt's rage dragging everyone down. But tonight, I realize, the burden is lifted because Kurt isn't here. Olympus had demanded he fly to LA immediately after wrapping for a Come To Jesus with Bobby about his disappearing act. Under any other circumstances, it would feel wrong to throw the wrap party without the director; but tonight in Kurt's absence, the world feels suddenly, mercifully buoyant.

After we'd made the rounds, Freddie secures us a chilled bottle of Sancerre and a cushy nook at the tail end of the dock—and I can't help but smile as I notice the bollard light atop the post, beaming steadily over the water. We settle into the muted lapping around us, the sun's slow belly dip.

I'm just getting cozy, just finally beginning to relax, when I notice the actress who played Rosemary hovering nearby. And even despite all that happened with Kurt, I feel a tug of sympathy and call out to her.

"What are you doing?" Freddie asks. "Her method acting went a bit far when she stole Kurt out from under you, don't you think?"

Still I shake my head, put on my most welcoming smile. "Will you come join us?"

She hesitates, then makes her way over. "Congratulations, Lila," she says. "Freddie, you, too."

"Cheers, hon," Freddie says, his tone unmistakable: let's play nice and keep our distance. But this seems to be lost on her. Her smile grows, and she slides onto the booth next to me. On my other side, I feel Freddie pinch my hip.

"I can't believe after all this time, it's really over," she says, then turns to me. "How do you feel?"

"Well . . ." I glance at Freddie. "I'm quite pleased with the film. And you did excellent work. I'm sure this will be a big moment for your career."

She breaks into her signature smile, and again, my breath catches. She really does remind me of my younger self, the sweet, innocent girl I used to be before all the trauma of my past. And despite everything, despite all the heartache and betrayal, I can't help it: I like her.

"You've always been so generous, Lila. Thank you." Then she leans in, whispers, "I just wanted to say—now that it's out in the open, and you're getting official writing credit—I'm so in awe of what you've done. You're a true champion of women; I can't tell you how much I admire you. I can only hope that when I'm older I'll be just like you."

Beside me, Freddie stifles a titter. "That's sweet of you to say," I reply. "Are you hoping to write, as well?"

She shakes her head. "Oh, I don't think so. I just mean . . . I guess I'd like to think myself a feminist. And I'm so grateful you've used your voice to do so much good for women." She looks out over the water. "I'm sure this hasn't been easy on you. But you've handled it all with such grace."

At this, Freddie scoffs, and she looks at him, startled—then flushes, grows quiet.

"I did want to talk to you before we parted ways," she begins, "about what happened with Kurt." Again, she glances at Freddie.

"It's alright," I say. "Anything to do with Kurt, you can say in front of Freddie." Freddie inhales, sets his jaw.

She nods. "I'm not naïve enough to think you hadn't realized. I'm just . . ." She hesitates, turns away. And when she turns back, I'm startled to see she's crying. "I'm so sorry, Lila. I've been miserable about it the whole time. I feel like I betrayed you—you, who I look up to more than anyone! I just felt so . . ." She shakes her head. ". . . trapped. I'd understand completely if you hated me."

I touch her shoulder. "I don't hate you."

She paws her face, smearing her makeup a little. "From the very beginning you've been so good to me. I wanted so badly to tell you right from the start, the first time it happened. It's just—with the film, with everything we're doing—it all felt too important. I didn't want anything to get in the way of that." She looks down. "I'm not trying to justify what happened, or make some sort of excuse. I just hope you'll understand how it happened—why it happened."

She attempts a wobbly smile, then buries her face in her hands. A few members of the crew begin to notice.

"Come on now," I say, rubbing her back. "I think you're giving yourself too much credit. I have a pretty good idea of what actually happened between you and Kurt, the sort of pressure he put on you."

She lifts her face. "You do?"

I give her a tiny smile. "I was in your shoes once, too, you know."

She blinks, eyes widening. And then grows very still.

Freddie clears his throat, and I know he thinks I'm divulging too much, that she isn't to be trusted. But I can't help it. I want to take care of her. I know Kurt: as soon as I leave him, the first thing he'll do is go after her again. I want to protect her from him.

"Listen," I say, leaning in. "I'm on your side—and I know it wasn't your fault. I just wish there was some way I could've stepped in and helped. I'm so sorry you had to go through that."

"So the whole time . . ." she says quietly, then looks up at me. ". . . you knew?"

I shake my head. "He did the exact same thing to me. In this industry, it's the price we women often have to pay to launch our careers."

She studies me a moment, at a loss. The only sound: the slow sloshing of water below us.

"Listen." I take her hand in mine. "Let's put this behind us, okay? There's so much to celebrate! Our incredible project is nearly done; and tonight is a very special night." I squeeze gently. "Tonight marks the end of a long and difficult chapter for both of us. But tomorrow—tomorrow is the real moment of reckoning." I watch her eyes widen as she comes to understand my meaning. "A fresh start," I say softly. "The chance to rewrite the narrative of our lives."

And my younger self smiles at me, her eyes filling with wonder, with hope . . .

—And even as I smile back, all I can think of is you, Jonah—because tomorrow, you and I will be together at last.

The three of us look to the horizon—past that clean, bright light at the end of our dock, which seems to burn stronger, stronger against the falling darkness—and I inhale, bid a silent goodbye to Montauk, to the film, to my life as I thought it would be. And then, in the blink of an eye, the blazing sun sinks below the surface, and the water fills with its blood.

———

Much later, in the dark of night, Freddie and I settle into our private car and begin the long ride back to the city. We're still feeling the high of the evening's festivities as we pass through each of the cozy, dusky Hamptons towns, discussing our hopes for the film's future. I solicit Freddie's opinion regarding the two alternate endings we'd shot: one which remains true to Fitzgerald's words, in which Dick fades slowly into obscurity. But the other, more dramatic ending for our film, I'd conceived of only days prior:

"I can't help it," I say now. "It feels so disappointing for Nicole to see Dick standing on the edge of that cliff, and have that regressive urge to go to him once more, only to have Tommy rein her in. It's so clearly the *male* version of events." I shake my head. "Fitzgerald got the idea for Gatsby's green light on the French Riviera, where *Tender* was originally set. And we've just shot our adaptation here, *on the slender riotous island that extends itself due east of New York*—a stone's throw from Gatsby's home. The melding of those worlds is all but begging for a nod. Just picture it: there Dick is, lost and alone, on the edge of a cliff . . . It wouldn't be difficult, would it, for Nicole to make his death look like suicide?"

We debate the implications of the two possible endings, but I have a clear preference. As you're the true aficionado, Jonah, I wonder what your take might be? Is it enough for Dick simply to fade into obscurity? Or is that letting him off the hook too easily? Wouldn't he, in fact, be lucking out, by being permitted to disappear? In the end, what's the just payment for Dick's crimes that would allow Nicole to walk away, a free woman?

As our adrenaline fades, we buzz up the privacy glass; and then, ever so quietly, I walk Freddie through the preparations for my secret departure, all of which I was only able to accomplish with your guidance. My excitement must have been apparent, because Freddie immediately guesses I'm not simply running *from* my life with Kurt, but also *to* someone else. And so I tell him my mystery man was the person he'd met at the gallery opening: I tell him all about you, Jonah, about us (*us!*), how we intend to be together. I gush about you, about our sessions, about your unrivaled reputation as a savior for survivors of domestic violence. But to my surprise, Freddie doesn't respond as I'd hoped.

"So let me get this straight," he says. "The guy specializes in working with battered women. He gets you to unload all your secrets about Kurt, gets you at your most vulnerable, and then he cheats on his fiancée and swoops in, promising to be your protector?"

I bristle. "You make him sound so manipulative."

"Well?"

"*Well*, he isn't! I was the one who confessed my feelings first. If anything, I seduced him."

"Lila, come on. He'd already identified your feelings for him as transference. Which they obviously are. And even so, he chose not to act professionally. He didn't stop you. Instead, he held out until you were at your most desperate, defenseless, and alone, in your new getaway pad that no one knows about except you, and then practically forced himself on you. Didn't he."

I grow quiet. "It didn't feel like that."

"Right. Just like you'd talked yourself into believing Kurt wasn't a sexual predator." He sighs. "I'm sorry, but your vision is skewed. You're letting these unreliable men convince you to trust them, and you're going in blind."

He threads his fingers in mine, squeezes. "Take it from someone who just got out of an abusive relationship. I made it to the other side, all because of you. Let me help you the way you helped me. I could get you away from all this. We could go off on an adventure together, anywhere you want. You could let yourself be alone for a bit. Allow the dust to settle, clear your head."

When I stay silent, he adds, "If nothing else, this is gross malpractice. The man should lose his license. He should never be allowed near another abused woman in his life."

"You don't know him!" I protest. "You make him out to be this terrible predator, but he isn't! I've fallen in love with him!"

"You only think you have." He grows quiet a moment. "Who even is this guy, anyway? What do you know about his background? His record?"

"Not much." I shrug. Then add: "We both went to Princeton."

Freddie blinks. "You didn't overlap, did you?"

"We did for a year, apparently. But neither of us realized until we did the math."

"Lila, you're too trusting. You always want to see the best in people.

But there are a lot of red flags with this guy. I have a bad feeling about all this—"

"Freddie, come on!" I exclaim. "Can't you please just be excited for me? I'm *happy*. I'm finally truly happy. And I know I can trust Jonah. So please just let it be."

He sighs. "Innocent until proven guilty," he says, then shakes his head. "I care about you; you know my intentions are good." He hesitates, then can't help himself: "Just let me do some digging, alright? Hopefully I'm wrong. Hopefully this guy has an immaculate record, and his intentions are as pure as you believe them to be. And then you'll have my full support, I promise."

. . . So there you have it. I hope this doesn't make you think ill of Freddie, whom I love so much. He's wrong about you, isn't he, Jonah? I confess I've been so desperate to escape my situation, and I've trusted you so completely, that I realize now I haven't for a moment questioned your integrity. I hope you don't think I'm doing so now. But I guess I *would* like your reassurance that you've been fully transparent with me from the start. Then I can sweep away this tiny seed of doubt that's been planted, and move forward with full confidence in trusting you, in trusting us. Please tell me I can?

Enough for now. Freddie is dozing off beside me, and on the horizon I see the city's twinkling lights as dawn begins to break. Whenever I make this drive home I think of that line from *Gatsby*, one I'm sure you love as much as I do: *The city seen from the Queensboro Bridge is always the city seen for the first time, in its first wild promise of all the mystery and the beauty in the world.* Anything could happen now, anything at all . . .

Even Gatsby could happen—

—Even you.

I've thought of you every moment since you texted about Maggie. I hope severing ties wasn't too terribly painful. Part of me hates myself for having split you apart. But I keep returning to my deepest, truest feeling: we are destined for one another.

Meet me at my pied-à-terre at sundown tomorrow. I have a special surprise in store. And then, at last—as your favorite author once wrote—we will look at each other with infinite hope as we cross over into the new sweet warm darkness.

x Lila

IX

Jonah woke with a smile on his face, his insides fluttering up in that feathery way they used to do on Christmas morning. Back then, he'd spring from his bed in his engine-red pajamas in search of Birdie—still in bed, mask morosely spread over her eyes, on this of all days? Or no: by the tree, perhaps sliding a final gift underneath? Or failing that, the kitchen: steaming coffee cupped between both palms, holiday station softly singing, as she gazed somewhere far away, somewhere Jonah could never seem to reach. Still he'd run to her and wrap his arms around her waist, his head burrowing into the softness he found there; say, "Merry Christmas, Birdie." And she'd start, brush away the errant tear that hadn't escaped his notice, kiss the top of his head. Whisper, "Merry Christmas, darling."

But that was long ago. He shook his head, tried to shut out the memory's thin, lingering sadness as it sighed and settled in, let the salve of Fitzgerald's words soothe his restless mind. *All the distress that he had ever known, the sorrow and the pain, had been because of women.*

He blinked his eyes open to reality, to the leaves stroking his window, the bright patch of sky beyond. The day had finally come. Today, at last, he'd commit himself completely to loving Lila Crayne.

He stretched his arms and legs wide across his empty bed, felt that shivery twitch of satisfaction when they'd reached their own capacity,

196

then followed the swimming spots in his vision across the ceiling until they settled and dissolved. All he had left was one more day, one more ordinary day of holding a safe space for his patients' secret griefs; and all the while, his private thoughts would swim upstream, against the current of their words, to Lila.

The final week had slipped by in an agitated blur, unremarkable save for the fresh wound of Maggie's departure from his life. After Jonah had returned from Lila's new home that night, he'd hurried to bed, praying for sleep to come swiftly; but the adrenaline of the night still crackled within, and dreams of Lila, of their imagined future together, burst dazzlingly before him to the quick drumbeat of his heart.

He was still awake when Maggie crept in around three from her night on the town, stumbling in her heels, swearing and giggling to herself. He watched through slitted lashes as she pulled off her shoes, then carried them dangling from her fingertips as she crept around the room in search of something in the dark. He listened through the bathroom door as she brushed her teeth, washed her face; then he'd turned his back, closed his eyes, so that when she flicked off the bathroom light and crept to bed, she'd shifted towards him beneath the sheets and put her arm around his waist, kissed the back of his neck, held him the way she knew he loved. He felt her hair sweep his skin, and in mere moments, the light flute of air through her nose came steady and cool against the knobby bone at the base of his neck. He could picture the sweet serenity of her expression as she held him, floating off into her dreams. And he tried to capture this, freeze it in his mind, as their final moment of closeness, when Mags was still happy, believing it was just a night like any other, just a single unremarkable night in the endless stream of nights before them for the rest of their life together.

He must've finally slid into sleep, because the next thing he knew, Mags was running her hand up and down the length of his torso, her fingers bumping along the gentle slopes of his abs, then reaching down farther, grazing over his cotton briefs and nudging below the thick band of elastic to scratch the delicate whorl of a nest there and wrap around the length of him, pleased by the readiness she'd found before he'd even woken up.

He was exhausted, not yet ready to relinquish sleep, and he felt a dry scratchiness to his tongue that extended all the way into his throat. His skin strung taut over his bones, his muscles tender, eyes bleary; but even so, her fingers running like water over him, the warmth of her touch, the hunger of her desire, pulled Jonah back to the surface, made him beg off the future in favor of losing himself to Maggie one final time.

He inhaled, stretched, and she hummed a little with happiness, pulled off his underwear and crawled her way back to him. He tried not to kiss her—his mouth tasted bitter, sour—but her lips were insistent, and finally he gave in. She spread her legs over him, pinning him down, her curls tickling his skin as she kissed his neck. He rolled her shirt up over her head and tossed it to the side, enjoying the full tilt of her breasts above him in the soft morning light.

Jonah ran his fingers through his own hair, scratched his scalp to wakefulness as she eased him inside her; but it seemed this morning she wanted to lead. And so he settled the meat of his palms onto her flanks, his thumbs pressing precisely upon each hip bone, and watched, as if in a dream, as she moved slowly above him, her eyes closed in pleasure, opening every now and again to lock onto his and smile.

And this was peace, wasn't it? This quiet room with the mingled scent of their sheets and shared shampoo, Maggie's hand soft upon his hair, the gentle rise and fall of her breasts—and then for a moment it was as though Lila was there, as though he were at rest in some sweeter and safer home than he had ever known . . .

With a slight pang, he realized all this would soon be destroyed. Maggie would never look at him this way again; and guilt swept through him once more. He felt his desire begin to waver, and so he tried to shake the feeling off, to focus only on the present; but a sudden wave of sadness overtook him, and he knew it would be mere moments before he'd lose it altogether. The only way to stay, he knew, would be to turn his thoughts away from Maggie, and onto Lila instead.

He closed his eyes to better focus on the fantasy, grabbed her wrists, pinned them tight at the small of her back, her spine arching violently in response, and he began to buck more strongly to spur himself to action. He was nearly there when he felt Maggie ever so slightly recoil.

"Jo," she said softly, and he opened his eyes. "Where did you go just now?"

"I'm right here," he said, but she shook her head.

"You're not." She pulled her wrists free, leaned her forearms against his chest, searched his eyes. "What's going on?"

He hesitated, and she pulled back a little—already beginning to understand. "Mags—"

But that seemed only to push her further. She drew away from him and retrieved her shirt, fumbling to turn it right side out, then pulled it on. Jonah watched her in silence, his heart pounding with dread, then pushed himself upright against the headboard as she folded her arms and looked at him.

"It's her," she said. "Isn't it."

"Mags—"

She stared at him, unblinking.

He grimaced, then said, "I can't do this anymore."

"Can't do what anymore," she repeated slowly, dangerously.

He looked at her, hating himself. Finally he managed the words. "I can't be with you, Mags. It's over."

She looked as though she'd been struck in the face. "What?"

"I wanted to make it work," he said. "But those feelings I had, those other feelings . . . they haven't gone away. She wants to be with me." He shook his head, struggling. "I feel like I don't have a choice."

"You don't have a *choice*?"

He spoke quietly. "I have to see this out, give it a chance. And in order to do that, I need to be fair to you and let you go."

"No, don't do that. This isn't about me. This is about you, Jonah, and what you want."

He nodded, ashamed. "You're right. I can't not try it with her. I'd regret it the rest of my life if I didn't try."

She hesitated. "When did this happen?"

He closed his eyes, lowered his head.

She let out a little laugh. "You were with her last night, weren't you? You lied to me."

He nodded.

"Did you sleep with her?" she asked, incredulous.

He shook his head.

"I don't believe you." She smiled sadly. "But I guess it doesn't matter, does it?"

"I'm so sorry," he said. "I know I could be making a huge mistake. Mags, I want you to know this has nothing to do with you. This is about me—my own baggage." He sighed, rubbed his forehead. "I think in some ways I'm still acting out the trauma of my mother—"

"Oh, enough with your fucking mother!" she cried. "You always do that. You always hide behind your pretentious psychoanalysis, as if that'll keep you safe. You can't blame your whole life on your mother, Jonah. So she was fucked-up—we all are! At some point you've got to take responsibility for your own mistakes."

She pressed the heels of her hands to her eyes, held them there a moment without breathing. "So that's it," she said. "You're done. We're done. All these years, this life we've built together. Our whole future. You're just going to throw it away for some fucking infatuation, because you're *curious* if there might be something there. Did I really mean so little?" She dropped her hands to look at him. "I mean, Jesus, Jonah! Am I really that easy for you to throw away? Do you even care? Are you even sad at all? Or are you just too excited to be with Lila Crayne?"

"Of course I care." He reached out to touch her knee. "I love you."

"Don't touch me." She pulled away, wrapping the sheet around her.

She stood at the foot of the bed, staring at him. "I knew it the day we moved into this house. Remember? I knew something wasn't right, that something was holding you back. And I gave you the choice to leave. But you promised me." Tears began to fill her eyes. "You promised I was everything you ever wanted. I was it for you; you were sure. And so I gave myself to you completely. But it was a lie, wasn't it? You weren't sure at all. You were always holding out for something better."

From the doorway, Zelda meowed and padded into the room, winding her tail about Maggie's ankles as she passed. Maggie inhaled at the unexpected touch, then looked around, seemed suddenly shaken to alertness. "I've got to get out of here."

She grabbed her phone and began to type, tears dripping from her chin and onto the screen.

"You don't have to leave right now, Mags," Jonah said. "Take your time. Let me help you find a new place. I want to."

She let out a dark laugh. "I'm sure you do. Thank you, Jonah, for being so generous, for not immediately kicking me to the curb. But don't worry: I'll get out of your way so you can make room for her. Though I don't know why you'd even bother; I'm sure her place is so much nicer."

She moved about the bedroom, pulling on clothes and throwing things haphazardly into a bag. Jonah lay back down and closed his eyes, made himself as still as possible, his ears pricked for her angry sighs, the wet sniffs of her nose, gummy sounds of her clogged throat; and he willed time to pass faster so that this agonizing end would be over.

At last, he heard her stop. He opened his eyes.

"I'll get the rest of my things at some point this week. Hopefully when you're not here," she added, then hoisted the bag over her shoulder.

"Maggie—"

She waited. "What?"

He looked at her, tried to think what he might possibly say to soften their ending, even the smallest bit.

She shook her head. "You're going to regret this," she said. "I hope for your sake you don't, but I have a feeling you will. But me? Even now, despite how sad and how fucking angry I am, Jonah? Already I'm grateful—to you, and to her." She paused. "I'd always wondered if there was another side to you, a darker side you'd hidden from me—and now I know I was right. For the first time, I feel like I'm seeing you for who you really are. Being with you has been the single biggest mistake of my life. And now it's finally over, and I can move on to the life I should've had all along."

———

After Maggie's departure, Jonah immediately texted Lila that he'd broken it off, that Maggie was gone. He waited for her response; but when he received only silence, his inner equilibrium began to falter. He found himself alternately filled with anticipation as the prospect of Lila drew nearer; then dreading that he'd made a terrible mistake. He wandered through the home Maggie had created for the two of them, acutely aware of her absence, and how empty his life suddenly was. He hated himself for the cruelty of what he'd done, how he'd so easily manipulated Maggie into a dead end of pain and misery from which he alone rebounded unscathed.

And what if it didn't go the way he hoped? What if Lila changed her mind, backed out of their plan? Or worse: what if, upon being with him, she decided she'd made a mistake? He might suffer two unrecoverable losses: he would have destroyed his future with Maggie for no reason at all, and his incorruptible dream of Lila Crayne might be extinguished for good.

Last night—Jonah's final night alone, before he and Lila would be together at last—had been yet another sleepless night. But at some point in the early hours, he'd felt more than seen a sudden glow through the thin skin of his lids, and reached for his phone to find Lila's final entry. Quickly, blearily, he'd read it, stomach flipping with her ardent affection; but when he reached her conversation with Freddie, panic poured over him in a great, hot flood. Was it possible Freddie might somehow uncover that he had indeed known her at Princeton, that he'd spent the first half of his senior year watching Lila from afar? No—how could he? And yet Lila had asked in her letter for his reassurance, for his word that she could trust him entirely. She had begun to doubt.

He knew he'd have to remind her of the evening they'd spent together eventually, in which they'd lost themselves so freely and fully to one another in the mysterious anonymity of the night; but to do it now, when they were so close to their happy ending? It would only be tempting fate. Though the encounter had been perfect, and his intentions always pure, she might understandably be upset that he'd neglected to mention it for so long. And even though it shouldn't be the case, discovering his lie of omission might give Lila pause—might even, god forbid, mean forsaking their future together. No; he'd tell her, and soon—but he couldn't tell her now.

As he printed a hard copy of her latest entry, he pulled out her patient file, which at some point that week, along with Jonah's framed Princeton photo, had made its way from his office to his bedside table. (The file would soon find its new home in the box hidden high in his closet, which contained innumerable keepsakes, including the *Gatsby* handkerchief Lila had given him, and most recently, the latest *Vogue*, with Lila and Kurt—*The Flapper and Her Philosopher*—gracing its cover. He imagined one day presenting her with his private collection, confessing he'd scanned the papers for years on the chance of glimpsing Lila's name, then watching her eyes fill with gratitude when she realized how steadfastly he'd loved her.)

Now he placed her printed letter behind all his notes from their sessions together, behind all the journal entries she'd sent him. Systematically, he reread each one, making sure for what seemed the hundredth time that he'd covered his tracks. He grimaced a little at the inaccuracy of his process notes, replete with misdirection and lies to cover up his longstanding love of Lila Crayne. He'd slipped up here and there, he knew, but those thoughtless, micro mistakes were surely harmless. He was finally nodding off just as dawn was beginning to break, Lila's papers sliding to the sides, soothed once more by his assurance that she was still unsuspecting. After all, it was right there in last night's letter, wasn't it? She loved him, and wanted above all to trust him completely; and he'd do anything not to break that trust.

————

At last, the morning of their secret elopement had arrived. The day was broiling—the hottest yet of the summer. The hours passed with excruciating slowness as Jonah waited for the evening's deliverance, imagining Lila: waking that morning with a smile on her face, thinking of him. Or Lila: packing up the rest of her things, the labeled boxes neatly stacked, bidding goodbye to her life on the Hudson, and to a new life with Jonah—hello! Then Lila: lingering dreamily in a bath (*good god*), scrubbing herself clean, smoothing lotion over her skin, all porcelain and pink, hair tousled to perfection, bright and shining and new. Lila: who might in moments succumb to a certain nervousness—this was a life-changing decision, after all—but would quickly shake off any doubt, secure in her certainty that the future she wanted, the future that was already here, could only be with Jonah.

When the workday was over and the sun in its slow blur was edging farther west, Jonah showered and shaved, dressed in his finest clothes, then pressed his way through the relentless beating heat to Lila's pied-à-terre.

In his fantasy, he pictured her having spent the whole day carefully crafting their new home. Of course it would still feel somewhat spare—plenty of room for their budding relationship to grow! But this time, there'd be a warmth to the space, the soft, subtle beginnings of roosting. Perhaps she'd picked a few bunches of daisies to brighten the space with their cheerful palate. Or perhaps she'd arrange a board of charcuterie and champagne: a light dinner before their more intimate celebration. He allowed for the fact that she might not have gotten around to purchasing furniture just yet—he knew she'd been busy in Montauk wrapping the film—but certainly there would be bedding of some sort, even if only a fluffy comforter spread upon the floor, where they'd wrap themselves into one another, secure in the knowledge they'd finally found their rightful home.

When he arrived a bit early, maybe twenty minutes till sunset, he let himself in, more confidently this time; but to his dismay, the house was still empty. As he made his way back down the hall, then up the stairs, despite the warm evening light, the space felt strangely unsettling. There was no evidence Lila had ever set foot there—even the candles had been stripped away. In its emptiness, it felt more like the ghost of a home, as though it had once been filled with a storied existence but was now barren, a mere fossil of its history.

A memory flickered in Jonah's mind: the summer after he'd graduated from Princeton. Birdie had recently died, and he'd had to sort through their affairs, boxing up his mother's art and a few cherished items to be locked away in storage, selling the rest for a price that was criminal, then putting his childhood home on the market. After it had sold, he'd walked through the empty house one final time: swept clean, painted over, gutted of all its memories. And perhaps because Birdie was gone, he'd felt that day that his home was pervaded with a certain melancholy beauty. He remembered having the distinct, uncanny feeling that if he simply searched harder, he might find his mother hiding there. And so he'd lingered in his hollowed-out home, hoping to feel his mother's presence once more; but he'd felt nothing—only the crushing realization he was utterly alone.

Now Jonah tiptoed through Lila's carriage house, telling himself he had every right to explore, and yet, for some reason, he couldn't shake the feeling he was trespassing.

The haunted atmosphere was making him too agitated, too jittery; and he didn't want to ruin the occasion by being in such a state. He swiped at his forehead, slick with sweat. So what if she was running late! She was an actor; wasn't that how actors were? Though he disliked lateness, it was certainly understandable—Lila must have had plenty to do in preparation. Still, as the minutes ticked past and his anxiety grew, he knew he had to force himself into a better headspace.

He stepped out to the balcony, shut the door behind him. Breathed.

It was better out here with the evening breeze, the sound of the trees, the soft shush of traffic. He'd watch the sunset, focus on steadying his breath, on keeping calm until Lila arrived.

But then the sun dipped low and was gone, the sky an empty, sanguine red in its wake. Still, perhaps he was rushing it; perhaps she was nearly there. He knew the exact route she'd choose, by foot or by car, imagined her traveling the whole way, counting every second it might take. Again and again he pictured it, like a snagging film looping endlessly over the same sequence, hoping each time she might suddenly arrive. And still: no Lila.

The sky was growing darker now. He'd texted her three times already, and no response. He ground his teeth a little, debating. No, screw it: he wouldn't worry about overstepping. They were going to be together, after all! He'd just call her and ask what was going on.

Lila's phone, however, went directly to voicemail, one he didn't recognize (*but what had it been before?* He struggled to remember. . . .): *The person you are calling is unavailable.* And then a beep.

"Lila, it's Jonah. Just checking in to see how you're doing. I'm at your place. Your new place, I mean. I've been here for a bit and, well . . . hope to see you soon. Let me know."

He hung up, heart rapid-fire. The automated message had only further unnerved him. Had he somehow called the wrong number? Or had Freddie uncovered something about him, and had she (*god*) blocked him? Had she decided not to leave Kurt, not to come at all? Was this it? Would he never hear from Lila Crayne again?

As he struggled not to spiral, a more likely, more dangerous reason for her silence entered his mind. Was it possible something had happened to her?

He waited there on the terrace, stewing miserably, till the sky had burnt itself black. He had to accept the fact that Lila wasn't coming. He sent her one final text saying he was heading home, but to please let him know she was okay. Then he groped his way through the silent mausoleum of a house, feeling all too keenly now that he was being watched, and hurried outside, shutting the door behind him.

Swept completely in the maelstrom of his mind, he set off towards Lila's apartment—as though, like Gatsby, he might keep watch below her window, and if Kurt tried any brutality, she'd send a signal by turning the light off and on. He stopped short when he realized where his feet were taking him, forced himself to turn home. He told himself he would hear from her, and soon; but he must do this right. He must wait.

But when Jonah turned onto his block on Horatio, he was startled to see the lights in his brownstone were on. Had he, in his distraction, left them on unwittingly? Then he saw a shadow of movement through the bedroom window, and his breath caught in his throat. Someone was inside.

He let himself in, heart battering. Called out, "Hello?"

What should he do? He looked down the hallway for something he might use to defend himself. Had Kurt broken in, and was he waiting for Jonah to return, so that he might take him unawares? Slowly, cautiously, he made his way to the bedroom, rounded the door, dreading what he might find—

"Mags."

He exhaled, so relieved at the sight of her there on the edge of the bed, sorting through papers, Zelda in her deep rumble curled in her lap. And for a single strange, desperate moment, Jonah wished none of this had ever happened, that Lila Crayne hadn't reentered his life, that he was simply coming back home, back to his life with Maggie.

She looked up, startled. "I wasn't sure whether you'd be home. But when I saw you weren't, I figured I might as well let myself in, do my packing while you were gone."

He glanced around. Sure enough, there were open boxes everywhere, clothes draped messily over the sides. It was happening. Maggie was leaving him for good, and he had only himself to blame.

He felt a sudden flare of anger. "Well, what are you taking?" he stammered. "Were you going to try to take Zelda, too, while I was out?"

She blinked, shook her head. "Jonah, no; I would never do that. Look, I was just going to pick up my own things now, and leave a list of the other bigger items I'd like to take with me. And we could sort out who gets what at some point in the future. But then I got distracted."

He shook his head, not understanding; but then he looked closer at the papers scattered across the bed. They were the contents of Lila's patient file.

"What the hell?" He snatched one of Lila's entries from her hands, incredulous, and frantically began to pick up the rest.

"I'm sorry," she said. "I know I had no right to read them. But it was just lying there, and I couldn't help myself. Jonah, we need to talk."

"What the fuck, Maggie?" he said, inadvertently ripping a paper in his upset. Thank god Lila's box was still hidden high in the closet, undiscovered. "This is beneath you."

"Jonah, please listen to me. I don't think Lila's been honest with you."

"What?" Was this some sad, perverse way of trying to get him back? "What the hell are you talking about?"

"Just hear me out, okay?" She brushed back her hair, eyes darting. "There are a lot of things in that file that don't add up. I lost track after a while, there were so many." Zelda slitted open her eyes, then stretched herself luxuriously over Maggie's thigh. "Like Zelda, for instance."

He shook his head. "Zelda?"

"Jonah, please don't look at me like that. Just listen. In her journal, Lila says she wants a cat, right? She talks about how much she loves cats. But the first time I met her in the hallway, right before her session? Her skin had broken out in this terrible rash, and she couldn't breathe very well. In your therapy notes from that day, you'd written she'd had a bad reaction to some makeup. But I remember distinctly that she'd asked me in the hall if we had a cat, and I told her about Zelda. She was really worried; she said in the past she'd had to go to the hospital she was so allergic."

Jonah rolled his eyes. "This is ridiculous, Maggie. It could've been a different day. And plenty of people who are allergic to cats still like them."

"Right, I know, but that's just the beginning. These notes are full of lies. Like the fact that she acted like her proposal to Kurt was spontaneous. But all the gossip rags state the opposite: apparently Lila asked Freddie James to tip the reporters off. She'd been planning the whole thing months in advance."

"Oh, so you're reading up on her now?" His heart was racing. "This is an invasion of privacy—hers and mine—and I'm not going to tolerate it. That's just cheap hearsay; and anyway, there are plenty of explanations, and I don't owe it to you to articulate them. It's possible, for instance, that she could've been feeling insecure. . . ."

"Then what about this?"

Maggie held up the inspiration for *Ícaro*: the framed photo of Jonah at Princeton from all those years ago.

He swallowed. "What about it?"

For a moment Maggie simply studied it in silence. "There was always something haunting about this photo," she said, "something captivating. I couldn't understand why you'd framed a dark, blurry picture, why you'd kept it so prominently displayed all these years. The mystery around it fascinated me. It inspired me; I felt when I was painting it that I was chasing down some sort of dream. I thought if I could understand this ridiculous photo, it might be the key to understanding you completely. But I never could unlock it. Until now."

She pointed to the blurred background, to the bright whip of golden-white light. "It's her," she said. "Isn't it."

He found he couldn't speak.

"I knew it," she said quietly, and shook her head. "You said in these notes you didn't know Lila at Princeton." She looked up at him. "Jonah. Why did you lie?"

His brain was reeling, his mouth dry, his breath shallow and rapid in his chest. He knew he was on the brink of a panic attack.

Maggie inhaled. "I saw her today."

His breath caught in his throat. "You what?"

"I was dropping off *Ícaro*, Jonah," she said, then shook her head. "I didn't have to, of course; but I wanted to. To—I don't know—put on a brave face? I wanted to look Lila Crayne in the eye and see if she felt any remorse for upending my life." She turned away, flushing, then continued. "But when I got there, she was . . . she was very upset. She asked me if I would stay and talk. And then she told me something—something I didn't want to believe was true—" Maggie swallowed, dared to look at him. "But then I saw the video."

"What video?" he said. "Maggie, what the fuck are you talking about?"

"God, I don't know *what* to believe anymore," Maggie said. "But Jonah, you have to stay away from her."

It was Maggie he couldn't trust, he realized. Maggie was the reason Lila hadn't shown up tonight, the reason she wasn't answering his texts or calls. In her desperation, Maggie had gone behind Jonah's back and approached Lila when she was at her most vulnerable, and scared her into abandoning her plans of being with him. She'd done her best to destroy their chances of being together so that she might win him back.

His phone dinged.

"Jonah?" Maggie pleaded.

He pulled his phone from his pocket and looked at the screen, saw a number he didn't recognize.

"Jonah, please!" Maggie said. "Something is wrong here. I can feel it. I don't want you to get hurt."

He unlocked his phone to read the text, and realized with a start that it was from Lila:

Jonah, he's here. I don't know what to do. HELP.

He looked up at Maggie. "Get out."

Her eyes widened. "What?"

"I know what you're doing," he said. "You're trying to keep us from being together. But this—what you've done tonight? This is a huge betrayal. You were right, Maggie: you were never my first choice. And now I know I deserve better than you. Now get out. I never want to see you again."

Maggie stood up, stunned. Tears filled her eyes. Jonah saw something else in her expression now, something altogether new. Fear.

"Did you not hear me?" he yelled. "Get the fuck out of my house! Now!"

For a minute they stood there, hating one another. But as he had loved the echo of himself in Maggie, so now what Jonah hated was only a mirror—his reflection strewn about the shattered night like broken bits of glass.

"I hope you get what you deserve," she whispered. She touched Zelda's head tenderly one final time, then ran out, slamming the door behind her.

Silence now, except for his heavy breath. Zelda caught his eye and sprang to her feet, spooked, then darted beneath the bed.

Should he call the police, send them to her apartment? No; he knew she wouldn't want to attract the media's attention. And besides: she'd asked for *him*. She wanted Jonah, wanted him to save her. It was the ultimate test, the final step to winning Lila at last.

211

There was no right answer, no safe way. But he knew he had no choice. It was time now for Jonah to take action. He'd do anything for Lila, would stop at nothing to protect her.

He swallowed and unlocked his phone, texted his response:

I'm on my way.

Act Three

WE MUST ALL TRY
TO BE GOOD

He flew through the night, his legs whisking weightless beneath him, soft clip of his oxfords echoing along the street. Ran faster than he'd ever run before, due west, the less trafficked path unencumbered by restaurants and bars. Legged it all the way to the silvery filmstrip of the Hudson, then hung a left and onward, closer and closer to Lila. Above him, the bleak and moonless sky, the stars long snuffed out by city smog. On and on like a ghost through the dark, lit in a breath by a lamppost—his own shadow chasing, eclipsing, overtaking him—then vanishing altogether, as though he'd never been there at all. Across West Street, couples, young families, small clusters of friends crowded the dressed-up piers, wandering up and down the city's edges to gaze at the water, at Jersey's bright and blocky coast. He dodged them like puddles, these people, all of them pulling blindly to the river, every last one ignorant of the crisis at hand.

Adrenaline coursed hot through Jonah's veins as he wondered what horrors might be happening to Lila at this very moment. He struggled to block these ghastly images out, reduce his worries to white noise. And he centered his thoughts on a single meditative chant, over and over to the rhythm of his run: *Lila. Lila. Lila.*

At last he reached her block. Her building towering before him seemed a fortress now, some terrible secret kept within its walls. He

215

tore down the side street, scanning the length of the road, unable to shake the stubborn sense that someone at that very moment might be watching his every move. And yet he found nothing: only the quiet, leafy street, tight line of empty cars, single pedestrian off in the distance. As if it were a summer evening just like any other. As if his world as he knew it weren't in this very moment about to change forever.

He approached the recessed entryway, glanced at the security cameras angled down as though aimed to fire. The front door itself a shining sheet of steel with a dead bolt; and next to it, a pin pad security system. There was, of course, no directory telling him which code he might punch for Lila Crayne; even the buttons themselves were unlabeled. There was only a third bulbous camera protruding from the wall like a single all-seeing eye. Jonah took a breath, tried the door handle.

Locked.

Such a fucking idiot, he said to himself. To have come all this way, only to have no clue how to get inside. Should he call Lila? Text her? He pulled out his phone, and his stomach leapt into his throat when he saw the same unknown number at the top of the screen.

Use the key.

The key? What key? He searched the entryway for any possible hiding spots in vain. There was no doormat, no potted plant or hidden ledge. The lines of the building were smooth, immaculate; there wasn't a crack or crevice to be found. And then a thought occurred.

He pulled the key to her pied-à-terre from his pocket. The idea was utterly nonsensical, ludicrously far-fetched. He dragged the teeth of the key over his thumb, debating. Time was ticking away, his chances of saving Lila slimmer by the second. He inserted the key into the dead bolt, turned it with a click.

The door opened.

Before him, a low-lit antechamber, industrial and cold. Directly opposite, a large freight elevator sat on its haunches, doors locked open as though waiting for him, its steely innards unremarkable save for the floor, a bright red tongue. He glanced back one final time to the comfort of the quiet street, its slow evening warmth. Told himself he could still turn around, still call the police and make his way back to the safety of his own home. But no: the last thing Lila would want would be the damning exposure of the police—and in their wake, the vulturous press. He gritted his teeth and pulled the door shut with a bang.

Though his breathing had settled, Jonah's heart maintained the quick patter of a light but steady rain. He stepped into the elevator and swallowed thickly. The buttons inside also unlabeled; but this time only six options, and he knew Lila's floor to be the top. He inhaled and pressed, then held his breath as the button illuminated and the iron doors slid shut.

As the elevator began its ascent with a quiet whir, Jonah took out his phone and pressed the volume and power buttons simultaneously, saw with relief the *Emergency SOS* option appear. He told himself he need only press those buttons and swipe, and help would be on the way. He slipped his phone back into his pocket, and heard it click against another object there:

His pocketknife.

He hadn't even thought of it till now, hadn't considered it might be wise to bring a weapon—and despite himself, he felt a small lift of relief. Kurt was bigger than he was, definitely stronger—but now he had something he could use, if it came to that.

But it won't, he told himself. He just needed to get to Lila and persuade Kurt to let her go.

The elevator stopped—seemed to hover in midair—and then the doors opened directly into Kurt and Lila's apartment.

All the lights had been killed. Before him, the sprawling great room with its twenty-foot ceilings, its vast wall of windows opening onto the dramatic sweep of empty balcony and the long ribbon of water beyond. In daylight, he imagined, the room must feel airy, drenched in sun— but now at night, a strange ambient urban light cast ghostly shadows through the dark; and those divine, farseeing windows had once again transformed into eyes, watching both within and without, keeping their silent vigil. *Ícaro*, he noticed, had already been hung, its massive body crawling across the length of the wall, suspended in the gloom. He shivered. Why had Lila had it delivered *here* instead of the pied-à-terre? Perhaps—possibly—to protect the whereabouts of her secret asylum?

To his left a stairway, likely leading up to their bedroom—the same stairway, Jonah remembered, that Kurt had thrown Lila down. At the far end of the room: a glossy bar, sparkling even in the dark with its crystal decanters, its shining amber innards. Deeper into the space: the dining room, then a hallway leading, no doubt, to the kitchen. All was still.

A muffled sound—*Lila?* It had been so fleeting he wondered whether he'd imagined it. But then he heard a soft scuff of movement from the direction of the kitchen. Someone was in there, trying to be quiet.

He began to move across the rug that covered the length of the living room. Scanned the bar for anything dangerous, anything Kurt might repurpose as a weapon against him, then reminded himself it needn't come to that. As he moved towards the kitchen, the hair on his forearms raised, and he felt he could sense someone was near, wondered if they sensed him, too. Muscles taut, hands at the ready, he crept through the empty dining room.

A flicker of light from the corner of his eye like a shadow swiftly cutting, and he froze, his gaze snapping through the pass-through to the open kitchen, gleaming in the dark. He tiptoed forward, sound of his heartbeat hot in his ears, focus locked on the darkened doorway slowly coming into view.

Through the shadows, the pale whites and silvers of the kitchen reflected a spectral light from the panel of windows on the far wall. At last he reached the doorframe and held his breath. Ever so slowly, he leaned in, then farther in still, till he had no choice but to step into the doorway, exposing himself.

"Jonah."

To his right, a few steps away: Kurt, leaning against the marble, arms folded across his chest.

"Lila told me you'd come." He shook his head. Cracked his knuckles. "I gotta say, I really wish you hadn't."

His stomach turned. What brutal punishment did Kurt have in mind? He cleared his throat. "Where's Lila?"

But Kurt ignored the question. "Listen: we don't have much time. I'll tell you everything, but I can't do it here."

He flicked his eyes upwards, and Jonah followed his gaze. Sure enough, in the upper corner: a nearly invisible tiny white globe. Lila must have installed cameras, he realized, as additional security against Kurt.

He swallowed, tried to relax his expression. He had the sudden absurd thought that they were actors in a scene, each of them performing his prescribed role, perfectly reciting the prewritten lines. He tried to shake away the notion as a nervous smile tugged at his lips. He must think clearly now.

"We need to move fast," Kurt continued. "The bathroom is the only place where there aren't—"

"You must think I'm an idiot."

"Will you listen to me?" Kurt whispered. "I don't give a fuck about you, man. But if you know what's good for you, you'll get the hell out of here." He reached out to put a hand on his shoulder, but Jonah jerked away.

"Don't touch me."

Behind Kurt, he noticed now: a knife block, stripped of its knives. *Where were they?*

"I'm not going anywhere till I speak to Lila," Jonah said, jaw clenched.

Kurt hesitated, studying him; then at last he sighed, shook his head. "You're going to regret this."

"Are you threatening me?"

"Again with the threats?" Kurt said. "Dude, I'm the good guy here."

"As far as I'm concerned, you deserve to be locked up for all you've done to Lila."

"Alright, fuck you, asshole," Kurt said, face darkening. "Last time I checked, *you're* the piece of shit who just broke into his patient's house— so if anyone's going to get locked up, it's you."

He inhaled sharply. He had to turn the conversation around, and fast.

"It's clear you're angry," he tried. "I know this situation is messy. But for the moment, can we please try to separate my personal involvement with Lila from my role as her therapist?"

"No, I don't think we can," Kurt said. "In fact, I don't think *you* can, either. I think you've committed gross malpractice."

"She doesn't love you!" he exploded. "She's leaving you. And I'm going to save her from you."

"From *me*?" Kurt laughed. "This is fucking incredible. Tell me: what have I ever done to Lila Crayne?"

"I know everything," he said. "I know you abused her. I saw the bruises, the marks."

"I never laid a finger on that woman," Kurt shot back. "I never hurt her. Not once."

"I don't have to listen to this." He turned, heart hammering, and began to walk out of the kitchen. "Lila?" he shouted, crossing through the dining room and back into the great room, the wide sweep of water shining darkly through the glass. "Lila?"

"She's not going to answer you," Kurt called from behind. "She's not going to come."

He whipped around. "Why not?" he demanded. "What have you done to her?"

"I thought therapists were supposed to be good listeners," he said, frowning. "I told you: I'm innocent. I haven't done a thing."

They'd come to an impasse. Jonah licked his lips, debating. "If you won't tell me where she is, then I have no choice," he said. "I'm calling the police."

He pulled his phone from his pocket. And in a flash, Kurt leapt forward and grabbed it from his hand, then threw it to the ground. Before Jonah could retrieve it, Kurt lifted his foot, slammed his heel down hard.

Jonah stared at his phone, shattered on the floor.

"I tried to help you, man," Kurt said. "I really did. But you wouldn't listen.

"So here's what's going to happen. You're going to stand there with your tiny dick in your hand, and you're going to keep good and quiet while *I* call the police and let them know there's an intruder in my home. And then I'm going to tell them that you aren't just any intruder: you're a manipulative motherfucker obsessed with his patient, and you stalked her all the way here and broke into her home, violating both her privacy and her safety. You'll be arrested, your practice will be destroyed, you'll end up in jail where you belong, and you'll never be allowed near Lila again."

Jonah stared at Kurt, thinking fast. It had escalated so quickly, was so much more than he could handle on his own. Should he try to get to Lila, only to have Kurt undoubtedly take him down? Or try to make a run for it, somehow get to the police first? But even if he managed to escape, Kurt would immediately place the call; and Jonah knew, much as it pained him to admit it, he had no solid argument against Kurt's case. If Kurt got to the police first, it would all be over.

What's more: if he left, wasn't he effectively putting himself before Lila, risking her life to save his own? How could she ever forgive him for such a betrayal? He'd already risked everything for her. What good would life be without her?

No. Somehow, he had to get to Lila. And he could not let Kurt make that call.

He knew what he had to do. Slowly, he raised his hands. "I understand. And I'll do exactly what you want. Alright?"

"Smart man." He walked over to Jonah. "There's no need for this to get messy, right?" Kurt turned away slightly as he reached into his pocket to pull out his phone. Jonah steeled himself.

And just as Kurt lifted his gaze, Jonah clenched his hand into a fist, reared back, and punched him in the nose with a sickening crack. Kurt stumbled backwards with a groan, one hand cupped to his broken nose, the blood pouring freely. Then he stood, and turned to face Jonah.

In the moment before the attack, Kurt's chest swelled, and Jonah realized just how much bigger, how much stronger Kurt was; he knew he was no match. With a growl Kurt lunged at Jonah, throwing him to the floor, then pinned him down and punched him hard in the face. His neck snapped back against the poured concrete floor and the world went blindingly bright, the sounds of the room suddenly hush; and for a moment he heard only the muffled beat of his own heart. He blinked, struggling to resurface. Kurt was bearing down, blood dripping, his face an ugly grimace.

"Come on now," he said. "Do you really think you stand a chance? I told you already: no one needs to get hurt. I don't want to do this to you, man. So why not stop now, before you make me do some real damage?"

In a swift move, Jonah jammed his knee into Kurt's groin. With a howl, Kurt toppled to the side, and Jonah scrambled to his feet, the world still swimming.

His knife. He fumbled for it in his pocket, then flipped it open as Kurt struggled to his feet.

"Don't come any closer," he warned, blade lifted.

Kurt's eyes widened when he saw it. "Jonah. Stop," he said. "Put the knife down. You don't want to do this."

But Jonah held it out, tightened his grip.

"I'm going to ask you one more time," he said. "Let Lila go."

Kurt shook his head. "You still don't understand, do you? That was never a possibility."

Before Jonah could process what he'd said, Kurt lunged to grab the knife, but Jonah slashed Kurt's cheek, and he stumbled back with a cry. He tripped over a table and fell, crashing to the floor, and Jonah followed. Directly behind Kurt, those immovable, all-seeing eyes—and through them: the water, churning hungrily in the dark. Jonah loomed over him, put the knife to his jugular—saw the fear in Kurt's eyes.

"You've given me no choice," Jonah said. "I would do anything for her. Anything."

"Wait," Kurt said, his voice a feverish whisper. "Listen to me. You don't know what you're doing. All this? It's not what it seems. There are things between Lila and me that you don't know. I'm not the enemy. We're both victims here."

He shook his head, heart racing. "What?"

Kurt nodded vehemently. "I swear to you. She's fucking insane. She's trapped us both. Please—don't do this—"

From behind: Lila, rushing towards him in a panic.

"Jonah, stop!"

He locked eyes with Kurt. Whispered: "For Lila."

And in a single swift motion, Jonah stabbed the knife deep into Kurt's neck, then drew it sharply across. Lila screamed.

Kurt's eyes bulged, a cascade of blood chuting from his neck to the floor. Shuddering, he began to look up; and just as his eyes met Jonah's, he collapsed to his side, a terrible gurgling sound guttering from his throat. Jonah watched, breathless, as the blood bubbled hotly from Kurt's neck, his mouth, his nose, his body twitching.

"Oh god," Jonah whispered, a stunned smile spreading across his face. There, before him: Kurt Royall, curled on the ground, dying.

Gradually the twitches grew smaller, less frequent, but still they persisted; and then at last, with a pitiful sigh, Kurt's body was still.

A strange, giddy glee rippling through him now. He'd done it: he'd saved her! The test was done—he'd sustained his will with violence. Let leniency walk in the wake of victory. Lila—his Lila—was free.

Then an awful sound, an animal sound—a violent tearing from Lila's throat. He turned to her, the knife clattering from his fingers to the ground.

"You killed him!" Her face twisted in agony. "Jonah—*why*?"

He grabbed her and pulled her into him, tried to still her shaking. "It's alright now," he whispered. "You're safe."

But when he drew back to look at her, she recoiled from him in terror. And then he noticed the blood smeared across her face, her chest. He looked down. He was soaked in Kurt's blood.

His stomach turned. He stepped back unsteadily, then sank into the nearest chair. Touched his hand to the back of his head—felt the warm stick of his own blood. He brought his fingers before his eyes, surprised at the brightness he found there.

Lila stumbled away, moaning, then threw herself over Kurt's body, began checking frantically for a pulse—

He squeezed his eyes shut. Something was terribly wrong. He'd done the right thing—he *knew* he had—and yet—she seemed so frightened now, so pained beyond the measure of her lot to bear. . . .

And then the memory of Kurt, of all that blood, began to fill his mind. And he suddenly became all too aware: the body was right there, mere feet away, lying lifeless upon the floor.

The panic setting in now, his heart racing faster. He squeezed his eyes tighter, pulled in air through his teeth, chest heaving, inhaled harder— harder still—

What should he do?

They should call the police—yes: they must get help. But then what? How could he make it clear he'd acted in self-defense?

As he struggled to formulate a plan, to slow his breath, to still his shaking hands—somewhere in the distance, a light metallic scrape, the quiet stick of feet upon the wet floor.

He opened his eyes.

Lila stood before him, her white slip soaked in blood.

And yet—

She was somehow different now from all the Lilas he'd known. This wasn't the vulnerable naïf from their therapy sessions—the flirtatious ingenue from the journal entries—the romantic heroine from her

224

pied-à-terre. *This* Lila, standing before him now—this Lila was altogether new.

"Lila?" he said softly. And then he sucked in his breath.

In one hand, she held his pocketknife. And in the other, an object indelibly imprinted in his memory from all those years ago . . .

A golden mask.

II

Princeton University. Though she'd already been there six months, the name still felt titillating to her tongue, the delicate ring of a silver bell. She, Lila Crayne, had been accepted to an Ivy League! Even now the very thought left her reeling. Before her, the future was spreading open its arms, an endless expanse of possibility.

Up until Princeton, her life had been razed and rebuilt just once before, back when Lila was only eight. Immediately following the death of her father, her mother had announced it was time for a change; a change would do them good. Karen had sold the ranch house in Reno, and they'd bid goodbye to their flat, arid existence and moved to the coast, to a place that was shiny and filled with promise: Santa Barbara.

With this home, her mother announced, they'd carve out a new way of living: a quiet, monastic existence, free from the influence of men. Twelve years of enduring her husband's rage had toughened Karen, changed her. She felt she'd learned the truth the hard way: at their core, all men were egotistical, heartless, and cruel. And if a woman were ever to impede a man's chosen path, and didn't immediately perfectly align with his narcissistic aims, she would be bludgeoned until she broke in acquiescence.

Karen swore she'd do her damnedest to protect her daughter—but she knew her influence could only go so far. So she made Lila take an oath never to let another man into her life. When all was said and done, Karen said, men would only hurt her, and strip her of her hard-won freedom. She must promise never to sacrifice that freedom again.

They found their fresh start in a mission home, with its inviting arched windows and cheerful, ruffled roof, a home that opened its doors directly to the Pacific. Lila could hardly believe it; already the dusty sweep of her past seemed so far away. Safe in their peaceful sanctum, Lila was taught that all she ever needed, all she'd ever need, was her mother.

Every day, she'd greet the early morning by stepping out onto the warm terrace and making her way to the water. In her new existence, the first items to be shucked were shoes. Tiny crystals of sand soon embedded themselves between her toes; and no matter how many showers she took, or how often she scraped her skin clean, still she'd spot them lingering, catching in the light. So much of her time was spent by the ocean that her skin itself began to appropriate some small piece of the sun, taking on its own glow. Any propensity for acne was slowly burned away, and her hair, darkest blond in its natural state, turned flaxen, a brilliant reflector of light.

Lila's hair became her defining feature, striking in the thick, salty mane of it. Ever since the move she'd let it grow long, its fringes just tickling her waist. She soon decided she hated pants, found them constricting and uncomfortable; no matter the season, she was quick to throw on a fluttery dress over her swimsuit, and even quicker to pull it over her head and run into the waves.

This was how she'd come into her own, how she'd learned to navigate the world. So when Lila arrived at Princeton, and first walked through the legendary FitzRandolph Gates, she'd felt as though she'd passed through a portal and into another sphere: the vast, sprawling grounds of a château, with its majestic architecture and imposing masonry, its gothic spires, its manicured landscapes and smart brick pathways teeming with equally smart and manicured students in their preppy polos, their swinging ponytails, cardigans with a tiny animal for an emblem.

They were so smooth, so sleek—the lot of them! Their hair held perfectly in place, the lines of their clothes deftly trimmed to their frames, the clean clip of movement and precise vertices of their silhouettes some complex mathematical equation she couldn't seem to crack. They were all so sophisticated, so effortlessly *of* this haut monde.

And here was Lila, in the middle of it all: unpolished and mussed, rolling from her bed with a deep stretch, hastily brushing through the soft tangles of her hair, throwing on a sun dress, even in the deepest winter months. How had she found herself amongst this entirely new species? She regarded them with curious fascination, without feeling any need to change herself to fit the mold; and they, in turn, pulled closer. Her uncanny otherness, her distinct deviation from the status quo, held a certain magnetic power. She made friends, and fast; and the ones who chose her were powerful, the elite of this utterly privileged world. She started spending her evenings at Ivy and Cottage, the most exclusive of Princeton's eating clubs, where she quickly became well-liked by their members, and began to receive invitations to their private gatherings.

And then there was the matter of the opposite sex. She'd sworn to her mother long ago that she'd never fall prey to their charms; but there were so many cute boys, and everywhere! In her classes, in her dorm, her dining hall, or crossing paths in the theater building, where she spent most evenings rehearsing for the fall play. Her innocent flirtations began to turn carnal on Friday and Saturday nights, when alcohol flowed freely at the eating clubs, and Lila found it wondrously easy to meet a tipsy, handsome boy all too eager to walk her home.

But despite this mild experimentation, Lila remained a romantic at heart, old-fashioned by nature. Oh, she'd dipped her toe a bit back in high school, under the watchful eye of her mother; but dates, as she'd known them, had never been more lickerish than a moonlight swim in the ocean, impassioned petting in the back of a parked car. And even now, when she'd find herself naked and ravenous in bed with a beautiful boy, toeing the delicious line of her virginity—even in the blinding heat of those moments, still she'd hit a full stop. She was holding out (she hated the term "saving herself," which smacked of Jesus-loving, Bible-thumping Christianity) for someone truly special, the first person with whom Lila would fall in love.

As she became more and more integrated into the elite social scene, Lila learned of St. A's (short for Saint Anthony Hall), the university's literary secret society. This, she discovered, was Princeton's aristocracy, realm of the blue bloods—far beyond the ranks of its eating clubs, never mind its paltry Greek life. Rumors around its inner workings remained mysterious; but from what Lila gleaned, St. A's skimmed the cream from the student body surface, choosing only those who displayed the most intellectual potential, while also occupying the most social prestige. No one knew exactly who its members were, though fingers tended to point to those in blazers, in oxford shirts and loafers, the slickest and sharpest—and often the most wealthy. Some students turned up their noses at the society, dismissing St. A's as pretentious and elitist; but in truth this was borne out of bitterness for not having been chosen.

This spring, for the very first time in history, St. A's was co-opting a long-held tradition from their fellow chapter at Yale, and would host the most highly anticipated social event of the year: the Pump and Slipper Ball. For well over a century now, the Pump and Slipper had found its way into a great many works of literature, including—on multiple occasions—writings by F. Scott Fitzgerald. This year, the ball would be an ode to *The Great Gatsby*—hosted at Cottage and set in the 1920s, complete with swing band and costumed attire. The intimate affair would mark the beginning of St. A's tapping process, when a handful of lucky underclassmen were selected as potential new members. These hopefuls would, over the course of the next few weeks, be whittled down to a chosen few, who would eventually be invited to join the society's ranks.

Invitations to the Pump and Slipper were near impossible to come by;

and Lila felt a quiet sense of triumph when she opened the door to her dorm one evening to find the signature creamy envelope awaiting her.

As Gatsby wrote to Nick,

The honour would be entirely ours if you would attend our little party.
You are most cordially invited to the Pump and Slipper Ball,
An eve of swank and revelry.
Dress to the nines in your finest Jazz Age attire.
Upon your arrival, you will be given a mask to wear.
Members of the society will be wearing a white mask,
All others offered black.
But if you've been tapped, the mask you receive will be brightly co-
loured.
Masks must remain on for the duration of the evening,
And no one shall disclose his identity—
Not even Jay Gatsby himself.
We await your attendance most fondly,
The Members of Saint Anthony

In the days that followed, it was all anyone could talk about. Armed with the possession of that simple little envelope, Lila's cachet in the world further amplified. She thrilled at its verboten nature, its aura of secrecy; and now that she might possibly be tapped, she found herself eagerly awaiting Friday night, when, upon her arrival, she might receive a colored mask.

The evening came at last, and Lila slipped on the dress she'd been saving for a special occasion. It was, in fact, her mother's dress, and perfect for the *Gatsby* theme: a silvery white flapper dress cut high upon her thighs, with fringe that shimmered in the light. She studied herself in the mirror one final time before leaving, a hopeful smile spreading across her face.

When she arrived at Cottage, she was greeted at the door by a man in a white mask.

"Lila Crayne," he said. "We meet at last."

She smiled shyly, studied his mouth, the only part of his face she could see. Something about him felt familiar. "I wish I could say the same, but I'm afraid I don't know who you are."

"All in good time." A twitch of a grin; then for a moment he turned away. When he returned to face her, he held a gold mask decorated with a delicate spray of shining pearls and a single fluttering plume.

"Congratulations, Lila," he said, mouth softening to a smile. "You've been tapped."

Cottage as she'd known it had been transformed. All its lights had been extinguished; tonight, the club was lit only by great clusters of pillared candles. The mansion she'd come to know so well felt suddenly mysterious, sensuous. Shadows flirted along the walls; in the distance, she heard a jazz band softly playing, piquant horns thrilling the air. And in the fore: the gathering guests, all incognito. She searched the room for another colored mask. So far, Lila was the only one.

Over the course of the cocktail hour the crowd swelled to about a hundred, and the space echoed brightly with laughter as the company milled and sipped and plucked up bite-sized canapés from flashing trays rounding the room. But despite the festive atmosphere, it was clear the members of St. A's were serious about maintaining anonymity: every few minutes, it seemed, another guest who tried to breach this rule was escorted out the door. It was hard to tell, but Lila thought she only counted ten colored masks (and all, she noted, were female), and fifteen white masks— almost all of whom were men. Rumor had it that this year there were only five spaces to fill. And she gathered she was meant to mingle with as many white masks as possible to better improve her odds.

She searched for the St. A's member who'd greeted her at the door (how did she know him? The riddle was driving her mad); but when she would spot him, it was always at a distance. She wondered if the fact that he didn't seem to be drinking helped set him apart—it seemed he only grew more correct as the fraternal hilarity increased. All the other white-masked members, however, were approaching Lila with startling frequency, discreetly proffering delicate bullet vials or tiny packets of fine white powder. When Lila would politely decline, they'd come back with various cocktail concoctions instead; and while no one pressured her, per se, she felt obliged to accept each glass that was slipped into her hand.

After an hour or two of drinking on a near empty stomach, her ability to make small talk was failing her. She noticed with quiet horror that she'd begun to slur a little; and from the corner of her eye, she spotted a girl in a purple mask clacketing quickly to the restroom to be sick. But the members of St. A's were gracious, didn't seem bothered or even surprised; and the more drunk Lila became, the more they helmed the conversation, subtly shifting the spotlight away and allowing her to laugh politely at the sidelines. And for this small mercy, she was grateful.

Eventually, music overtook conversation, and everyone migrated to the ballroom to hear the band in full swing. Before long, they were all packing onto the dance floor, tipsily testing their footing with the Charleston. At the height of this revelry, all lighting was extinguished and a black light switched on, and Lila and the rest of the tapped underclassmen were guided to the center of the room—a bright pistil of glowing girls, with their sweet, bare shoulders and ambrosial hair—and in the periphery, watching: the members of St. A's, kept anonymous by their identical white masks. By now, Lila's drunkenness had begun to fade, and she felt herself to be in finest fettle. She'd hit that delightfully sweet spot, in well enough control of her faculties, yet loose enough to dance without inhibition. She felt so deliciously, unabashedly free—freer than she'd felt all year. As she danced, she sensed the St. A's men watching from the shadows, recognized that distinctly singular energy of the piercing male gaze; but in this moment she relished it, hoping that what they saw, they liked.

As they swung deeper into the night, the atmosphere began to turn rousing and wild. Before, she'd idly clasped hands with the women beside her, let the men spin her around in an impromptu swing; but now people were beginning to pair off, coupling in corners or even right there on the dance floor, sloshing up against her with an anonymous partner for the night. She closed her eyes, tried to lose herself to the music as she danced; but now she, too, was beginning to feel that wanton pull.

"We meet again." That voice in her ear, low and smooth. She turned: *him*. He smiled, and his teeth glowed. "What do you think of the Pump and Slipper?"

She bit her lip, raked a hand through the wilderness of her hair. "I feel like I've been dropped into one of Fitzgerald's famous parties. I keep hoping I'll get to meet Gatsby himself."

He grinned. "Perhaps you already have."

He was looking at her the way every girl wanted to be looked at. He had such a good-looking mouth, she noticed again—would she ever . . . ?

"I like to think myself a Fitzgerald aficionado," he continued, and she found she had to bite down on her smile. His elaborate formality of speech just missed being absurd; it seemed he was picking his words with great care. "I've read his entire oeuvre. Do you enjoy his work?"

She looked up into his eyes, and her insides feathered. "I'm embarrassed to admit I've only read *Gatsby*."

"Then I'd say you ought to get to know him better." Delicately, he took her hands and placed them onto his shoulders, and around them the world blurred and slowed. "He had the *power of recreating, by spring in darkness, that illusion of young romantic love to which women look forever forward and forever back*."

"You make a compelling argument."

He smiled. "He was a member of this club, you know," he told her. "Fitzgerald finished his first novel here at Cottage about a century ago. A page of his manuscript is framed in the library. I can show it to you later, if you'd like."

"I'd love that."

"*You've made an enormous impression,*" he murmured into her ear, and she felt her stomach flip. Despite herself, despite not even knowing who he was or what he looked like, or maybe *because* she didn't know, she felt drawn irresistibly in. Their bodies began to move to the music, the rhythm slinging them together, and she held tight, enjoying the feel of his hands on her waist, the warmth of his body against hers. He was tall, and quite slim; but even so, he was strong. She felt something stirring within her, a warm, tingling rise.

He was a good dancer, sure on his feet and commanding—a man who knew how to take control. She laughed as he spun her out, then in, then out again, whirling her beneath his arm, around his back, then whipping her in once more, the world around her reeling. At some point, they'd taken over the room—her dress, his mask, glowing in the darkness—and surrounding them now on the edges, the men in white masks had gathered. Out of the corner of her eye, a camera's sudden, startling flash—her senses overwhelmed as the roar of the crowd pummeled the air, howling them on to the final violent flourish. Hearts racing, chests expanding, they hugged one another; and around them, the white masks waited in silence.

He licked his lips, pushed back his hair. "Fitzgerald famously said that when he married Zelda, he married the heroine of his stories. You remind me of her."

"Which one?" she laughed lightly. "Daisy?"

But his eyes remained upon her, unblinking. "You remind me of all his heroines, wrapped into one."

In that moment, she realized suddenly she knew who he was. Jonah.

First day of second semester: Intro to Anthropology. Lila had noticed him right away—she'd glimpsed him on occasion around campus, striding long-limbed across the quad, or studying at a thick-waxed table in Firestone, or in line for a midnight slice of pizza after an evening at The Street. Wherever he was, he'd always pulled her eye.

He was cute, no doubt about it. Handsome, in a slender, bookish way, as though he'd been pulled directly from an older, more romantic world. He was always wearing something warm and nubby, no matter the weather: an argyle sweater, herringbone jacket, softly buffed corduroy. He fit perfectly in a place like Princeton. More than the preppy lacrosse players or lanky water polo boys, attractive in their muscled lines and self-assured gait, Jonah seemed to Lila a true intellect, someone with a powerful mind, someone with promise. He was quiet, mysterious, seemed always serious and lost in thought. And yet: there was something about him that made her feel he was just as aware of her existence as she was of his. It drove her a bit crazy, in fact: and often she'd wonder if this romanticized awareness of one another was a mere concoction of her overactive imagination. Though she'd never caught him looking her way, still she couldn't shake the feeling he was watching her.

She was surprised, then, to discover him in the same lecture hall on their first day back from break. Her mysterious crush was here, in an intro course of all places? Maybe this was a sign the two of them were destined to meet. And now, tonight, she finally had her chance.

The music changed to something slower. He pulled her in tight. She looked up at him, and he whispered, "One of my favorite quotes of his is, *the biography of every woman begins with the first kiss that counts.*" He looked deep into Lila's eyes. "What do you think?"

Had she known then what would happen next, reverberating unremittingly through the years to come and changing the woman Lila was forever, she would have pulled away, would have left him then and there. But she didn't know, and in that moment she allowed herself not to think, to be led by innocent impulse. She stood up on tiptoe, one hand wrapping delicately around his neck—and she gave him her answer.

He reacted in full, just as she'd hoped, and met her mouth with his, then eased her over to a nearby wall. She could sense the overwhelming magnitude of his desire, and thrilled at the influence it gave her. This—this absolute *power*—this was altogether new. Each breath, each slight, subtle gesture transformed into a delicious way to tease him, knowing he was slave to her every whim. It was astounding! How was this mysterious, sophisticated senior now rendered powerless by his passion for *her*?

"I've been watching you all year," he said softly, and at this she delighted—she'd been right!—and bit down upon his lip. He pulled back momentarily, then met her eyes and grinned, kissed her deeper.

At some point she must have sensed they were being watched; and when she opened her eyes, she started. While the rest of the room had resumed its intoxicated spin, several of the white masks remained eerily still, their collective eyes fixed upon Lila. *What did they want?*

He must have noticed the change in her, because he glanced over his shoulder. His shoulders tightened when he saw them.

"God dammit."

Her heart quickened. "What?"

He shook his head, then glanced at her. Hesitated. "There are a few guys in St. A's that fancy themselves the society's intelligentsia. They— god, it's vile—they have this tradition, this 'game' they like to play." Again, he hesitated.

She slipped her hand into his. "Tell me."

He clenched his jaw. Swallowed. "They take a vote to determine the hottest girl who's been tapped. And then . . ."

"What?"

He looked at her with a pained expression. "Please don't make me say it." He closed his eyes. "They're assholes. They think they deserve to get whatever they want. I've tried to stop them, but . . ." He shook his head. "Let's just say, they're determined as hell."

He looked down at her then, and she realized: tonight, they wanted *her*.

She began to panic. "But I don't—"

He touched her cheek. "Of course," he said, shaking his head. "Listen, I won't let it happen to you, alright? But these guys are fucking cunning." His eyes narrowed. "You didn't take a drink from any of them, did you?"

Her heart accelerated as she struggled to remember. "I'm not sure—"

236

"Fuck," he said under his breath, then looked at her. "I need to get you out of here, away from them. I know a place where you'll be safe."

She looked into his open, trustworthy eyes. "Take me," she whispered.

Gently, he obeyed, and took her by the hand and pulled her away, past the pulsing crowd to the stairs leading to the mansion's upper floors, where only club members were allowed. He began to climb, then looked back when he felt her hesitate. "It's going to be okay," he said. "You can trust me."

She looked at her hand in his, searched his eyes. "I know," she whispered.

Up they climbed to the second level, the music growing fainter through the floorboards. All the while, she continued to look over her shoulder, terrified of what she might find—a white mask emerging like a ghost in the dark—but each time she dared herself to look, she found nothing. As she followed Jonah, she studied his tall frame, his beautiful hands, the feel of his fingers around her own. She wondered at this sudden intimacy with a total stranger, felt so fiercely grateful to him for daring to protect her, to take her somewhere safe. Past the empty library, then through a door to a dark and narrow hallway, quieter still. Was he an officer at the club, and was he taking her to the sanctuary of his own room? He turned again and, pulling a key from his pocket, unlocked a mottled wooden door. It creaked open to reveal a thin tongue of steps. Without looking back, he began to climb.

It was blindingly dark now, and Lila found she had to follow the sound of his shoes, stumbling a little, the sound of her breath loud in her own ears. And just as she wondered if the climb would ever end— they arrived. He let go of her hand and walked across the black room to the small window before them and pushed it open. With a sudden woosh of cold, the rest of the world came flooding in—the sounds of the party below, the twinkling lights strung over the grass, the smell of the soft spring night.

"It's alright now," he said. "They'll never think to come up here."

She turned to him.

"Are you okay?" he asked.

She breathed, nodded. "Thank you," she whispered.

He smiled sweetly, cocked his head, hands reaching out to her face; and before she knew what was happening, he'd pulled off her mask. She shivered, felt suddenly exposed. Through the window the jazz floated in as though from another world. She reached for his mask so that she, too, might see him at last, but he pulled back.

"I can't," he said with a look of chagrin. "Those stupid rules still apply."

What a wonderful song, she thought abstractedly, trembling. Everything could still *be* wonderful tonight, she told herself—most of all this romantic scene, the inevitable held just at bay, looming charmingly close. The future vista of her life still seemed in that moment an unending succession of scenes like this: under pale starlight, in the backs of low, cozy cars stopped under sheltering trees . . . only the boy might change—and this one was so nice . . .

He took her hand in his, kissed her upturned palm. Then his lips met her neck as he slipped the straps from her shoulders, her dress puddling upon the floor. She stood before him, shivering. Here, in this quiet attic room, they were so completely alone.

"God, you're beautiful," he said.

And as he took her in, eyes glistening from behind his mask in the moonlight, she realized: he still thought she didn't know who he was.

She felt instinctively—suddenly—that something was terribly wrong. Something was telling Lila she wasn't safe. She should get out—*now*. That was the moment she should have known.

He kissed her hard then, a kiss like a fist. The strength of his grip was startling; it frightened her. He groaned a little as he pressed himself against her, his strength and size threatening to swallow her whole. The tables were somehow turning now; and for the first time, she felt powerless. He shook off his jacket as he kissed her, pulled away his tie, began to unbutton his shirt.

"Let's go slow," she pleaded.

He paused, smiled a little. "Don't worry," he said. "You're safe now."

He moved into her again, and she tried to return his kiss, but still she couldn't shake the cold prickling within. Again the kissing became more insistent, and she recoiled. It was all wrong, the clip of their intimacy a train streaking through the night, and she felt there was nothing she could do to stop it. Off came his shirt, the shoes kicked away, his pants unzipped. He ran his hands through the thick mane of her hair, held fast and tugged, looking deep in her eyes.

"You like that?" he asked, and she nodded a little. She did—didn't she? "Let's lie down," he said, then lifted her weightlessly and eased her upon the dusty rug.

He followed her down, then began to kiss his way up her body, and she tried as best she could to lose herself to his touch.

There were silences in that stretch of time as murmurous as sound. There were pauses that seemed about to shatter—only to be snatched back to oblivion by the tightening of his grip, and the remembered sense that she was still resting there: a caught, gossamer feather, drifted out in the dark.

When his eyes reached hers, he pushed her shoulders against the ground, pinning her in place. She couldn't move if she wanted to.

His hand inside her now, his fingers long and sure—she turned away, eyes shut tight—and he bit her neck hard. She gasped, heart hammering. Then a shift, a sudden pressure.

"I'm not ready," she said.

"You don't need to be nervous," he said. "You can trust me."

He stroked her cheek, eyes glittering in the dark. "Alright?" he whispered. And before she could answer, he wrapped his fingers around her neck and thrust himself in.

She cried out with the first bright rip, dug her fingernails into his back. She felt him inside her, and the sharpness began to mellow, but still: this wasn't what she wanted. "Please," she whispered.

He smiled darkly through his mask, a smile that would haunt her for years—as if they'd been in some perverse and ecstatic alliance the entire time—as if this were a secret they shared, and this were all some twisted game. Then he gently turned her over, pulled her in by her hips, and forced himself deeper.

"You're safe now," he whispered again; and what was the point in resisting? With a whimper, she gave in, tears streaming down her face; and she let him have what he wanted.

He had taken her under false pretenses, had deliberately given her a sense of security—let her fully believe that he could and would take care of her. And he'd made the most of his time—took what he could get, ravenously and unscrupulously. He took Lila that still spring night—took her, because he had no real right to touch her hand.

When it was over, he fell beside her, his chest rising and falling heavily. And he pulled her into him, and wrapped his body around hers, warm puff of his breath in her hair soon slowing to a deeper rhythm. And she closed her eyes, tried to take comfort in being held, tried to convince herself that in breaking her childhood oath, she'd gotten what she'd deserved. But she knew it wasn't true.

She woke a few hours later, naked and alone, a tender throbbing between her legs. Outside, the early morning sky was just diluting to a milky grey. She looked around the grim attic space: bulky furniture in slipcovers furry with dust, piles of clutter in the corners, the frightening stillness of a forgotten space. Her heart began to pound. How could he have left her there? She needed to get out, back to the safety of her own bed, where she could pull down the shades and up the covers, lose herself to darkness and try to forget.

She stumbled into her clothes and slipped on her gold mask once more, as though it might protect her somehow. Then she palmed the wall as she made her way down the steep steps and pushed open the door with a creak. She looked down the hallway of the upper floor, saw with relief it was empty; but at the end of the hall, the dull murmur of

240

voices. The swinging doors of the library had been closed, but through their cutout windows, she could see the lights were on. To get out, she'd have to walk past the library and risk being seen. She fixed her gaze ahead, hurried down the hall; but as she was passing by, she couldn't help but look in.

The members of St. A's had gathered around a table in discussion, tipping onto the hind legs of their chairs, slumped forward in exhaustion, even sprawled lazily on the floor. All their masks had been discarded, the vacant white faces strewn onto the tabletop or dangling blindly from their wrists. Without the masks, they all looked so terribly plain, so dull: their faces splotchy, the scant women's makeup running, every last one of them tired and puffy and hungover. In Lila's stomach, a sudden swill of disgust.

And then she saw him, presiding at the far end. He'd swiveled his mask onto the back of his head, lending the illusion of a man with two faces, an all-seeing god, gazing at once into future and past.

He said something final; and as chairs were scraped back, Lila bolted down the stairs, through the main entryway, and out into the frigid early-morning air.

She was almost to the road when she heard him call her name. She hesitated, then turned to face him.

Once again, he'd returned his mask to his face. Seeing him now in the thin bright air, he looked disheveled and dazed—absurd, really—as though he'd simply lost his way. As he continued down the path, she found she had to fight the impulse to flee.

"I didn't want to wake you. Are you alright?" That smile again—she would never forget it. He reached to touch her shoulder and she shivered.

"I'm fine," she said. "Just drank a bit too much."

He cocked his head. "I hope you had a nice evening?"

"Of course," she said. Then added impulsively, "Although at a certain point, my memory gets a bit fuzzy."

He froze; and for the first time, his smile faltered. "You don't remember what happened?"

She averted her gaze. "Should I?"

He hesitated; and from behind his mask, she thought she glimpsed hurt in his eyes. But then he shook his head, and the smile returned. "It's alright," he said. "We had a wonderful time, you and I."

She blinked, startled. Then, before she could stop herself, she began to reach for his mask.

He stepped back. For a moment they remained silent, watching one another.

She forced her mouth into a smile. "Don't I get to know who you are?"

At this he let out a little laugh. And then he leaned forward, kissed her cheek, and she forced herself not to pull away.

"You'll have to wait until next time to find out," he whispered.

———

In the wake of that terrible night, Lila summoned the courage to confide in a few girlfriends about what had happened to her, and she was shocked to discover that, at some point, each one of them had been a victim of assault. But as she recounted what had happened, she began to doubt. Was Jonah even aware he'd done anything wrong? Had it (*truly*) been rape? She knew of course that she hadn't *wanted* to have sex with him; but had she let him know loud enough, hard enough? Or had she given mixed signals? Was she, in fact, partially to blame?

When she asked their advice as to what action she should take, the friends were unanimous: there was no point in Lila reporting it. If she was already shaky on her own narrative, then she had no real ground to stand on. And besides, in their experience, the men always found a way out. Reporting it would only bring Lila more shame, more humiliation. The best solution, they said, was to put it behind her, try to forget. In the end, Lila felt so brittle, so weary and frightened, that she capitulated. She didn't report him.

That same week, Jonah had gotten the call from home, and he'd left

Princeton to take care of his mother. He finished the remainder of his studies remotely, and graduated in absentia. Lila had waited in dread for the day he might reach out; but that day never came. She only heard his name once more that spring, when it was announced he'd won Princeton's most prestigious senior prize for his thesis on Fitzgerald's *Tender Is the Night*.

She understood then just how alone she was. The world wasn't going to look out for her, she realized. It was up to Lila to find a way to help herself.

In a reckless act of retaliation, Lila stole the university's only copy of Jonah's thesis, and then realized: she was now in possession of a way to process her trauma. And as she pored over his magnum opus, puzzling through the thesis as a means of understanding its author, an idea sparked within her. She began a new private creative endeavor, rewriting Fitzgerald's story to give Nicole the just ending she deserved—a secret riposte to the misogynist text Jonah Gabriel so revered.

In time she'd find this rage adaptation wasn't enough. She'd never cared one way or the other about Fitzgerald, after all—she'd only ever cared about undoing the man who worshipped him. Lila would realize eventually that she'd have to author her own independent ending to find the closure she so desperately sought. But in the moment—even as she set out to invent her own way of healing—Lila Crayne had begun to learn a valuable lesson:

Revenge tasted sweet.

III

She grips the mask with both her hands—glint of gilded armor in the dark—and looks in horror upon Kurt's body, lying in a slowly spreading pool of black blood.

"We have to call the police," Jonah is saying now, "and make it clear it was an accident."

She takes him in—rubbing his palms on his thighs, his skin stained pink with blood—and her expression turns to disgust. "It wasn't an accident," she says.

His eyes widen. "Lila, we need to get help—"

She shakes her head, trembling. "What good would that possibly do?" she says. "Nothing can bring him back. Nothing can ever undo what you've done."

"What *I* . . . ?" He shakes his head. "What are you talking about?"

She swallows—seems to will herself to stay strong, to do everything in her power now to see her plan through and give Jonah the ending he deserves.

She rounds the velvet wingback, sinks into its mouth.

"This was a setup, Jonah," she says quietly. "A trap."

And with sudden swiftness, all color bleeds from his face.

"You took something from me that night at Princeton, something I can never get back. And for thirteen years, you've gotten off scot-free.

But now?" She looks again at Kurt, seems to strengthen her resolve. "Now you're going to pay.

"Do you understand how terrible it was, living with the trauma of your assault?"

"*Assault?*" he says. "Lila, I—"

"Shut up," she says, shaking her head. "For once in your life, Jonah, you're going to shut the fuck up and listen. It's my turn to do the talking." Again, her gaze snaps to Kurt's body. She closes her eyes, trying to drive the terrible image away.

"For years, the nightmare of what you'd done replayed itself. I felt so powerless, so vulnerable. I kept questioning myself, doubting myself. Telling myself I was somehow to blame. In time, I learned to push it to a corner of my mind—but I was never able to heal entirely. I thought I never would.

"But then one day, about three years ago, I got an email from a young actress, an undergrad at Yale. At first I didn't pay it much attention. *Waiting Game* had just come out—I figured maybe she was a fan. But her message was strangely cryptic: she said we had someone in common, and asked if I would help her." She swallows, tries to steady her breath. "I agreed to meet her in person, and noticed immediately we looked uncannily alike. And then she told me her story, and the parallels were impossible to ignore. Her freshman year at Yale, she'd been tapped by the St. A's chapter there; and at *their* Pump and Slipper, she'd been raped by a man in a mask."

He closes his eyes. "Oh god."

She wipes her hands over and over on her blood-soaked slip. "I didn't need to hear anything more. I knew it must've been you. She was so traumatized that she'd dropped out of Yale altogether. Her life was falling apart. But at her therapist's suggestion, she reached out to me, because her only clue as to who you were was that you'd bragged to her that you'd spent a romantic night with me. She hoped that maybe, just maybe, I might know who you were. I looked you up, and discovered

245

you were indeed at Yale then, getting your PhD. All she wanted was your name, so she could report you for raping her."

"Wait a minute, Lila," Jonah says, frantic. "That isn't—"

"You can't imagine how terrible I felt." She closes her eyes. "My doubt had kept me silent all those years; and it was my doubt that had allowed you to get away with it all over again. This was, in part, *my fault*." She looks at him. "But the story she told me of what you'd done? There was no *room* for doubt. You raped her—just like you raped me."

He shakes his head. "How could you say that? Lila, how could you possibly think—"

"I realized then reporting you wouldn't be good enough. Too many years had passed, and neither of us had done rape kits. We had no evidence, no witnesses. . . . It could easily turn into a battle of 'he said, she said,' and I had no interest in trying to convince anyone of what I *knew* you'd done." She hugs herself, shaking. "All my life I'd been bludgeoned into believing it was a man's world, where men like you could get away with whatever you wanted, without having to pay for your crimes. I decided I wasn't going to allow it any longer. I convinced her to hold off on reporting you. And I came up with a way for both of us to get the justice we deserved."

She turns again to Kurt, and tears fill her eyes. "Up until then, I'd been happy with my arrangement with Kurt." She kneels beside his body, and the tears start to trip down her cheeks. "Of course our beginnings had been fraught; but we'd moved beyond that, shifting our relationship into one that benefited both of us—publicly, professionally . . . even sexually." She takes his hand, strokes it softly, the ring gleaming in the dark. "An open relationship—which was fine by me; I didn't care what he did, as long as we maintained the façade." She kisses his hand, then eases the ring from his finger, unclasps her necklace, and returns the ring to its rightful place. "My career had skyrocketed, the public loved us—but there was no real connection, no heart. And then I realized: this was my chance for a new beginning.

"I realized I needed Kurt's help with an important film—a passion project. His name would all but guarantee it got made. But I knew he'd never agree to it, especially not if he knew I'd written it." She wipes her hands on her thighs, then picks up the knife and stands—forces her eyes from Kurt's body. "So I turned the tables, threatening to leak that he'd coerced me into sex to get cast in *Waiting Game*. He panicked, and tried to keep me quiet by promising whatever I desired." She swallows. Lifts her chin. "For over two years I kept our relationship afloat. I was in complete control of his personal and professional life—Kurt was asking 'how high?' before I ever said 'jump.' And it was all worth it, because our film had been greenlit—a project I knew you wouldn't be able to resist."

She turns to Jonah. "*Tender Is the Night*, adapted in secret by Lila Crayne? A book written by your favorite author, and the subject of your thesis?"

He closes his eyes. "Oh god."

She crosses to the bookshelf, slides his pocketknife out of reach onto the top step of the staircase above, then pulls the tome from the ledge. "Your thesis was invaluable, the perfect manual for the argument I wanted to disprove."

"*You* stole it?"

"Of course I did. I've had it all along." She studies him. "All these years. You really thought you were going to get me, didn't you? Did you honestly think you were being covert? You were so obvious, so amateur. I mean, running by my apartment every day? My team wanted to serve you with a restraining order the very first week, but I convinced them to hold off."

She rakes back her hair, turned sticky with blood. Shivers. "Innocent, helpless girl of your dreams working on your passion project comes knocking on your door? Caught in a terribly abusive relationship, and only you can save her?" She shakes her head. "Kurt never hit me; not once. He liked to play rough; but he was never violent."

"But the bruises . . ."

"It's amazing what film makeup can do, isn't it?" Her temple pulses. "But my favorite moment was our 'breakthrough,' when you *miraculously* unlocked a childhood trauma I'd never actually repressed."

At this he blinks. "You mean . . . ?"

"I'm an actor, Jonah—a good one. I'd remembered the car crash all along. Mother and I don't keep secrets from one another. We never have."

"Lila, please! Why are you doing this?"

"When Kurt quit the film, everything clicked into place. Do you know what Mother texted him—how we got him back? I offered him his freedom, if he'd help me trap you."

He moans softly.

"I never needed to escape Kurt; I used him as *bait*, so that you could feel like the hero, swooping in to save me. And you ran straight into the trap."

She inhales sharply—looks down as Kurt's blood seeps between her toes. Her breathing quickens, and again and again she presses her palms against the fabric of her slip, desperate to be rid of the blood.

"I swore to Kurt if he snared you tonight, I'd frame you as the manipulative, jealous predator, and him the hero defending me. I'd never tell a soul about the women he'd coerced, and he could walk away forever. As a guarantee, I gave him photos Freddie had taken of Dom and me in what looked like a romantic embrace; we'd leak them afterwards as proof of my infidelity. All he had to do was wait for you to break in, corner you, and call the cops—the laws protecting women are so inadequate, nothing less would suffice. We'd hidden all the weapons; and I assured him that even if you did get physical, you were no match. I swore he wouldn't get hurt."

Here her voice catches, her eyes blur.

"I never wanted him to die," she whispers. "I thought once we had you trapped, we'd simply turn you in and go our separate ways. I never thought you might actually *kill* him."

For a moment she studies Jonah, a single tear slipping down her cheek. Then she shakes her head, brushes at her face. And folds her arms in resolve.

"But you *did* kill him—and that only confirms how horrible you are. All I did was give you the rope to hang yourself; but now you've framed yourself as a murderer."

"I'm not a murderer!" he cries out. "It was self-defense! I thought he was going to kill me!"

"I saw you, Jonah!" she says, incredulous. "I saw what you did. Your life was never in danger—he didn't have a weapon! And he kept telling you to put the knife down. You didn't have to kill him, but you *did*." She shakes her head. "The authorities will never believe you, anyway—not when they find all the evidence."

His eyes widen. "What evidence?"

"I recorded all our sessions. I have evidence of every moment you crossed a line. Our text exchanges. My journal entries, which paint me in a *very* vulnerable state, and demonstrate clear signs of transference." She lets out a little laugh. "I gave you so many outs! So many opportunities to do the right thing this time around. I never would've gone through with it if you had. But *you*—you just continued to prove your own guilt. You didn't have to take me on as your patient and lie about our history. When I told you I'd been raped, you could've admitted the man who'd raped me was *you*."

"But I didn't—"

"That's right: you didn't. Once again, you concealed your identity." She folds her arms. "You didn't have to allow our relationship to turn physical. And you didn't have to cheat on Maggie—and yet: you did."

She walks across the room. "Then there's the footage of you lurking around my apartment. The testimonials from my security team. Oh, and Freddie and Dom—I told them you'd been stalking me, and they promised to help protect me from you." She reaches the coffee table and picks up a remote and aims it at the wide-screen on the wall. "And then there's this."

249

The TV flashes on, blinding in the dark. A fuzzy black-and-white picture fills the screen—security footage: two stamps of dark matter in a wash of light grey. Then one of them shifts, and Jonah sucks in his breath.

"I tried to re-create the atmosphere of St. A's that night at my pied-à-terre. I thought you'd want to relive it, and I was right: you replicated almost every single step. See? You kissed me hard, and held me in place as I tried to push you away. You pulled my hair, forced me to the ground. And there I am, trying to escape." The camera cuts to an interior angle as Lila crawls across the floor, Jonah following. "You pinned my shoulders so I couldn't move, then grabbed me by the throat and held me in place. And then you pushed my face to the side as you got ready to force yourself inside me." She turns off the TV with a click.

"There's no sound in that video!" he cries. "You wanted me to kiss you—you begged me to! I didn't do anything to you against your will."

"The footage tells a different story, though, doesn't it?" She sits in her chair, grips its bloody arms to steady herself. "All evidence points to a clean narrative: back at Princeton you were obsessed with me, and raped me, thinking I wouldn't find out who you were. Now, years later, you concealed our history and violated all protocol when you accepted me, a vulnerable movie star, as your patient, to pursue your own agenda. And when at last you'd manipulated me into seeing you as the answer to my problems, and seduced me into becoming romantically involved, Kurt became the only remaining impediment to having me once and for all. So tonight, in a frighteningly unhinged state, you killed my fiancé in a fit of jealous rage."

She shakes her head. "Maybe if you'd been able to see past your own ego, you might've caught on a lot sooner. Now *Maggie*—Maggie was paying attention. She knew something was awry, didn't she?"

He grimaces, shuts his eyes.

"Should've listened to her when you had the chance." She lowers her voice. "Thank god I saved her from you."

"Maggie loves me!" His eyes widen. "She'd vouch for me. Maggie would take my side."

"Would she?" She cocks her head. "I talked to her today, just to be sure. When she arrived to deliver the painting, I was weeping, beside myself—clearly traumatized. I told her you'd been stalking me, and that recently, you'd even assaulted me. I showed her the video—the one you just watched. I promised I was getting help for myself; but that for her own safety, she should stay away from you too."

"She didn't buy it," he insists. "She said she didn't know who to believe."

"Of course she did. She's smart, like I said. So she probably tried to prevent you from coming here, right? At which point—let me guess—you assumed she was a jealous, conniving bitch, trying to keep us apart. So you said something unforgivable, something that made Maggie realize just how little she meant to you all along. Am I getting warm?"

But he shakes his head. "Your story doesn't track. If you thought I'd assaulted you, why would you seek me out for therapy? Either you knew who I was or you didn't. You can't have it both ways."

She smiles sadly. "Are you sure?"

Then she closes her eyes, presses her palms to her ears. Her shoulders curve and rise, hands needling together—and when she blinks her eyes open they widen, glistening. "Your Honor, I had no recollection of that night. If Jonah hadn't shown me how to unlock the memories I'd repressed, I don't know if I *ever* would've remembered. I might never have realized he'd purposefully hunted me down and was trapping me all over again."

She blinks, wipes at her eyes. Then turns to Jonah, her mouth a thin, grim line. "It's my word against yours—and finally, the world's going to take the woman's side. Because with all the damning evidence, who do you honestly think they're going to believe?"

"Lila, *please* don't do this!" he begs. "I know you! This isn't who you are!"

"You have no fucking idea who I am," she shoots back. "*This* is the real me, Jonah. What—you don't like this version? Am I threatening to you? You want me to be your sweet, infantilized patient again? Or how about the goofy, sexy pen pal, instead? I'm curious: which fantasy was your favorite? Everything you *think* you know about me, everything you've seen up till now—our therapy sessions, the journal entries, that night at my pied-à-terre?—it was all a performance. A lie. You think I'm unrecognizable?" She shakes her head. "You don't know me at all."

He sucks in his breath—but then, very quietly: "What about that night at Princeton? Wasn't that you, back then?"

Her eyes narrow.

"That *was* you, I think—the woman I fell in love with." A pause. "The woman I still love."

For a moment, they study one another in silence.

"If you really love me," Lila says, "admit what you did to me."

He hesitates. "What?"

She seems to brace herself. "I want you to admit that you raped me. Why can't you just acknowledge it after all these years?"

She stands before him, waiting. Directly behind, *Ícaro* looms in relief, the painting an epic reincarnation of Jonah's only memento: a dark, blurred photo of the two of them together that night. She stands before him, pallid and fragile and trembling. With rage?

Or—is it possible—*fear*?

"There's been a terrible misunderstanding," he begins slowly. "What you say I did to you that night . . . I would never have done that to anyone."

She blinks, startled.

"I don't mean to discount your experience. But Lila . . . I think you might be misremembering."

"I didn't want to sleep with you," she says firmly. "You forced me against my will."

"It's so painful to hear you say that. Because for me . . ." He looks at her. "It was the best night of my life."

252

In the distance, thunder rumbles.

"I know I've made some terrible, unforgivable mistakes. I shouldn't have taken you on as a patient. I should've told you I remembered you. It was morally and ethically wrong, I *know*. But—" He looks at her. "I've thought about you all these years, hoping our paths might cross again. So when you came back into my life, I saw it as my only chance." He wipes at his eyes. "God, Lila—all these years, I've been in love with you!"

A wild clap of thunder. And through the windows' pansophic eyes, the cracked vault of sky appears backlit in a sudden, jagged flash.

The room sinks back to darkness, only the white of Lila's slip lingering in the lightning's glow. He watches as she picks up the mask, turns it in her palms.

"You took off *my* mask," she says slowly, "but you never took off yours."

"Because of those stupid rules . . ."

She looks at him. "But what about the next morning?"

He hesitates.

"If you'd really thought that night had been perfect," she continues, "you would've wanted to make sure I knew who you were in the light of day. But you kept your mask on. You were protecting your identity, because some part of you knew you'd done something wrong."

"It makes sense you'd see it that way, but that wasn't why I kept it on. I think . . ." He lifts his hands. "I was in shock. I thought we'd shared this perfect night; and then I find out you didn't remember at all? I was humiliated."

She shakes her head. "But you lied to me about what happened—"

"I didn't," he insists. "I just said we'd had a good time—I thought that was true! I had no *idea* it might not be. I didn't want to embarrass you further by giving you the play-by-play of a night you couldn't remember. It never occurred to me you might've been lying."

She opens her mouth to protest.

"But that doesn't matter," he says quickly. "Of course I should've told

SWEET FURY

you everything. I was just so embarrassed, and I acted like a coward.
As for what *did* happen that night—I just wish you'd said something. I
really thought you wanted it as much as I did."

"I tried to stop you—"

He tilts his head. "Did you?"

Her eyes begin to fill.

"I'm so sorry I misread the signals. But Lila, you never told me you
didn't want to have sex. At least, I don't think you did." He studies her.
"I guess I thought if you didn't want to, you would've told me explicitly.
But I don't remember you ever saying 'no.' Am I wrong?"

She watches Kurt's blood creep around them.

He lifts his hand. "It doesn't matter. You didn't want it. All *I'm* saying
is: I truly didn't know. If I'd known, I would never—"

"But it happened more than once," she insists. "You did it again—"

"I remember that other woman," he says, "the freshman at Yale. It was
about four years ago. I'd been invited, as a member of St. A's Princeton
chapter, to attend Yale's Pump and Slipper. She came up to me, right at
the start. She was charming, almost as pretty as you. We hit it off and
had a few drinks . . . and it's true we spent the night together. I cheated
on Maggie that night; but I also confessed to Maggie right after it happened. I took responsibility for my mistake.

"But as for what *really* happened that night at Yale?" He takes a step
towards her. "That girl lied to you. *She* was the one who initiated; she
wanted it more than I did." He pauses. "Thinking back on it now—
maybe she expected something more? But of course I wasn't going
to leave Maggie. So maybe she contacted you because she wanted to
hurt me and get revenge. You said it yourself: her life was a mess. She
was unwell."

He takes a step closer. "Lila, think of my work—my calling. I don't
prey upon women—I help them! Think of all the women I've helped
over the years. Think of Brielle." He hesitates, then adds, "Think of how
I saved *you*, all those years ago."

Her chin begins to quiver.

"Don't you remember those men, and all the drinks you'd accepted?" His voice almost a whisper now. "The only reason I took you upstairs was to protect you. I thought you wanted to get away from them. Didn't you?"

A tear slides down her cheek. "Of course I did."

"I was more than attracted to you; I was beginning to fall in love with you. But that night, with those men – I just wanted to keep you safe."

Gently, he lifts his hands. "I know what it is you want to hear. And I want to give you what you need to heal. But . . ." He shakes his head. "I just can't admit to something I had no knowledge or intention of. I won't say I raped you, Lila. I could never admit to that."

Silence spreads between them.

And then from above: another voice, shivering through the air— "You're lying."

She steps into view on the landing above, picking up the pocketknife from the top of the stairs, and Jonah sucks in his breath.

"Celia?"

"The press release runs tomorrow," Lila murmurs, watching Celia warily, "announcing Celia as Rosemary."

"You raped us, Jonah," Celia whispers.

"I didn't—"

"You did!" Celia cries. "I know you did—because you used the same trap *twice*."

He freezes.

"I wasn't pursuing you that night," she continues. "I wasn't even interested in you! You wouldn't leave me alone. You did your ridiculous Fitzgerald routine, and then you told me I looked exactly like Lila Crayne—that you'd known her a long time ago." Her hand finds the banister, grips it tight. "There were other men flirting with me, and you didn't like that. So you pulled me aside and told me you'd overheard them talking about all the unspeakable things they wanted to do to me. You were concerned—had I accepted any drinks from

255

them?" Her voice catches. "God, I was terrified! I wanted to get out of there immediately. But you said I shouldn't leave, because they might follow me. You knew a place where I'd be safe, where I could wait until they'd left."

Her voice barely a whisper. "Once you got me alone, you were a completely different person. I told you I didn't want to have sex; the whole time, I *begged* you to stop. But it didn't matter. You acted like you didn't even hear me. You kept shushing me, telling me not to worry. Telling me I was safe."

"The other men . . ." Lila whispers, eyes widening with the revelation. "That was a lie? But—" She turns to Celia. "But you never told me—"

"You never *let* me." Celia shakes her head. "You didn't care about the details of my story—you only cared about what happened to you."

Then Celia turns back to Jonah, and deals the final blow: "There never were any other men who wanted to hurt either of us, were there. The only man who wanted to hurt us was you."

"You're acting like it was premeditated," he stutters. "It was just a made-up story—a stupid pickup line—"

"It was a trap," she insists. "A trap you used twice. You wanted to have us. It didn't matter whether we wanted it too."

In a flash, his expression morphs. "This was never about you." He turns back to Lila. "You have to understand—we'd been drinking, and . . . god, she looks just like you!"

Lila remains silent.

"If you want me to admit to assaulting *her*—if that's what you need me to say—?" He lets the suggestion linger. "But Lila, you have to believe me: I never raped *you*!"

Celia looks to Lila, staring at Jonah in disbelief.

"Everyone makes mistakes, don't they?" he stammers on. "I just wanted to relive my time with *you*. I wanted to reclaim the memory of our perfect night—the night you told me you'd forgotten. It was never about her. It was only ever about—"

"Lila," Celia finishes, brushing angrily at her tears. "Believe me, I got that loud and clear. You didn't give a shit about me. You just used me to pretend I was her."

"I loved her!" He turns again to Lila. "I know I shouldn't have told you that story about the men—I *know* that! But Lila, I couldn't believe it was finally happening! And I didn't trust you'd want to be with me. I wanted to give you a reason to stay—to know that with me, you'd always be safe. Lila—" He paws at his face. "I love you."

"That isn't love," Lila says. "It's possession." Then she shakes her head. "Give up, Jonah. It's time now for us to get the justice we deserve."

But at this, Celia lets out an incredulous laugh.

"This was never about justice," she says. "This was always only about Lila Crayne."

Lila's eyes narrow. "What are you talking about?"

Celia sucks in her breath. "The first time we met, face-to-face, you promised me Jonah would be convicted for what he'd done to us. But you needed more time to collect evidence, find out if there were other victims. . . . You promised you'd do everything in your power to craft an irrefutable, airtight argument to prove his guilt; and once you did, we'd go to the police together and report him. *Two women are stronger than one*, you said."

Lila glances at Jonah. "Celia—"

"In the meantime, you'd get your film made. And you generously offered to convince Kurt to let me audition." She inhales. "You warned me Kurt could be difficult in casting; but it would mean *so much* to you if I got the role. You'd feel like you were making things right for me now. We could become real friends as we gathered evidence for Jonah's arrest."

Celia braces herself. "Even after last night, when I found out you'd known Kurt would force me to have sex with him—even then I tried to convince myself you must've had no choice; otherwise, how could you have let something so terrible happen to me?"

257

Lila's eyes widen. "But Celia, I didn't—"

"When I showed up uninvited tonight, you had no time, no choice, but to hide me away. And I heard everything, Lila. You'd been blackmailing Kurt for years! It would've cost you nothing to keep me safe."

At this Lila hesitates, and Celia lets out a little gasp of a laugh.

"You probably *liked* that I kept him distracted, didn't you? All through filming, he harassed me; and out of sheer trust in you, I stayed silent. I even felt guilty, like I was some sort of homewrecker! You hadn't told me, of course, that your relationship was a lie."

Lila shakes her head. "I'm so sorry," she says. "I didn't realize. I thought you knew the sex was transactional, that you knew this was what it would take to launch your career. I thought you'd willingly agreed."

"Just because you were okay letting him do that to you doesn't mean I would be. It doesn't make it okay. And it sure as hell doesn't make it any less traumatic. Why didn't you warn me explicitly? We both know the answer: because discussing it might jeopardize your plans. So you stayed silent and let it happen. Because to you, I was a worthwhile sacrifice."

Lila clasps her hands. "Celia, that isn't true—"

"Stop acting," Celia says. "I know this is just another one of your performances."

"I'm not acting!" Lila cries. "I swear I'm telling the truth."

"I trusted you," Celia says. "I was sure we were on the same side. We'd shared the same trauma—how could we not be allies? Did you even care that Jonah had raped me too? Or was I just a pawn, the catalyst that set into motion your secret hellish plan?"

Celia takes in the devastation around her. "Kurt's death?" she says, then looks at Jonah. "And framing him as a killer?" Her voice barely a whisper. "Even *he* doesn't deserve that. You *made* him into a murderer, Lila. You're just as responsible for Kurt's death as he is—maybe more. You alone created this nightmare. If I'd known this was what you were *actually* planning, I never would've wanted a part in it. Kurt is dead because of you."

"I didn't mean for him to die!" Lila cries, wringing her slip. "It was an accident!"

"Kurt's life was a risk you were willing to take. Collateral damage—just like me."

"Celia, please just listen." Her eyes dart to Jonah. "We didn't have any evidence! We both knew he'd raped us, but we had no way of showing it. All I did was create the proof."

"With *lies*." Celia looks at her. "Do you even realize what you've done? The faked abuse with Kurt—pretending your fiancé regularly assaulted you? Do you care how far back you'd set the real victims, if those lies ever came to light?"

"Those lies were just to trap *him*," she says, glancing at Jonah. "And that tape I made? Jonah *did* assault me. It happened; we're just talking about *when* it happened."

Celia shakes her head. "You created false evidence."

"I gave him another chance!" Lila pleads. "All I did was give him the opportunity to create the evidence we needed to bring him to justice."

"Justice can't be built upon lies," Celia says. "This is entrapment."

"Celia, please!" Lila begs. "We're so close to getting everything we wanted—"

"Everything *you* wanted," she shoots back. "What about what *I* want?"

"Don't you want to see him locked up for life?"

"You promised I could testify!"

Lila opens her mouth to respond, but nothing comes out.

"I spent years in therapy working through what he'd done," Celia says. "Testifying was the closure I needed. I *need* to be able to stand up in court and recount the nightmare I lived through, and look the man who raped me directly in the eye. I want to set an example for other women—show them they don't have to be afraid to come forward and tell the truth! But how can I possibly do that now? How could I testify under oath without risking everything coming out in the open? Can you honestly tell me there's still a way in your genius plan for me to take the stand?"

Lila gazes at her, helpless.

"You're just as bad as he is," Celia whispers. "When will you learn to look out for other women?"

She walks over to Lila—stops inches from her face. "I recorded everything tonight," she says, gripping the knife tight. "Just like you would've done, right?" She hesitates. "If I wanted to, I could take you down—couldn't I?"

She studies Lila. Waits.

"I'm done with your bullshit," Celia says finally. "It's time to put an end to this, once and for all." Then she pulls her phone from a pocket of her dress.

"Celia, please!" Lila cries. "I want you to have the justice you deserve. Please, I'm begging you: what can I do?"

"After all the promises you've broken? Nothing could ever make me trust you again." She begins to dial.

"Wait!" Jonah cries, and the women turn. "What if I were to tell you I have something to offer? Something you'd want?"

Celia's grip on the knife tightens. "What are you talking about?"

He licks his lips. "My patients."

"What?" Lila says quietly.

He inhales. "Almost all my patients are victims of abuse. It doesn't have to end here with me. I can give you everything: their names, their notes, their personal information, recordings of their sessions . . . everything you need to ruin their abusers' lives forever. Don't you want to take down *those* men, and give their victims the justice they deserve?"

The women watch him, completely still.

"You can still make this go away," he tells Lila, gesturing to Kurt's body. "You can still frame it that he was a violent, abusive partner, and I came to your rescue and killed him in self-defense." He swallows. "I'll give you everything if, in return, you'll let me go free."

He waits.

260

"Oh Jonah," Lila says. "You think I'm some sort of black widow. But my motives were always pure—and my fight ends here, with you. And in offering to sacrifice your patients so that you don't have to pay for your crimes? You've only further condemned yourself."

"You're both insane," Celia whispers. "I've got to get out of here—"

Lila lunges suddenly for the phone, and Celia leaps back with a startled cry.

"Come on, Celia," Lila says. "Just give me the phone."

"Fuck you," she says, clutching it tight. "The police can deal with this now. And you won't have time to mastermind your way out."

Jonah turns away, reeling. His legs begin to give, and he leans forward to steady himself against the sliding door.

"Celia—" Lila cries, "—stop!"

Then, almost imperceptibly: the distant ring, the operator's voice. And then Celia speaks: a perfect imitation of Lila.

"Please help me. Someone's been stabbed. He's . . . oh god, I think he's dead."

The operator responds, and Celia chokes out the address—adds, "Please hurry. *Please*"—then ends the call.

"What did you think?" Her voice empty. "Did my performance do you justice?"

And with a harsh, broken shout, Jonah hurls himself across the room. He throws her to the floor, phone and knife flying from her fingers, then clambers on top—

And he wraps his hands around Celia's throat.

"What are you doing?!" Lila screams.

He squeezes harder, bears down, and the noise Celia emits clots into a strange scraping rasp, her eyes bulging wide, delicate skin swelling red—deepening to purple—

"I'll kill her, Lila," he says through gritted teeth. "I'll do it for you."

"What?!" Lila cries.

"I'll save you from her—" he says, "—and damn myself."

261

"Jonah—"

"Take me," he insists. "Let me take the fall."

Lila opens her mouth to cry out again, then inhales—

Hesitates.

Celia's heels thud in the blood with a hollow clopping sound—the sound of an animal, a doll. Her nails scrape at Jonah's back, then seem to forget their own aim as they impotently claw the air. He grimaces with the effort—or is it a smile now tugging his lips?

"Shhh," he instructs, then shushes her again. Her eyelids begin to droop, her eyes swooping backwards, and the job is almost done—

"Let her go."

Lila picks up the knife, places its blade to Jonah's neck.

He looks up at her. "But—"

She presses in, and a bead pops to the surface. "Take your hands off her, Jonah," she says, "or I swear to god I'll kill you."

At last he releases, and Celia gasps, choking on air, then curls into herself with a guttural groan. Between her legs: a dark, wet blooming.

Slowly, he lifts his bloodied hands and gazes at her in despair.

"It was for you," he whispers. "It was all for you—"

"Enough," Lila says.

Celia holds her throat tenderly. She looks up at Lila, undone.

"It's over now, Jonah," Lila says. "I don't care if you never admit to what you did. I know the truth—I'll never doubt it again. And for me, that's enough."

———

He stands and walks to the balcony, and slides the door open to a shimmering rush of rain. He steps out, and it bears down on him in great cold sheets, sluicing the pinkish blood down the length of his body and onto the terrace below.

The sky beginning to lighten: dawn soon. He leans his elbows onto the rail and looks out at the water's corrugated surface, the rain flowing freely down his face.

His gaze travels to the street below, to the tree where he'd stopped to rest each morning. He blinks as he sees someone hovering in the shadows, watching—

He blinks again—the ashen, fantastic figure is gone.

The smile fades from his face, till it's so small it's nearly imperceptible. He waits, lips parting. And through the soundproof wall of glass, he doesn't hear the women's quiet conference, doesn't notice as Celia slips from the scene to absolve herself of abetment; and Lila wipes the knife handle clean, tosses it to the corner, and readies herself for her final performance.

He will hear the sirens, though: at first so faint he'll think he's imagined them, then swelling to overwhelm the air as trumpets would. And by some trick of the ear, the eye, the sound will link itself inextricably to the green lights of Jersey as they blink out, one by one. Then, for a single transitory enchanted moment, he'll hold his breath, his arms stretching farther into the dark, and it will seem to Jonah as though the sound is heralding from across the water, the call of salvation, the beckoning home———

He'll be ready for them, when they come.

CODA

W inter, now.

She heads west—past the barren saplings, the tight shutters and empty windows, black in the bleak January light. When she reaches the highway, she pauses just a moment at his tree, then makes her way to the end of the pier.

After the film's sweeping success, the trial's smooth conclusion, she'd been sure it was finally over. Jonah had been sentenced to a life in prison; in the eyes of the nation, America's Sweetheart had risen to become their hero. At last, she'd gotten the justice she deserved.

But then she'd received Maggie's letter. Maggie was convinced Jonah had been wronged, and she'd asked Lila if they could meet in private. All Maggie wanted, all she'd ever cared about, was the truth.

She knows what she must do; it's unfortunate, but it's the only way. In mere minutes Maggie will arrive, and Lila will present her with a foolproof story that will absolve her completely. And then, finally, she'll walk away free—

But of course, someone else must take the fall.

Celia.

A sharp wild brace throttles the air, and she draws in a deep breath of it, unutterably aware of her identity with her country—our country—before melting indistinguishably into it again.

And already her thoughts are whipping across the water—past the scattered constellations of slowly rotting pylons—past, even, the yielding, bloodless sun—

They are bound for somewhere altogether new—somewhere distant, and yet unseen—flying faster, faster, even as they're borne back into the past. Still they'll remain steadfast in their aim, and—very soon now—she will feel once again the familiar, inexorable embrace of that sweet warm darkness, which has always been, will always be, her destiny . . .

But there in the gloaming, two women approach: slips of shadow gliding down the pier. In the blonde one's hands: the golden mask. The brunette will tap her phone: silently, it begins to record. The perfect triangle converges, bears down. Perhaps she'll sense them then—or perhaps the women will whisper her name in the dark—

And she'll turn.

ACKNOWLEDGMENTS

To my dream team of strong, kind women at WME: Suzanne Gluck and Andrea Blatt, when I accepted your offer back in 2021 to become a throuple, it was one of the smartest decisions I ever made. You are the best agents an author could hope for. Thank you for your keen guidance and unfailing support; it's because of you that I can now call myself a writer. Jill Gillett and Nicole Weinroth, I pinch myself every time I remember that you're turning my dreams of bringing *Sweet Fury* to the silver screen into a reality. It's an honor to be in cahoots with you both. Caitlin Mahoney and Suzy Ball, fiercely representing *Sweet Fury* beyond the US to the world at large—you are powerhouse women, both of you, and I feel so grateful to be in your safe and expert hands.

To my Simon & Schuster family: first and foremost, my genius editor, Carina Guiterman. Carina, you are beyond my wildest dreams. You are wise, thoughtful, perceptive, and so humble and kind. I knew from the day we met that I'd found a kindred spirit. From the start, you understood *Sweet Fury* in the way I'd only hoped someone else might, and I knew in my gut I could trust you completely. Thank you for making me a better writer; I'm thrilled we're in this for the long haul. Tim O'Connell, I was blown away by your ardent support from the very beginning. Thank you for your kindness, and your belief in me. Jonathan Karp, I am humbled that you care so much about the success of this book. Thank you for inviting me to call Simon & Schuster my home. Danielle Prielipp and Maggie Southard, thank you for putting your hearts and souls behind bringing *Sweet Fury* to the world at large. Sophia Benz, thank you for your infinite patience with my technological ineptitude! Stacey Sakal and Kayley Hoffman, thank you for your careful close reads of the final drafts, ensuring all my (overused!) en dashes became em dashes in the end. Lisa Rivlin, thank you for the time and care you put into ensuring my book landed in a safe space.

To my international families: I must single out Imogen Nelson at Transworld, whose belief in and passion for *Sweet Fury* brought me to happy tears. I was blessed with two editors for this editorial process, and Imogen, your sharp insights and thoughtful notes made this book so much stronger. I'm so lucky to be in partnership with you. And to the rest of my growing international family at Alfaguara, AST, AW Bruna, Companhia das Letras, Dook, Fischer, Gyldendal Norsk, HarperFrance, Hayakawa, Keter, Libri Könyvkiadó, Mondadori, Otava, and Trei: I'm still in utter shock that you loved this book enough to bring it to your respective countries. Thank you.

When I graduated from Princeton in 2009, I founded an informal writers' group with some of my former classmates, with the admittedly selfish aim of keeping me accountable and forcing me to write regularly while I pursued a career in theater. Little did I know this group would become my backbone over the years, and the best group of friends, editors, and supporters I could ever wish for. Sixteen years later, all five of us can now say we are published authors. Laura Hankin, my little lump of clam, thank you for lending your talents as you taught me to craft the twists and turns of a zippy, plot-driven novel. Lovell Holder, my unbelievably generous friend, how many hours did we while away over the phone in which you oh so patiently helped me troubleshoot the litany of riddles in this book? I don't deserve you, dear one. Blair Hurley, literary wonder woman, thank you above all for introducing me to *Tender Is the Night.* Without you, Fitzgerald never would have found his way into this book. And Daria Lavelle, my plot doctor: you are a veritable genius when it comes to plotting, and I've learned so much from you. I truly mean it when I say this book would not exist without the four of you.

To my legal team at Davis + Gilbert: Ashima Dayal, Samantha Rothaus, Alexa Singh, and Jordan Thompson, thank you for your invaluable help, your wisdom, and your tenacity. You allowed me to feel protected and safe. Above all, thank you to my hero, Paavana Kumar—one of the smartest and most talented women I know, who had my back when I was at my lowest.

Jonathan Warren, thank you for lending your expert eye to my book, and ensuring I (sort of!) sounded like I knew what I was talking about when adopting the voice of a therapist.

Anna Pitoniak, thank you for patiently indulging my endless list of naive questions, for your sage advice, and for your genuine support.

Stacy Testa, you believed in this book from the very beginning. Thank you for your tremendous generosity, and for being the most trustworthy compass. I am so thankful for our friendship.

Alex Ulyett, thank you for your early read of this book, and for always being there to clue me in on the inner machinations of the publishing world. Most of all, thank you for being the best friend I could ever hope for.

Harrison Hill, thank you for holding my hand in the trenches as our respective debuts were bought and published. I'm so grateful to share in this journey with you.

Stephanie Lieberman, you were the first person to hear the kernel of the idea that eventually became *Sweet Fury.* Thank you for telling me that this was a story that needed to be told; it's because of you that I began writing this book. Molly Steinblatt and Adam Hobbins, thank you for your early notes and encouragement.

Mom and Dad, thank you for your unconditional love, and for

believing in me my whole life as I pursued the life of an artist, in all its various iterations. I wouldn't be here without your support and encouragement.

Finally, to Ben, the best and kindest man I know. You believed in me and in this book even when I'd lost all hope. I love you more with every year that passes, and thank my lucky stars for you, my Benny, most of all.

ABOUT THE AUTHOR

S ash Bischoff is a writer and director living in New York. *Sweet Fury* is her first novel.